W9-AYH-616

continued . . .

"A fabulous combination of vampire lore, parental angst, romance, and mystery. I loved this book!"
—Jackie Kessler, author of *The Road to Hell*

"All I can say is *wow*! I was totally immersed in this story, to the point that I tuned everything and everybody out the whole entire evening. Now that's what I call a good book. Michele can't write the next one fast enough for me!"
—The Best Reviews

"A winning follow-up to *I'm the Vampire, That's Why* filled with humor, supernatural romance, and truly evil villains."
—*Booklist*

"Had me laughing from beginning to end. . . . The humor and tension blended together perfectly."
—Romance Divas

I'm the Vampire, That's Why

"From the first sentence, Michele grabbed me and didn't let me go! A vampire mom? PTA meetings? A sulky teenager? Throw in a gorgeous, ridiculously hot hero and you've got the paranormal romance of the year. Get this one *now*."
—MaryJanice Davidson

"Hot, hilarious, one helluva ride. . . . Michele Bardsley weaves a sexily delicious tale spun from the heart."
—L. A. Banks

"A fun, fun read!"
—Rosemary Laurey

"Michele Bardsley has penned the funniest, quirkiest, coolest vampire tale you'll ever read. It's hot and funny and sad and wonderful, the kind of story you can't put down and won't forget. Definitely one for the keeper shelf."
—Kate Douglas

"An amusing vampire romance . . . a terrific contemporary tale."
—The Best Reviews

"A great read."
—Once Upon a Romance Reviews

"A marvelous introduction to the world of vampires and werewolves . . . funny and filled with explosive sexual tension."
—The Romance Readers Connection

OTHER BOOKS BY MICHELE BARDSLEY

Paranormal Romances

Come Hell or High Water
Over My Dead Body
Because Your Vampire Said So
Wait Till Your Vampire Gets Home
Don't Talk Back to Your Vampire
I'm the Vampire, That's Why

Erotica

Cupid Inc.
Fantasyland

Cross Your Heart

A Broken Heart Novel

MICHELE BARDSLEY

A SIGNET ECLIPSE BOOK

SIGNET ECLIPSE
Published by New American Library, a division of
Penguin Group (USA) Inc., 375 Hudson Street,
New York, New York 10014, USA
Penguin Group (Canada), 90 Eglinton Avenue East, Suite 700, Toronto,
Ontario M4P 2Y3, Canada (a division of Pearson Penguin Canada Inc.)
Penguin Books Ltd., 80 Strand, London WC2R 0RL, England
Penguin Ireland, 25 St. Stephen's Green, Dublin 2,
Ireland (a division of Penguin Books Ltd.)
Penguin Group (Australia), 250 Camberwell Road, Camberwell, Victoria 3124,
Australia (a division of Pearson Australia Group Pty. Ltd.)
Penguin Books India Pvt. Ltd., 11 Community Centre, Panchsheel Park,
New Delhi - 110 017, India
Penguin Group (NZ), 67 Apollo Drive, Rosedale, North Shore 0632,
New Zealand (a division of Pearson New Zealand Ltd.)
Penguin Books (South Africa) (Pty.) Ltd., 24 Sturdee Avenue,
Rosebank, Johannesburg 2196, South Africa

Penguin Books Ltd., Registered Offices:
80 Strand, London WC2R 0RL, England

First published by Signet Eclipse, an imprint of New American Library,
a division of Penguin Group (USA) Inc.

First Printing, September 2010
10 9 8 7 6 5 4 3 2 1

To Daddy and Linda . . .
and to Aunt Rosie and Uncle Benny . . .
and to all my Arkansas family

ACKNOWLEDGMENTS

I'd like to thank Laura Cifelli, Jesse Feldman, and Team NAL for being awesome. I just write the words. They do everything else.

I can't let a book go by without a shout-out to my wonderful agent, Stephanie Kip Rostan (who puts up with a lot), and to Monika Verma (who makes accountants tremble). Smoooooooooches!

You know why my life doesn't suck (even when it does)? 'Cause Renee George, Dakota Cassidy, and Terri Smythe are my very best friends. They know when to hold my hand and when to kick my ass. I adore you all.

I also need to say a big ol' thank you to my Minions, who gather online to support me (and insult me, as needed). I heart you.

And finally, to all the readers out there who keep me in vodka and chocolate . . . thank you, thank you, thank you.

For him I sing,
I raise the present into the past,
(As some perennial tree out of its roots, the present on
the past,)
With time and space I him dilate and fuse immortal
laws
To make himself by them the law unto himself.
—Walt Whitman, *Leaves of Grass*

What's the point of saving the world if you can't get
a little nookie once in a while, huh?
—Dean Winchester, *Supernatural*, "Hunted"

A NOTE FROM THE AUTHOR

At the start of *Cross Your Heart*, the seventh book in the Broken Heart series, five years have passed since the Consortium vampires rolled into town. The parakind community has been attacked by Wraiths (rogue vampires with bad tempers), Ancient vampires who've gone all *droch fola* (soulless), a dark mage were-dragon, a secret military paraterrorist group, and a bitch demon named Lilith and her Pit-dwelling posse.

So, you know, it hasn't been easy. Our heroes and heroines have prevailed, and, with Queen Patricia Marchand ruling both vampires and lycanthropes and the Council running the town (along with the Consortium's input, of course), Broken Heart has managed to finally become a haven for parakind. Werewolves, vampires, fairies, witches, wizards, pixies, and, hell, even zombies are welcome in Broken Heart.

You'd think with all the trials and tribulations our citizens have been through, all the obstacles to love that they've conquered—and, hey, some of those vampire parents even managed to raise their mortal children to adulthood—that they would finally get some freaking peace and quiet.

Yeah. Not so much.

Evil isn't always an outside force trying to steal or

smash its way in. It isn't always a pissed-off demon, a sociopathic mage, or a soulless Ancient. Sometimes evil is hidden within. This kind of malevolence has patience. And purpose.

It's just waiting, quietly, insidiously, to be unleashed.

The Curse of Broken Heart

It is said that beautiful and feisty Mary McCree drowned herself in the creek near her farm. She had loved her husband so much that his infidelity drove her mad with grief, and she could not live with his betrayal.

Before she waded into the water and met her death, she cursed this place and all who lived in it, swearing that anyone who dared to love would eventually know the depth of her own heartbreak.

Whether or not Mary McCree uttered such a curse is unknown, but she did commit suicide by drowning and her husband was accused of infidelity. No one really knows if, as town lore indicts, Mary's daughter shamed the founding fathers into naming the town Broken Heart, so that everyone would remember the suffering of Mary McCree.

Statistics have shown that Broken Heart had the highest divorce and unwed-mother rates in Oklahoma.

At least until the vampires arrived and took over the town, remaking it into a parakind community.

And if harmony was fickle, at least romantic love prevailed.

The curse of Broken Heart was no more.

Or so it seemed.

Chapter 1

"You wanna make out?" asked the man standing on my welcome mat. He cocked a pierced eyebrow at me, leaned on the doorjamb, and tucked his hands into his pockets. The gesture flexed his muscled, tattooed arms, drawing attention to the six-pack abs defined by his tight T-shirt.

He was gorgeous and youthful and impetuous.

"Rand, you make me feel old." I caved in to the smile flirting with my lips. "And I'm immortal."

His grin widened. "Aw, Lizzie. You're tops in my book."

"Don't call me Lizzie. It's puerile." I opened the door and gestured for him to enter. "C'mon. It's ready."

Now twenty-two, Rand moved to Broken Heart when he was seventeen. As a human, he was a rarity in a town filled with paranormal residents. He was also the expert on the care and feeding of dragons.

I was forty-three when Lorcan O'Halloran, or rather the beast he'd become, attacked and killed me and ten other residents of Broken Heart, Oklahoma. He suffered from the Taint, a disease that reduced the infected vampire to a crazed and rabid state. A cure had recently been discovered, thanks in large part to the revelation of its origins: demon poison. Our resident scientist, Dr. Stan Michaels, himself a Turn-blood, had figured out a real and lasting cure. The Taint was no more.

Every vampire got strength, speed, glamour, and—unless our heads were chopped off or sunlight got us—immortality. There were eight vampire Families, each with their own particular power. I was from the Family Zela, and our ability was to manipulate and control any metallic substance.

As a human, I hadn't been able to conquer my vanity about getting older. Going under the knife, taking the injection, getting the acid peel . . . I had done them all. However, becoming undead rid me of crow's-feet, stretch marks, and cellulite, and forestalled other atrocities of the aging process.

"I'll make tea," I said as he stepped inside and shut the door.

"Earl Grey?" he asked.

"Of course."

Though I enjoyed my solitary lifestyle, I couldn't resist having a cuppa with whoever crossed my threshold. Thanks to an accidental fairy wish, vampires within the borders of Broken Heart could eat again and drink liquids other than blood. I had missed taking tea and had been pleased to reestablish the routine.

My old Victorian opened into a wide foyer. Straight ahead was the staircase to the upper floor. On the left side was entrance to the formal living room. On the right side was a smaller room, the parlor, where I typically entertained visitors.

Rand paused by the antique hall tree. He studied it, then glanced at me. "New?"

"Yes. It's French. Hand-carved oak. Circa 1870. See the hooks? They're cherubs." The darkened wood had been polished with beeswax. I'd fallen in love with the piece merely from its picture. eBay was a glorious boon for vampires. "The bench seat opens." I flipped it up and we looked down into the emptiness.

Rand shook his head. "You've got a thing for old stuff."

"So do you." I tweaked his earlobe, and he laughed.

The kitchen was accessed through a narrow door at the back of the parlor. While Rand took a seat at the small table I used for tea service, I went to the kitchen and put on the kettle.

"Hey, I forgot!" Rand called from the parlor. "Patsy gave me something for you. Said they found it in the attic and it belongs to you."

I poked my head into the parlor. "I've told her a hundred times that whatever she finds, she can have or toss out."

He shrugged. "I'll go get it."

While Rand went to get whatever it was, I returned to the kitchen and cleaned up a mess I'd made earlier during a botched attempt at making scones. I heard the front door open and shut, and then Rand's steps in the foyer.

"Elizabeth."

A man's voice seemed to come from right behind me.

It vibrated with fury. I swore I felt big male hands creep around my neck.

Startled, I whirled around, my hand pressed against my chest. My palm flattened over the spot where my heart no longer beat.

Nobody was there.

The kitchen was small. I'd kept it simple during the renovation, thinking it pointless for me to even have one. The cabinets were whitewashed, the countertops and walls a cheery yellow, and the floor, like the rest of the house, was polished oak. About the only place for someone to hide was the pantry. I opened the door but saw only the fully stocked shelves and, in the back, cleaning equipment neatly aligned on wall hooks.

Unnerved, I returned to the stove and opened the cabinet that held my tea stashes. I pulled down a tin and pried its lid off, and looked down into the dark loose leaves. They smelled strong and fragrant, like good tea should.

"Elizabeth." The voice was stronger now. Insistent. I had excellent hearing, thanks to my vampire ears, but this wasn't someone speaking from a distance. The man calling my name did not like me. I had the uneasy feeling he wanted to hurt me. Foreboding sat in my belly as solid and heavy as an iron weight.

Pain throbbed around my neck.

"Hey, you need help?"

I yelped, dropping the tin. It bounced and rolled, its contents spilling onto the floor.

"Shit," said Rand. "I didn't mean to scare you." He crossed to the mess and picked up the container. "I don't think there's much left."

"I have another one." I hesitated. "Did you hear anyone just now?"

He frowned. "Who?" He glanced around the kitchen the same way I had. "You think someone's in the house?"

I shook my head, feeling foolish. "Never mind. I'm being silly."

"You're a lot of things, Lizzie, but silly isn't one of 'em." He grimaced. "I mean, you know, that you're mature." He slapped a hand against his forehead. "I'm not saying you're not fun, just that you're serious."

His face went red. I swallowed my laugh and reached for the second tin of Earl Grey so he wouldn't see my amused expression.

"Maybe you should stop complimenting me," I offered, "and go get the broom."

"Yeah," he said, sounding relieved. "I'll clean up the mess. No prob."

"Where's the all-important thing?" I asked.

"I left it inside the hall tree."

"Why on earth would you do that?"

"So you'd have a surprise to open."

I stared at him, but he shrugged and grinned. Then he went to the pantry, grabbed the broom, and busied himself with cleaning up.

Later, we settled at the table with our tea and conversation. However, I didn't want to torment Rand for too long. He'd come to my home for a singular purpose.

"Here." I slid the velvet box across the table and Rand accepted it.

His face had a look of wonder, and if I wasn't mistaken, an edge of panic. I suppressed my smile as he flipped open the box. His mouth fell open and his eyes went wide.

It was gratifying to see his reaction to my work.

He plucked the ring from its silk confines and studied it. "I knew you did great work, Lizzie. But . . . wow. This is art."

"Thank you," I said modestly.

Rand had procured silver and gold for me, and a small rare dragonfire gem—deep purple in color, passionate in promise. Two dragons, one silver, one gold, stretched in a circle from joined tails to snouts pressing against the oval stone.

Rand was in love with MaryBeth Beauchamp, a vampire who'd been Turned at the tender age of eighteen. I suppose she would be twenty-three now, if vampires counted years. (Thank goodness they didn't!) She was a nice girl, and the official full-time nanny for Queen Patricia's triplets.

Queen Patricia, whom most of us knew as Patsy Donovan, had once been the town's only beautician. Then Gabriel Marchand arrived with his band of outcasts and revealed a prophecy: Patsy would become queen of the vampires, effectively ending the reign of the Council of Ancients. And if that bombshell weren't enough, she would also be given rule of the lycanthropes.

Patsy was no longer undead. I had never quite comprehended the process that had given her life. Magic— and there was a lot of magic in Broken Heart—was the only explanation. Not only did she wield seven of the eight powers of the Ancients, she had become like Gabriel: *loup de sang.* They were blood-drinking lycans—a true combination of vampire and werewolf. Most vampires could not shape-shift. *Most* because previous attempts at Taint cures had given a very few vampires the ability to take wolf forms.

Broken Heart was a very interesting place to live.

I sipped my tea and watched Rand study the ring. He was smiling—and looking a little less green around the gills. I wondered if he might be imagining MaryBeth's reaction. Would she scream? Shout yes and throw her arms around his neck? Kiss him senseless? I had to admit that my inner romantic loved the potential scenarios.

When Rand approached me about making an engagement ring for MaryBeth, I asked him about his concept of forever. He was human, after all. Then he explained that as a handler of dragons, he fell within their protection—and one gift given was immortality. He said he'd probably stop aging completely around thirty human years, which was the same for dragon shifters.

So, he and MaryBeth would truly have forever. Or at least a century. Oh, that's not cynicism. Vampires didn't have one-night stands—because sex equaled an instant hundred-year commitment to our bedmates. Needless to say, most of us were very careful. In my case, I avoided dating, though I sometimes yearned for the emotional and physical intimacy of a relationship.

Ah, well. Love was for the young, and all that.

"Well?" I prodded.

"It's perfect," Rand said. He dragged his gaze from the ring to me, and grinned. "Now, all she has to do is say yes."

"How could she not, darling?" I looked into my teacup and squinted at the leaves clinging to the ceramic. I knew nothing about reading tea leaves, but Rand didn't really need me to. "I predict you will both have a long and happy life together."

He reached across the table and took my hand. "What about you, Lizzie?"

"I will also have a long and happy life," I said, looking away from his sincere gaze. The shadow of his concern for my own love life fluttered in my stomach. I had it good. I didn't need a relationship to feel complete. Of course, this was not a concept Rand would understand. I squeezed his hand and let go. "When will you propose?"

"I gotta make sure everything's just right." He closed the lid to the velvet box. "Thanks again."

I stood on the porch steps and waved good-bye. Rand drove a white Ford truck, a rather mundane vehicle for a man with such a wild nature. Soon, he would give Mary-Beth the ring, and his love. I hoped she returned the favor. It was a difficult thing to do, to entrust one's heart to someone else.

Or so I suspected.

I had never really been in love.

I married Henry Bretton when I was twenty-two, in the fall after I graduated from the University of Tulsa. Not for love, though I certainly enjoyed his company and found him an amiable companion. No, I married the man my parents picked for me because I understood the limitations of my own life, and certainly the figurative dangling scissors they held over the line to my trust fund.

In my late twenties, I discussed with my husband the possibility of having children. I wanted a baby, maybe even two, or three. Unfortunately, our attempts ended when I found out endometriosis had made me infertile.

We'd been discussing the possibilities of adoption when Henry felt compelled to confess that he already had a daughter.

The month before Henry married me, he had a one-night sexual romp with a Las Vegas showgirl named Trinie. Nine months and one DNA test later he was the reluctant father of a baby girl. His solution to this problem was to throw money: at Trinie, at the baby girl she named Venice, at those willing to cover up such a delicate situation.

I was aware my husband enjoyed extramarital activities, but he'd always been discreet. It was a terrible blow to learn he had a child, one he'd kept hidden not only from me but the world.

After that, Henry and I never again discussed adoption. We kept separate bedrooms, and though he continued having affairs, I never took a lover. I kept busy with planning parties, chairing committees, heading charities, and mixing martinis. According to my mother, a dry martini and a good cry could fix damn near anything.

This was probably the point at which a discerning woman would've filed for divorce and perhaps searched for a more suitable mate, if not a more suitable life. However, I was comfortable in my role as Mrs. Bretton, and, for the most part, I enjoyed my life. If the kind of love found between the pages of my beloved romance novels was not mine to be had, then I accepted it.

I was the one who insisted Henry publicly claim his daughter.

It's understandable that Venice grew up with a skewed

sense of self-esteem and a damaged moral compass. She was embarrassed to have a showgirl mother, and desperate for the attention of the wealthy father who'd emotionally abandoned her.

The drama started in her early teens. Kicked out of boarding schools. Arrested for underage drinking. Photographed with a lifted skirt—and no panties.

Henry was mortified by his daughter's behavior. He shipped Trinie and Venice off to Europe. Anytime Venice ended up in the tabloids, he'd pack them off to another country.

When Venice was seventeen, her mother died in a car accident in France. Henry had no choice but to bring the girl into our home.

Venice never realized she didn't have to compete with me for her father's affection. I wanted so much to be a good stepmother. But every time I reached out to her, she ignored me, or worse, she viciously rejected any show of kindness.

Venice became the fashionable club girl. Famous only for being famous. With her father's money, she started a perfume line and then a clothing line. She acted in a few bit parts of low-grade horror movies. Then Henry financed her return to France, and she left without so much as a good-bye.

Not long after my forty-third birthday, Henry died of heart failure.

I found myself facing the prospect of creating a life all my own—without parental expectations to accede or husbandly indiscretions to ignore.

I left New York after the funeral. I dropped every

obligation, abandoned every project. I spent the next couple of months at my parents' home, completely out of sorts. Mother plied me with martinis, and Father, with portfolio advice. My parents loved me, but they weren't emotional people—so their suggestions were meant to fix me, not comfort me.

I think it was a relief for all of us when they took an anniversary trip to Europe.

Then the family lawyers called to tell us about a generous offer for the old Silverstone estate in Broken Heart, and the plans to inventory the home. I took on this project myself. It was busywork, but I didn't care. I needed to do something productive.

The mansion and its once-luxurious gardens had been abandoned for nearly five decades, ever since my great-uncle Josiah Silverstone, my grandfather's brother, left Oklahoma for the Alaskan wilds.

My grandfather and his brother apparently had a falling out, but I had never been curious enough about the family drama to ask questions. I knew only that my grandfather came to Tulsa, married, built his own home, and raised his family within it.

I recall meeting Uncle Josiah once. When I was eight years old, I accompanied my grandparents on an Alaskan cruise, and we met my great-uncle for lunch in Juneau. He struck me as a very lonely man but, at the same time, was prickly and unkind. I didn't much like him, which was another reason I didn't pay attention to his life, or his death.

While Uncle Josiah lived, no one paid much attention to his estate moldering in Broken Heart. It didn't seem to bother my grandfather that his childhood home might be going to rot and ruin, so no one else had cause to worry about it, either.

When my great-uncle died, I remember how my grandfather grumbled about his brother's unusual will. Of course, I was still young and didn't understand much about probates or trusts. Uncle Josiah left the care of his estate to the family lawyers, and in his will stated that no one of Silverstone descent be allowed to live in or own the home.

Of course, these were the details I learned as an adult, and as I became familiar with the house and all its inherent problems. After a discussion with my father, we decided to take the offer by the mysterious Consortium, a powerful corporate think tank, but before they garnered full ownership, we—and by *we*, my father meant me— would inventory the place for whatever family treasures might be left.

The Consortium turned out to play an even bigger role in my life than simply buying the Silverstone house and lands.

I had never been told why Uncle Josiah abandoned the manse, or why he insisted no one occupy it. I was just grateful for a project—and I was nothing if not a woman who could organize.

On my first evening in town, Lorcan found me outside Broken Heart's one and only motel (now demolished). I'd been trying to coax a can of Sprite from the uncooperative soda machine. What can I say? All the modern technology in the world—and still no machines that dispensed chilled vodka and green olives.

Ah, but I was talking about Lorcan. Violent and insensible from the Taint, he threw me against the wall, tore open my neck, and sucked every drop of blood from me.

It was not a pleasant way to die.

I woke up undead—courtesy of the Consortium, which turned out to be an organization created by vampires who wanted to better the world. The idea was that, eventually, the Consortium would reach out to the human world so that, one day, parakind and mankind could live together—as they once had centuries ago. In the meanwhile, the Consortium's technological and medical breakthroughs were filtered to the humans via a complex network of businesses. Most humans employed by Consortium-owned companies would be shocked to know their bosses were vampires, werewolves, and fairies.

Not only had the Consortium purchased the mansion; they'd also been secretly buying up homes and businesses in town. Part of their motivation had been to create a parakind community, but magic and prophecy had brought them to Broken Heart. Odd, isn't it, how a small town in Oklahoma became so important to creatures most humans believe are mythological? In any case, the Consortium ousted most of the human residents, and did indeed create a haven for paranormal beings. However, it didn't seem we were any closer to bridging the gap between humans and ourselves.

For a while, my friend Jessica and her husband, Patrick, as well as their children, lived there. Eventually, they moved back to Jessica's old house on Sanderson Street. Now the mansion is occupied by Patsy, Gabriel, and their darling four-year-old triplets.

After I was Turned, I could hardly return to Tulsa or even to New York. Aside from the Consortium's encouragements for new vampires to stay within its protection, I found myself rather intrigued by the idea of being part of this new community. My parents were surprised when I told them I wanted to stay in Broken Heart, but they didn't question my choice. They certainly don't know that I'm a vampire. My parents travel a lot, and even when they're in town, they have many societal obligations. When I do manage a visit, I do so at night, and only for a little while.

I renovated the lovely old Victorian to suit me, and settled down into the life of a well-to-do bloodsucker.

I very much wanted to be a mother, and I will always regret never knowing the experience, the joys or the sorrows. I had hoped to have a little piece of it with Venice. No matter how small the slice of motherhood she might've allowed me, I would've been so much the happier for it.

Alas, motherhood had never really been an option for me.

I was not holding out for romantic love, either, and certainly not the giddy, passionate, moon-eyed kind that seemed to afflict so many of Broken Heart's residents.

What was that saying? Oh, yes. We were the sum total of our experiences. Sometimes, I felt more subtracted from than added to.

Thunder boomed.

Startled, I looked up into the cloud-swirled sky. It was nearing mid-September, and still warm by Oklahoma standards. The suddenness of the storm didn't concern me. The attitude of Oklahoma weather could be summed up thusly: *I'll do whatever I damn well like.* Come to think of it, that was also the attitude of the state's residents. Especially the ones in Broken Heart.

I shook off my pensive mood. Sunrise was in less than two hours. Like everything about my unlife, I embrace the sudden sleep that affects all vampires. I usually prepare for bed earlier than necessary, and read until I pass out.

My guilty pleasures are romance novels. Though I don't even dream of finding that kind of love in my own life, I very much enjoy reading about it. Happily-ever-after gives me a thrill of satisfaction. I enjoy every novel, and, when finished with one, I'm eager for the next.

The rain began in earnest, and, suddenly chilled, I went inside.

I paused by the hall tree. Thinking about Rand's silliness, hiding whatever object Patsy had discovered, I tugged up the seat.

Foreboding shot through me like a poisoned arrow. I knelt down and picked up the silver box. Uneasiness quelled my admiration of its simplistic beauty. As strange as it sounds, I felt like I was touching something evil. Something wrong.

I removed the lid.

Empty.

It was only a small square, maybe a couple inches around. Its dark blue silk lining pegged it as a jewelry container. I imagined it had once held a ring.

Then I saw my name was engraved on the lid.

Seeing the name made me shiver.

Elizabeth was a family name passed down through generations. It was likely that this item belonged to my great-grandmother, who was married to Jeremiah Silverstone. She'd died not long after their second child was born.

The box was tarnished, obviously old. I stared at the lid, and frowned. If the "Elizabeth" on the lid referred to my ancestor, and this was a family heirloom . . . then why did it feel like I was holding plutonium? It didn't belong here. It wasn't mine. And I had the strangest urge to chuck it out the front door.

Instead, I left it on the tea table in the parlor, and, fighting off a rousing case of the heebie-jeebies, locked up the house and retired to my bedroom.

The storm raged with a ferocity that made me distinctly uncomfortable. I lay among my pillows with the covers pulled up to my chin, like a child frightened of closet monsters. I tried to focus on the novel, but my gaze kept wandering to the flickering light of my bedside lamp.

We vampires didn't do coffins, but crypts were another matter. I had created my bedroom in the basement of the house as a precaution against sunlight. I added a full bathroom down here as well, with a Jacuzzi tub and a steam shower. Everything was luxurious, from the rich green, gold, and bronze colors of my decor to the Egyptian cotton sheets and towels.

Beautiful interior design and luxuriant materials, however, did not offer the kind of comfort I currently needed. I was too much the woman alone in her creaky old house—the horror-movie heroine stalked by an ax-wielding maniac.

I gulped.

I couldn't shake off my trepidation. No amount of

self-lecturing about my maturity or vampire skills (as my friend Jessica would say, I totally kick ass) or reminders to myself of protections (werewolves, Invisishield, neighbors) helped. Granted, my neighbors weren't exactly close. I lived on three acres, two acres of which were all woods. I had blazed my own trails hiking through there numerous times, but now the closeness of the forest merely represented optimal hiding places for the nefarious.

I badly wanted to hear another person's voice, but I would feel utterly ridiculous if I gave in to such an urge. How would I explain such a phone call to my friends?

It was still an hour away from sunrise.

I decided to make some jasmine tea to calm my nerves. I gave in to cowardice and used vampire speed to zip from my bed to the staircase that led directly into the kitchen.

The rain pounded like fists against the windows, making them rattle. I set the water to boil and wandered around, flipping on all the lights. I stopped in the parlor, my gaze falling on the little silver box. There it was, on the table where Rand and I had enjoyed our tea.

"Elizabeth!"

I whirled around. The man's angry voice didn't emanate from any obvious source. I reached out with my vampire senses and felt no one. Nothing. My own powers didn't include communing with the dead-*dead*. The very idea of a spirit roaming my house gave me the willies.

I snatched up the box, thinking I should just toss it into the trash. Would doing so end this nonsense? I was disturbed by its presence, and equally disturbed by my fear of it—and that voice.

"Elizabeth!" The scream pummeled my ears. *"You betrayed me!"*

"Who are you?" I cried.

I felt a pair of big male hands encompass my throat, and squeeze.

Chapter 2

I choked, backing away.

What was going on? Why were the sensations so strong? No one was in the room with me. But I'd lived in Broken Heart too long to discount even the craziest explanation. Ghosts. Demons. Invisible men.

Panic fluttered.

"S-stop!" I yelled. The violence of the act terrified me. I couldn't die from strangulation; I didn't need to breathe. But my windpipe could be crushed and my neck broken. Healing from such injuries would be terribly unpleasant.

"*Elizabeth.*" My name was a despairing sob, and the hands squeezed harder.

I moved out of the parlor and into my foyer. I couldn't turn around. I couldn't run. I couldn't escape.

I put my own hands to my throat and felt nothing, not even the barest outline of fingers—and yet it felt as if nails dug into my flesh. My throat threatened to collapse against the tremendous pressure.

I dropped the box.

Instantly, the strangulation ceased.

I fell to my knees and rubbed my bruised throat. I couldn't quite ease the ache, or the terror.

My gaze fell on the box, and I scrambled back from it. Whatever was trying to hurt me was using the jewelry container as the connection.

I sat there, trying to gather my courage, and I heard another voice, and with it an urge so fervid, I scrambled to my feet.

"I'm here," said a weeping female. *"Please find me. Please."*

A detailed image pierced my mind: Ringed by pine trees, an irregular stone marked the spot. Nearby was a fallen oak, and there, a path I often walked.

I knew this place.

I had to go.

"Yes," cried the voice. *"Hurry. Find me."*

I turned blindly for the front door and wrenched it opened, stumbling onto the porch.

The sunrise. How long did I have? Forty minutes? Less? Not long. Probably not long enough.

I felt compelled, as if my legs were obeying someone else's commands. Rain slapped at me, cold and stinging. Thunder cracked and lightning zigzagged from roiling black clouds.

I used my vampire speed to go around the house and make the trek to the woods. I had to slow down, though, because the path was strewn with fallen logs, stones, and holes. Still, I went as quickly as I could, grateful my supernatural vision let me penetrate the thick darkness.

I'm not sure how long it actually took to find the

area, maybe ten or fifteen minutes. I snaked through the trees, slipping through mud and puddles until I finally found the exact location. The storm was relentless, but I ignored its brutality. I dropped to my knees and started to dig.

Faster. Faster. *Faster.*

Wet soil flew in all directions, spattering me and assaulting my mouth. Rain stung my eyes, but I couldn't stop.

"Find her," I murmured. "Find her before he does."

Then the earth gave up its secret.

The female voice muttering in my mind faded away, and I was left alone in her grave.

"Oh, my God." My fingers slid over the skull. No vampire could cry—in a literal sense. But even without the satisfactory discharge of tears, I found myself weeping. I did not know the woman, but I felt a soul-deep sorrow for her death.

Her murder.

I heard a low, long growl. The disturbing noise came from my right. I would've pegged it as one of the lycanthropes who often did security rounds in their wolf forms. Yet, it sounded catlike.

Why would a were-cat be out here? There were only a few who lived in town, and they mostly kept to themselves. Turned out cats weren't social creatures, whether pet or shifter.

Then I heard other noises, and these came from the left.

Still the storm raged, giving cover to those who were apparently sneaking up on me.

Why? Who?

Someone else was in the woods with me. The violent spirit? My heart skipped a phantom beat. If the ghost, or whatever it was, had followed me into the woods, then my theory about its connection to the jewelry box was incorrect. If this was someone, or something, else, then their purpose was unknown. I owned this land, including the wooded area, and didn't expect anyone to be out here—certainly not in this storm.

More bones were being washed clean, but I couldn't take them all with me. I estimated that I had about twenty minutes before daybreak. I'd have to hurry to make it back to my house. I loathed leaving the rest of this poor soul here, but I could return in the evening to retrieve the remains.

I kept the skull close, and struggled out of the pit I'd dug.

The rain dampened my senses, but I could still hear something big moving in the woods. Most large animals in Broken Heart were shifters. A security lycan wouldn't try to hide its presence from me. Another series of cat yowls interrupted my ruminations.

My instincts screamed at me to get going. I hurried to the path, but my foot caught on debris and I tripped.

Oh, perfect. I landed on my side, splashing into an icy puddle. I spit out the nasty water as the skull rolled out of my grasp. I really was the heroine in a horror movie, waiting for the ax-wielding maniac to cut me down. What kind of moron left the safety of her home to follow a ghostly voice to a grave? At night? In a vicious storm?

So long as I was making idiotic choices, I decided I wouldn't leave the woods without the skull. I needed

something to show for my efforts, and, by God, the
woman deserved whatever closure I could give her. I
saw my ghoulish prize at the edge of the path, lodged
into a scraggly bush. I crawled to it and yanked it out.
Then I rose unsteadily to my feet, triumphant.

I stilled.

A cat, and, my goodness, was *that* an understate-
ment, crouched on the path four or five feet away from
me. He—and I couldn't help but think of it as *he*—
was massive, with sleek black fur and green-gold eyes.
He growled—a warning to me to stay put, or so I assumed. His muscles rippled under that glorious coat as
he moved into a pouncing stance. I gulped. A shifter, I
hoped. Otherwise, I'd have to believe a jaguar had been
living in Broken Heart without anyone noticing.

His unstaring gaze looked beyond me, his nostrils
flaring.

Fear pulsed through me, but I couldn't get my legs
to move. Even if I could tap into my vampire speed,
there were too many obstacles in the woods. I took an
unsteady step back, and he yowled.

I stopped.

The rain pounded me. My nightgown was plastered
against me, offering no shield, no warmth. My toes sunk
into the slick, cold mud. My hair lashed my face and
neck.

Seconds ticked by.

The dawn was coming—I felt it in my waning strength
and rising panic. I had to either risk the jag's attack or
risk roasting in the sunlight.

The cat roared: a terrible, fierce sound that sliced
right through me.

Something hard smacked me on the back of the head.

Pain spiked all the way down my spine, and I went down to my knees, my gaze on the beautiful, angry jag.

He tore down the path toward me.

My vision grayed as I fell forward.

The cat launched over me, and I marveled at his grace, at the power he so wonderfully exhibited. He knocked something—no, someone—over, and I heard sounds of a struggle.

Then I passed out.

"Lady? Aw, hell. C'mon, sweetheart. Wake up."

As I assimilated the unfamiliar male voice, I felt the sting of a light slap on my cheek. My eyes flew open.

"Stop that immediately!" I demanded.

His hazel eyes widened, and then he grinned. "No problem, princess. You wanna get up now?"

"Certainly." I took his proffered hand and struggled to my feet. I felt dizzy and light-headed. It had stopped raining, although the sky rumbled ominously. "Where's my skull?"

"Attached to your neck."

"Don't be ridiculous," I snapped. "I mean the one I dropped."

One brown eyebrow winged upward. I realized several important things right then. One, I didn't know this man. Two, he was quite handsome, with skin the color of caramel. And three, he was unaccountably naked and very, very well built.

And endowed by the gods.

Did I just look at his . . . his . . . *package*? Embarrassment shot through me, and I averted my gaze. Ah. I spotted the skull grinning up at me from a shallow puddle. I scooped it up and turned to the gorgeous nude man. For a moment, I couldn't get my throat to work. Finally, I managed a crisp "Thank you for your assistance."

I marched away.

He followed.

"You're welcome," he said lazily. "Anything else I can . . . assist you with?"

His sensually charged question nearly made me trip again. What the— Really? Sexual innuendoes *now*? And why did I feel like my cheeks had been dipped in lava? Vampires didn't blush.

I stopped, and turned to glare at him. "Are you a nudist?" I asked in a frosty tone.

"With the right person."

His gaze let me know that I could be the right person. Was he insane? I was muddy, my hair was a mess, and my clothing . . . Oh! I looked down and it was exactly as I feared. My satin nightgown was plastered to my body, outlining every curve and showcasing my turgid nipples. Oh, sweet heaven. If I waited long enough, maybe lightning would strike me.

I felt suddenly woozy, and, for a moment, I wondered if the man had rendered me nigh unconscious with his virility. Then I realized that was not the case at all. *Sunrise.* "H-how long was I out?"

"Five or six minutes," he said. "You didn't even ask about the creep who whacked you. What are you doing out here?"

"These are my woods. I can go wherever I like." I paused. "What creep?"

"I didn't get a good look. But he just about kicked my ass." Fury lurked in his eyes. "That doesn't happen too often."

Someone had followed me. Or had been here already. Had they known I was looking for . . . well, whomever I found? Were they compelled by the same intuition, the same sorrowful begging? If they'd arrived for the same purpose I did, then they wouldn't have struck me. Could a ghost do such a thing?

No. My rescuer had fought someone. This someone was either in the woods to find the grave, to hurt me, or for some other reason. Had I been mistaken for a predator?

The very idea was laughable.

However, now I knew who, or rather what, this man was.

"Most women I know collect purses and shoes." He glanced at the skull, then at me.

"I'm not most women." Alas, I did love shopping for shoes. "You're the jaguar."

He hesitated, as if considering whether or not to admit it, and then nodded. "You don't seem surprised."

"New in town, aren't you?" Wooziness made me sway. The man grabbed my elbow to steady me. "I must get home before the sun rises."

"Why? You turn into a pumpkin?"

"I die." I felt sluggish. As a shifter, he seemed to have a limited knowledge of parakind—and didn't seem aware of my undeadness. Did I risk telling him I was a vampire? No. I'd risked enough already. "I have a severe allergy to the sunlight."

We hadn't yet made it out of the woods. It was getting too close to sunrise and I felt as weak as a newborn kitten. "I hate to ask a favor so soon after you saved my life," I said, "but would you mind helping me to my house?"

"You always talk so prissy?"

"Excuse me?" I asked.

"It's just kinda hot, is all."

"Hot?"

"You know. Sexy."

"My way of speaking has never been described in quite that way."

"Better stop talkin' all fancy, princess, or I just might kiss you."

I don't know how he managed to turn "princess" into an endearment that offered both complaint and compliment. My gaze dropped to his mouth, and I watched his lips curve into a delicious smile. A dark yearning wound through me, and I looked up at him, feeling rather stunned.

"Promise you'll look at me that way tomorrow," he said.

"I'll do no such thing."

He laughed, and the sound vibrated all the way through me. "By the way, I'm Tez. Tez Jones."

"That's the most suspect name I've ever heard," I said, which garnered another laugh from the so-called Tez. I bristled. Then I straightened and inclined my head. "I'm Elizabeth Bretton."

"Perfect name for you. Sounds *prissy*," he said. "You live in the Victorian house up the hill, right?"

"Yes." He'd done enough snooping around to realize my house wasn't too far. Yet, he hadn't known that

I lived there. I simply had to trust him. Either that, or risk being exposed to the sun. I was too weak to use my vampire speed to get home.

He scooped me into his arms, and I yelped.

"Better hang on, Ellie Bee."

"Ellie Bee!" I repeated, horrified. I looped one arm around his neck, and clung to the skull with my free hand. "That's a terrible nickname. Don't you dare call me that again."

"Seriously. I'm gonna kiss you."

He ran all the way to my house.

Tez refused to put me down, not until he'd tucked me into bed himself. No amount of protests would make the man leave or do as I bid. I had no choice but to accede to his wishes, which I must say was rather unusual. I was used to being fully in charge of my own life; not even Henry had argued with me.

I was filthy, but I had no time to shower—and I'd rather walk into the dawn than allow Tez to undress me while I was passed out. So, there I was, caked in mud, hair wet, and gown ruined, and I didn't even care. I hadn't even the merest second to shed my nightie.

Tez pulled the covers up to my chin and tucked me in. I refused to give up the skull, so Tez propped it ghoulishly onto the pillows next to me.

Then it was simply too late to worry about Tez or his intentions.

I fell into dreamless vampire sleep.

When I awoke in the darkened room, I was met with the gaping stare of a dirt-crusted skull.

I screamed.

"Princess!" I heard Tez's cry all the way from upstairs. Then he was hurrying down into my room, where he smacked into something and cursed a blue streak. "Damn it! Where's the light switch in this mausoleum?"

Trembling, I flipped on my bedside lamp and saw Tez rubbing his shins.

"I thought cats had excellent night vision." I flinched at the rudeness of my tone, but I was off-kilter. At least he wasn't naked anymore. No, he was wearing the matching robe to my ruined nightgown. I tugged the covers back up to my shoulders. I felt grimy. My sheets were now as ruined as my clothing. I wanted a shower. And blood. And to regain some control.

"Screaming women tend to make me panic." He grinned. "Okay, not *all* screaming women." His gaze flicked to the skull sitting on the pillows. "You having morning-after regrets?"

"Your humor leaves much to be desired, Mr. Jones." I leveled him with a suspicious look. "*If* that's your real name."

"My real name is Tezozomoc Abraham Elvis Jones."

I blinked. "I see why you prefer Tez."

He laughed. He started to cross the room, but I held up my hand. "I'm sure you understand my need for caution, Mr. Jones. I don't know you, or your purpose. And I only have your word that you—" I couldn't get over what he was wearing. "The only suitable attire you could find was my robe?"

"I didn't want to leave you alone. I ditched my clothes in my car, which is still parked by the Thrifty Sip. I didn't want to dig through your stuff," he said. "Well, except your panty drawer. I couldn't resist. Nice undies, Ellie Bee."

"Mr. Jones!" I struggled to regain my composure. The robe fit atrociously. It didn't even close at the top; he had too much chest and too many muscles. On me, it swept my ankles; on him, it barely reached his knees. The belt, cinched around his waist, just added to the ridiculousness. I tried to stop staring at his chest. I'm afraid I wasn't successful. Of course, the natural progression of my line of sight led me straight to his groin. I had excellent recall. He certainly was gifted in that particular area.

"You keep looking at me like that, princess, I might forget my manners."

I wouldn't pretend I didn't know what he meant, and I couldn't deny that a small part of me wanted to shuck off the covers and lead him into the shower with me. It had been rather a long time since I'd been in a relationship. I was, much to my own shock, thinking of sex. Hot, sweaty, oh-my-God sex. I couldn't recall ever being seized by pure lust before. It was exhilarating.

"That's it. I'm coming over there."

"Don't you dare!" I glared at him, but he hadn't moved. He was giving me a smoky look, though, one edged with amusement, so he knew I was flustered and thought it was funny. What was wrong with me? I didn't even know this man!

"Did you really go through my underwear?" I asked tartly.

"Yep. I even picked out a few of my favorite pairs. I put 'em on top." He shook his head. "I was a little disappointed with the available colors. No red?"

"I refuse to discuss my lingerie with you. And I do not appreciate your assumption that you're going to see me in my undergarments. Ever." I paused and tried to gather my wits. And tone down my ... well, lust. My gaze meandered along the robe again. Wow. He was really built. "Could you find no other appropriate attire?"

He grinned at me, and my stomach took a peculiar dive. "I love that mouth of yours, princess. Go on. Talk pretty to me."

"You're insufferable."

"Aw. I bet you say that to all the jaguars."

Would nothing stop his rampant flirting? I had the insane urge to smile at him, but instead I rolled my eyes. I did not want to encourage his bad behavior. Much. "Please go upstairs, Mr. Jones. We'll talk after I take a shower."

"You need help scrubbing your back?"

"No," I said primly. He opened his mouth and I lifted my hand in a *stop* gesture. "Nor do I need help washing any of my other parts."

"My morning is really starting to suck." He sighed at me, then turned and deliberately sashayed away.

I couldn't quell my laughter.

He flashed another grin at me over his pink-clad shoulder. I tried to think of something else I could offer him to wear, but I wasn't a sweatpants kind of girl—and I had no men's clothing. Aside from Tez draping himself toga-style in a tablecloth or sheet, the robe was the best option. I swear, it had nothing to do with the way the material clung to his rather impressive buttocks.

Tez took the stairs two at a time. After I heard the door shut, I went up and locked it. I must admit, at least to myself, that I rather liked Tez. More than I should, given that we had just met—and under the oddest circumstances. However, continued trust was another issue. It had to be earned.

I put in a call to Damian, a lycanthrope who was in charge of town security, and asked him to drop by. Then I took a scalding shower.

Mud caked my skin. It took two good scrubbings to feel clean—and I used half a bottle of shampoo on my hair. By the time I finished up, nearly half an hour had passed. I dressed in a pair of beige pants and a cowl-neck top in dark brown. I blew my hair dry and pushed back the mass of blond curls with a tortoiseshell headband. I put in my diamond earrings and slipped on a pair of beaded mules.

I gently picked up the pillow on which the skull rested and carried it upstairs.

Tez and Damian were in the kitchen.

Tez leaned on the counter near the stove with his arms crossed. A bruise stained his cheek and a cut slivered the skin above his eye. My robe was torn across the shoulders, too.

Damian sat on a barstool by the island. He had a shiner, and a sullen expression. He rubbed his scraped and swollen knuckles.

"What happened?" I put the pillow with its cargo onto the counter closest to Tez. I turned and glared at Tez, then at Damian. I hadn't heard the ruckus, so it must have been a brief, if brutal, altercation.

"He hit me," answered Damian. "So, I hit him back, *Liebling*. His skull is like marble."

"Tez!" I studied his banged-up face.

"I didn't know who he was," he said. He squinted at me. "Still don't. He says you called him."

"Of course I did." I supposed it might've helped matters if I'd thought to inform Tez about Damian's imminent arrival, or had told the werewolf to expect to meet a were-jag. It didn't occur to me that Damian would arrive so quickly. I really was off my game today.

Well. Enough was enough. I needed to get control of the situation—and myself. I made up two bags of ice, and gave one to Damian. I slapped Tez's hand out of the way and pushed the bag onto his bruised cheek.

"Ow! Careful, princess."

I ignored him and focused on pressing the ice pack carefully against his injury. "Damian is the head of security. We must tell him about the skeleton I found and the attack." I glanced apologetically at Tez. "I'm sorry I forgot to tell you"—I paused to look over my shoulder and smiled at Damian—"or you, about other."

"You wearing the black ones?" Tez asked, as if he didn't even hear me.

I gaped at him.

His gaze dropped to my waist and he spent an inordinate amount of time perusing my southern region. "'Cause I really liked those."

"Must you insist on embarrassing me?" I hissed.

"I dunno. Are you really embarrassed?"

I wasn't. Not much. I was actually both irritated and thrilled that he flirted so outrageously with me and didn't care who was watching. Then I had another flash of insight: He was letting Damian know of his interest in me. It was the testosterone-filled equivalent of yelling, "Dibs!"

Now I was completely irritated.

"Cotton panties, full-cheek coverage," I said, plopping the ice bag into his hand. "Beige. With an extra-wide waistband."

"You are a cruel woman."

I sniffed, and turned toward the lycanthrope. If I didn't know better, I'd say something like amusement sparkled in Damian's eyes. But he smiled so rarely and seemed to take everything so seriously that everyone had decided he didn't have a sense of humor.

"I found a dead body last night," I said.

Damian's eyes went wide.

"Bones," corrected Tez. "Old bones. Buried in the woods." He reached over and patted the top of the skull. "See? She brought back a souvenir."

"Oh. That's different," said Damian. "You know we find graves every now and again—usually family plots that are unmarked or have lost their headstones. Eva told us that sometime in the 1920s, the town moved its cemetery to the current location. Not every body made it."

Tez snorted a laugh.

I slanted him a look.

"What? I like gallows humor."

Damian frowned, as if he didn't quite get the joke. I sighed. "I think I should talk to Patsy." I explained to him about the disembodied voice and the choking incident. He looked concerned, but I'm almost positive it was because he was worried about the security issues of an unknown and violent assailant. Damian was very good at his job, and didn't let pesky emotion get in the way of performing his duties.

"What about him?" asked Damian.

We both turned to look at Tez.

"I have an invite," said Tez. He turned around and bared his shoulder, revealing a tattoo: a red heart with double swords piercing it.

"It's a temporary tattoo," said Damian, "developed by Brady and Dr. Michaels. It allows prospective residents to pass through the Invisi-shield. After ten days, the tattoo dissolves"—he sent a narrowed looked to Tez—"and so does the invitation."

The Invisi-shield was a creation of technological genius and old-world magic. All the residents' DNA codes were programmed within it, which allowed us to go in and out without problems. Anyone who didn't belong in Broken Heart couldn't get through the shield and would set off the alarms.

"You didn't come to the checkpoint," accused Damian. "Who sent you the tattoo?"

"Alpha Calphon," said Tez, referring to the leader of the were-cats. He shrugged. "Believe me, I was just as surprised as anyone to find out there was a whole town full of paranormal beings in the middle of Nowhere, Oklahoma. I wanted to check out things for myself."

"Before you revealed yourself?" I asked. "You're not anywhere near the were-cat commune. It's on the far side of town, well past the main living areas of the other residents."

He tapped the side of his nose. "I followed this . . . straight to you."

Well, what did that mean? His gaze was dark and intense, and I felt branded by the heat of those hazel eyes. *Mine,* he seemed to say.

How ridiculous.

I pressed a hand against my stomach to still the feeling of butterflies taking wing there. He made me crazy, that were-jaguar.

He gave me the once-over. "What exactly are you, princess?"

"Vampire," I said.

"Really?" He studied my mouth, probably to see my fangs, which only appeared when I fed. Or got really angry. I pressed my lips together and glared at him.

He grinned. "Didn't figure vampires were real."

"But shifters are normal?" I asked, amazed he knew so little about the paranormal world. How could he believe shifting into a jaguar was stranger than meeting someone undead?

"Always been a shifter," he said. "Never met anyone else like me."

"And what are you?" asked Damian. "You do not smell like the other cats."

"He's a jaguar," I said. Oddly, I sounded rather proud, as though his other form were mine to gloat about.

"That's impossible." Damian stood and wrapped his fingers around my wrist. I got the impression he planned to yank me behind him and do something silly. Like hit Tez again.

Tez leaned against the counter, looking unaccountably masculine in my pink satin robe, and pressed the ice bag to his cheek. His expression was inscrutable.

"Damian—"

"No, Elizabeth. He's a liar." Damian pulled me, but I resisted. I glanced at him, surprised at the fury in his gaze. "Jaguar shifters are extinct."

Chapter 3

"I saw him in his jaguar form." I gently removed myself from Damian's protective grip. "He saved my life, and I will not think ill of him"—I slanted a glance at Tez, who was smirking—"unless he gives me reason to do so."

His smirk widened into a grin.

"I'll believe him when I see him shift," said Damian.

"You first, cupcake," drawled Tez.

Damian's eyes narrowed. He stepped past me with clenched fists. I gripped his shoulder and hauled him back. Having vampiric strength was certainly advantageous when dealing with an angry werewolf.

"Enough, boys," I said. "Damian, I think it would be wise for us both to talk to Patsy. Would you make those arrangements? Perhaps take a look at the woods to see if you can determine who might've attacked me?"

Damian looked as though he wanted to protest, but his duty to the safety of Broken Heart, and me, won out over his animal instincts. "Yes, *Liebling*. I'll call Patsy and update her as well." He nodded good-bye to me, launched one last fulminating glare at Tez, and left.

Whew.

"I'm starving," said Tez. "You gonna feed me?"

I rolled my eyes. "Why am I in charge of your . . . your . . ." I waved my hand around, agitated by his caveman attitude. "Gustatory pleasures?"

Tez dropped the bag of ice into the sink, then sauntered toward me. I wasn't sure how I felt about the look in his eyes. It seemed just as fulminating as Damian's, but in a much more sexually combustible way.

"What was that you said again?" he asked. "About my pleasures?"

Once again, he was scrambling my good sense. He was the biggest flirt I'd ever met, and everything about the man was designed to make a woman crazed with lust. I'd had far too many inappropriate thoughts about him already.

He managed to back me against the kitchen island, a smile playing on his lips as his gaze sparkled with a mixture of humor and desire. *Oh. My.*

I needed to retrieve control of the situation. "I'll drop you off at the Old Sass Café while I attend to my own breakfast."

"And what do you eat?" His gaze suggested he had a menu in mind, though I doubted it consisted of the carotid artery.

"I'm a vampire. I drink blood."

"Huh. Not sure how I feel about you gnawing necks. Especially another guy's." He stood mere inches from me. He wore his hair short on the sides, and spiked on the top. It was almost militaristic, but the look fit him perfectly. He was too sexy. I felt my pulse stutter, which was ridiculous because I had no pulse.

"We hardly know each other," I said. "So, your opinion about my dining options is irrelevant." His gaze darkened even more, and he leaned forward. I licked my lips. I liked the way he was looking at me, and I liked the way I felt. In this moment, I was the only woman in the world; and this man, this gorgeous man, wanted only me. So, as Tez had asked earlier, I decided to talk pretty to him. "Yes. Your opinion simply doesn't count. Neither does your inexplicable ire about the gender of my donors."

"Jesus. That vocabulary of yours makes me hot." His gaze went unnaturally still—a rather eerie reminder of how his jaguar self looked right before it pounced. "But that snotty tone of yours is what really gets me hard."

My stomach dropped to my toes, and I swear I could feel the pounding of my undead heart. It was nonsense, of course, but I almost felt alive around Tez. He didn't appear to care very much about manners or politically correct behavior. Of course, the citizens of Broken Heart weren't the type to beat around the bush. I'd grown to like the direct way most people talked to each other; it was far better than dancing around expected behaviors in polite company. It seemed that Tez would fit in just fine in our little town. Tez's particular brand of directness was . . . well, rather a turn-on (there, I said it). I swallowed the knot—or was that my heart?—in my throat. "You're very earthy."

He grinned again, but the gesture was more a feral parting of his lips, and a show of a lot of white teeth. Yet another predatory move that unnerved me. I wasn't used to such intense attention, especially not from a man. "Say that thing about gusta-whatever."

I couldn't resist playing the game, even if I wasn't sure about the rules. I looked at him through my lashes. "You mean . . . gustatory pleasures?"

He leaned down and sucked on my lower lip. I was stunned by his action, and found myself too flabbergasted to protest such an intimate gesture. He swept a thumb over my swollen lip. "You taste like cinnamon."

"It's my gloss." *Oh, excellent comeback, Elizabeth.* I stifled a groan of embarrassment. Obviously I was ill-prepared for flirting. I needed one of those "For Dummies" guides—then again, I didn't think there was a book available that would teach me how to deal with Tez.

"Hmm. I like it." He leaned in to smell my hair. "You gonna introduce me to your meal?"

His closeness discombobulated me. He was doing it on purpose, to keep me off guard. "What would be the point?"

"To see if he's better looking than me."

Hah. An opening I could use.

"He's utterly gorgeous," I said with a dreamy sigh. Well! Maybe I could play the coquette. "Sometimes, I sit on his lap, wrap my arms around those big, broad shoulders, and just . . . *lick*." I looked at Tez, and smiled. "We should go now, so I can suck on his delicious neck."

"I might have to kill this guy," said Tez, his eyes glinting with humor. He leaned down and tugged my earlobe between his teeth. I felt his tongue trace the inner shell of my ear, which made me tingle all the way to my toes. Then he whispered, "You really are a cruel woman."

I pushed him, and, to my relief, he backed up a couple of steps. "Just remember that," I said primly.

"Oh, I will," he said, baring that feral grin. "I like it down and dirty. Rough. Hard. Mean." His toothy grin widened. "I think you're the perfect woman for me."

I drove Tez to his car, parked at the Thrifty Sip. The convenience store had been abandoned for a long time, and due to an accidental dragon fire, it was now just a burned-out shell. I gave Tez directions to the Old Sass Café and agreed to meet him there in a half an hour. He had no problem shedding the robe and redressing right there next to his car.

I'd already seen him naked, and I very much enjoyed staring at his impressive form. The problem, of course, was resisting the urge to touch all those muscles. Not to mention the things my mouth wanted to do him.

I looked in my rearview mirror. "Who *are* you?" I whispered. "Where's proper Elizabeth Silverstone Bretton?"

I left before Tez witnessed my drooling—and encouraged me to do something about it. I had lust issues, and I wasn't quite sure what to do about my overwhelming attraction. I couldn't recall ever imagining a lover falling into a vat of chocolate, which I then laved from him, ankles to lips. What about Tez inspired such fantastical thoughts?

For a vampire with lack of body temperature, I felt unaccountably hot.

I drove to my donor's home, a five-bedroom ranch on Sanderson Street. Donors often shared domiciles since the turnover rate was so high; most spent limited time as vampire meals. Of course, humans who left Broken Heart had their memories wiped (and new memories implanted). Some stuck around for the long haul, though, and had homes of their own.

Although some vampires preferred seeking out the same donors, I enjoyed the variety. I arrived at approximately the same time each evening and dined on whoever was available. Had I been given the choice to Turn or to die, I would've chosen Turning. Granted, there were sacrifices, but there were also wonderful benefits, and I embraced my vampire nature. Certainly, I sometimes thought about what life would've been like had I not become undead. In the more than five years since Henry's death, if I had not become a vampire, what would I have done with my life? Despite Henry's libidinous behavior, I did love him. We didn't have the everlasting love I so often read about in my favorite books, but his passing did put my life into a tailspin. Maybe I would've traveled or found someone new to love or . . . well, the possibilities were many. But I couldn't dwell on the life I didn't get to have. I loved Broken Heart and its quirky residents, and I loved my vampire gifts. I did wish, however, that I had a larger purpose, a bigger role to fulfill in this world in which I now lived. But I had yet to figure what, exactly, would make me feel more useful.

When I arrived at the donor house, Harold Panner met me at the door. He was in his forties with thinning blond hair and a slight paunch. He loved all variations of brown and beige, which frankly did nothing for his coloring. He needed more jeweled tones, more blue, green, or even purple. Harold had been a real estate agent in Tulsa who'd lost nearly everything—his job, his home, and his wife. He'd been on the precipice of suicide when

Patrick O'Halloran found him and invited him to become a donor.

I liked Harold. He was nice. We sat in the kitchen and talked for a little while. Then he shyly offered his neck, and I took my pint. Vampire saliva had a numbing agent to prevent pain, and healing properties to erase the marks left by our fangs.

After the feeding was over, Harold walked me to the door. He shook my hand, his eyes bright—pleasure was often a residual effect of feeding—and we said our good-byes.

"Elizabeth!" called a familiar voice. I paused on the sidewalk and looked down the street. My friends Jessica and Patrick live just a couple houses away. Patrick O'Halloran was the twin of Lorcan, the vampire who, crazed with the Taint, had killed me and ten others. Patrick and Lorcan were also the sons of Ruadan, the very first of our kind. Lorcan and Patrick had founded the Consortium more than five hundred years ago. However, the current leader of the organization was Ivan Taganov. He didn't spend a lot of time in Broken Heart, partially because the woman he'd nearly mated with had fallen in love with someone else, and . . . well, I think he just didn't like Broken Heart. However, he had to drop in every now and again since the majority of the Consortium's work was done here. He was a big man, a little overwhelming in both looks and nature. He seemed to have perfected the scowl, too.

Jessica waved at me, then continued to survey a deep gouge in her lawn. Curiosity got the better of me. I joined her and we studied the odd slash in her otherwise perfect yard. "What happened?"

"I don't know," said Jess. "It looks like a monster comma. I mean, did God reach down with a giant finger and make a punctuation mark in my grass?"

"Perhaps Bryan . . . ?"

"He's in Stillwater. He's got a girlfriend, and he wanted to spend the weekend with her." Her tone held both worry and pride. Bryan knew how to keep our secrets, so the worry must be related to the fact her son was grown and dating. She was proud of him for going to college, but I got the impression she wasn't quite ready to let go.

Broken Heart had its own night school with one teacher, Eva O'Halloran. She was the town historian, and colibrarian of the substantial Consortium archives— duties that she shared with her husband, Lorcan (yes, *that* Lorcan). Since Broken Heart technically doesn't exist, the Consortium set up an accredited online high school so children who graduate from their studies could attend college. Bryan had chosen to attend Oklahoma State University, OSU, and was working on a journalism degree.

"Jenny wants a Vespa," said Jessica. Her gaze narrowed. "Does that look Vespa-like to you? Like maybe a girl who didn't know what the hell she was doing on a freaking Vespa spun through a perfectly landscaped yard?"

I knew better than to answer such questions.

"She's fourteen," I said. "Too young to drive around a scooter."

"She also has her stepfather wrapped around her pinky. And this is Broken Heart where rules for normal people don't apply." She rolled her eyes. Then she glanced at me. "Before I track down my family and solve the mystery of the lawn comma, tell me about the jaguar hottie."

I shouldn't have been surprised that she already knew about Tez. The small-town grapevine worked even faster on a paranormal scale. I shrugged. "He was invited to town by the were-cat alpha."

"Why?"

I blinked. I hadn't even thought to ask Tez why he'd been invited. I had assumed he merely was interested in living among his own kind. But then, he hadn't petitioned to live here. *Hmm.*

"I don't know. But Tez was in the woods behind my house. He saved me from an attacker."

"Attacker?" Jessica looked shocked. "Who the hell would want to hurt you?"

I shook my head. "I don't remember much."

"Wait. What were you doing out in the woods anyway?" She turned to fully face me, her expression filled with concern.

I felt like I'd entered the conversation at the wrong end. I started over, explaining everything from the moment I received the odd little box, to the ghostly attack, to the female voice urging me to go to the woods—less than an hour before dawn. "I found her grave," I summed up. "And dug her up."

Jessica's mouth dropped open. "Holy freaking shit."

"The bones are old," I said. "Damian thinks someone buried a dead relative in the woods. Or perhaps I uncovered a family cemetery."

"Is that what you think?"

"No," I said reluctantly. "I have no proof. Just . . . feelings. I think she was murdered, Jess."

"You gonna talk to Patsy?" She wiggled her fingers as if casting a spell. "She can kick any ghost's ass."

I hoped that was true. I wasn't too thrilled about facing the entity again. Being attacked by something unseen was terrifying—even for a vampire.

"I'm definitely going to consult with Patsy. Right now, I need to meet up with Tez."

"Tez. That's his name?" asked Jessica. One eyebrow winged upward. "Seriously?"

I held up my palm. "Swear."

"Mo chroi." Patrick hovered above us. Literally. As a vampire from the Family Ruadan, who were part *Sidhe*, or fairy, he had the ability to fly. He landed softly on the ground next to his wife.

"Elizabeth," he said in his Irish-tinted voice. "How are you?"

"I'm very well," I said. "And you?"

"I'm—" His words stalled as he looked at his wife. Jessica sent him a sizzling look of fury, and his gaze slid guiltily to the mark in the lawn.

"I'll see you later," I trilled. Then I hurried to my car.

When I arrived at the Old Sass Café, I found Tez ensconced in a booth with two vaguely familiar young women. Tez patted the seat next to him, his eyes gleaming. I had yet to determine what, exactly, made his eyes sparkle like that. Nothing good, I was sure. His werewolf-inflicted facial injuries had already healed. I slid in next to him, planting my large purse between us.

"Good evening," I said to the ladies. "I'm Elizabeth Bretton."

"Tawny," said the red-haired vixen on the left. Her

eyes glittered with challenge. She wore a low-cut blouse showing off perfect cleavage. She tossed a flirtatious grin at Tez. I slanted a look at him. He grinned. He was enjoying the attention. The man was such a . . . a hound. Oh, you know what I mean.

"I'm Serri," said the woman on the right. She was a brunette with gorgeous caramel highlights and a green gaze that was much friendlier. "We heard about Tez's arrival and couldn't wait to meet him."

"Turns out I'm very rare," said Tez in a voice that was filled with innuendo.

I resisted the urge to kick him in the ankle. Did he have to sound so I'll-eat-you-up-my-pretty?

"You should come meet the rest of the clan. After all, *we*"—Tawny tossed a glare in my direction—"are your kind."

"We've never met a jaguar," said Serri, sending her friend a cutting look. "As far as any of the clans are aware, the were-jags died out long ago."

"Well, there was at least one around thirty-four years ago hanging out in the Mexican jungles," said Tez.

"And he mated with a human female?" asked Serri. Her and Tawny's expressions both held disbelief.

"Probably didn't have much choice," said Tez. "Especially if ol' Pops was the last jag shifter."

"Human and were-cat unions don't usually produce offspring," said Serri skeptically. "At least none that I've ever heard of."

"Perhaps only were-jags can mate with humans." I smiled at Tez. "Your mother must've been very special."

"Or just convenient." Tez smiled back, but his attempt at levity didn't take the edge off his bitter tone.

I was taken aback. His paternal-inspired anger added a new layer to this man, who was flirtatious, sexy, dutiful, and far too macho. I wondered what it had been like for him growing up with a human mother, knowing that his father had abandoned her and the child she carried. Tez had his secrets . . . but didn't we all?

My cell rang. I plucked the iPhone from my purse and answered.

"I heard you had a real interesting morning," said Patsy. "Those dawn shenanigans can get you killed, you know."

"I'll try to cut down on my aberrant behavior."

Tez's hand snaked out and squeezed my thigh. I'd have to remember to use "aberrant behavior" in the future—and not just in conversation. I lightly slapped at his hand and he removed it, but I could still feel the lingering heat of his fingers. It was surely a phantom sensation because I was wearing pants and my undead flesh didn't retain warmth.

"Well, can you come on by?" asked Patsy. "And bring the cat man with you. I gotta show you something, Elizabeth. It's some crazy shit, too."

"You've spoken to Damian?" I asked.

"Yeah. He'll need you to lead him to the location of the . . . er, find. And if you got a ghost, I'll talk to the bastard. But first, come by here."

"I'll bring the box," I said. "I think he's attached to it somehow."

"Peachy. Like I don't have enough assholes to deal with." She blew out a breath. "Don't worry, Elizabeth. I'll take care of whoever's bothering you."

"Thank you." We said our good-byes. I looked at

Tez. "That was Queen Patricia. She asked us to drop by. However, I have to return to the house before we see her."

"Okay. I'll follow you out there." He nodded toward his new friends. "Ladies."

"Calphon is hosting a welcome party for you so you can meet the clan," said Tawny. "Do you need a place to stay? We have a very comfortable . . . couch."

Her gaze was all daggers as she stared at me. She cast a sultry look at Tez, and, I swear, she simpered. *Goodness*.

"That's sweet of you," said Tez, "but I already have digs lined up." He pulled out a couple of business cards and handed one to each of the women. "Look forward to meeting the rest of the cats."

Serri looked down at the card. "You're a cop?"

Surprised, I paused in gathering my purse and stared at Tez.

"Yeah," he said. "I'm a homicide detective with the Tampa Police Department." He looked at me with raised brows. "We leaving, or what?"

I scooted out of the seat and Tez followed me. He put his hand on the small of my back, then smiled down at the were-cats. "Nice to meet you both."

"We'll see you soon, Tez," said Tawny.

I gave them a little wave, then turned and headed out of the diner. I felt perplexed by my feelings. My jealousy was absurd! Tez could spend time with whomever he chose. And certainly any woman, particularly a cat shifter, would be interested in him.

We stopped on the sidewalk. My Lexus was about three cars down from Tez's Honda in the front parking area.

"You're a homicide detective?" I asked. "And you're only thirty-four?"

"Thirty-three," he said. "And yeah, I'm with the murder squad. Only I'm on sabbatical." He frowned at me. "Why the interest in my age?"

If I hadn't died at the age of forty-three, I would be celebrating my forty-eighth birthday in a couple of months. That would make me nearly fifteen years older than Tez. I could hardly see Patrick holding his four-thousand-years-plus against Jessica, so it wasn't particularly fair for me to consider the years between me and Tez. Still, I felt old and I would've preferred to feel age-*less. Damn*. What was I doing even worrying about our age difference? It wasn't as though we were, or would be, a couple.

"You're not doing that woman's math in your head, are you?" he asked. "Vampires don't age, so you can't do addition."

"You have no idea what I'm thinking," I said, mortified that he'd guessed at my thoughts.

"Shit. You are doing math." He shook his head, his lips quirking. "Whatever the problem is, you need to get over it, princess. 'Cause I'm not letting you being undead and me being a shifter get in the way of us."

"You've decided that, have you?"

"God, I love that snotty tone." He stepped closer, his gaze hot. "Yeah, I've decided. Now, you just need to decide, and we can move on."

"Are you aware that sleeping with a vampire basically means you're married for the next century?"

"Sleeping with," he whispered, "or fucking?"

His coarse language sent a dark thrill shooting through

me. He knew it, too, because his lips pulled into that feral grin—the one that all but said he'd enjoy knocking over every obstacle I put in his way. For what? Sex? Well, I couldn't have sex, not in the traditional ways—though, lovemaking certainly didn't have to rely on penetration. *Good Lord.* I couldn't believe I was even having these sorts of thoughts.

Tez was corrupting me . . . and I liked it.

"If you have intercourse with me," I said, "then you're my husband for the next hundred years. And you can't have sex with anyone else, either." I looked at him down my nose and pursed my lips, casting him a superior gaze. Jessica had once described this look as "snooty bitch."

"I so want to bend you over right now."

Shock nearly buckled my knees. "Tez!" I gaped at him. "Don't you have a filter between your brain and your mouth?"

"Yeah. But I don't use it much. As for a hundred years of being hitched to you, I don't see the down side." He tweaked my nose. "But I guess *you* need time to think about it. C'mon, I'll follow you to your house."

I was still flummoxed by his assertions—and his bold sexual statements. "I don't need an escort."

"I know," he said. "You're tough as nails, Ellie Bee. Still. I'll park at your place. No reason for us to drive two cars to meet Queen What's-her-face. Anyway, I need to stow my stuff."

"Stow your . . ." I trailed off and stared at him. "Where, exactly, are you staying in Broken Heart?"

"With you."

"I don't recall issuing an invitation."

"You don't?" He reached for a loose curl and tugged

on it. "It was in the woods last night. You know, when some wack-job tried to off you."

The way he played with the strand of hair made me feel tingly. I had the oddest impression that he planned to sweep me into his arms and kiss me. My stomach squeezed, and I found myself licking my lips—as though preparing for that kiss. His gaze wandered around my mouth, and I felt the blood rushing away from my head. (Except that I really had very little blood to rush.) Around Tez, I felt keenly off balance. The strange thing, however, was how much I enjoyed that sensation of free-falling.

I cleared my throat, and plucked the curl from his blunt fingertips. I skewered him with another haughty look. "Are you saying that I don't know how to protect myself?"

"Nope. I'm saying, ain't nobody gonna kill my girl." He turned me around, aimed me toward my car, and patted my buttocks. "Meet you at the house, Ellie Bee."

For the love of heaven! How could this man's chauvinistic behavior make me weak-kneed? It was such a primal response. I hadn't felt in control of my emotions since I met Tez. Why not just live in a cave and wait for him to cudgel me with a club? *Humph.* Would I also cherish him dragging me along by my hair? I tried to feel offended, I really did. But those un-Elizabeth-like naughty thrills kept getting in the way. Whatever was I going to do about him?

I glanced over my shoulder, but Tez was already sliding into his car. I heard him whistling and instantly recognized the Elvis song "Don't Be Cruel."

* * *

We arrived at my house, and while Tez unloaded two duffels from the trunk of his car, I went inside. I unearthed a hatbox from my closet, layered it with tissue paper, and returned to the kitchen. The skull rested on its silk pillow, sadly regal, and I wondered again about to whom it belonged—and why she had wanted me to find her. As I placed the skull inside the hatbox, Tez walked into the kitchen with his gear and ambled toward the door that led to my bedroom.

"Excuse me, but where do you think you're going?" I asked.

"I figured I'd put my underwear in with yours. That way they could all get to know each other." One brown eyebrow lifted. "Unless you want to make some formal introductions right now?"

I ignored the sexual taunt. Oh, all right. I pretended to ignore it. My body had other reactions, but I took control. Barely. "You're not living with me," I said icily. "You're visiting."

He studied me, spending an inordinate amount of time on my breasts, and then he sighed. "Which room you giving me?"

"Gentleman's choice."

He grinned.

"Any room you like *upstairs*. Mine is off limits."

His look seemed to say *We'll see about that*, and he said nothing. He pressed something into my hands: the jewelry container I'd dropped in the foyer last night. It felt cold, and fear slicked my spine. "Oh. Thanks."

He studied me, frowning. "What?"

"It's just . . . um, nothing. I need to bring this to Patsy and see if she can sense the spirit that tried to hurt me."

"Murdering ghosts? I don't get it. Christ. This is one fucked-up little town," he said, shaking his head. "I'll see you in a sec." He sauntered away. A moment later, I heard him climbing the stairs. He was whistling "Don't Be Cruel" again.

I smiled.

"Elizabeth."

The angry male voice startled me. I looked up, shocked to see a huge wavering shadow. It exuded a terrible chill that stabbed at me like tiny knives.

Something hard and sharp and cold punched me in the chest.

I flew across the kitchen, smacking into the pantry door. Big male hands enclosed my throat and squeezed.

"You love me," whispered a man's anguished voice. "I'll make you remember that you're mine. *I'll make you remember, Elizabeth.*"

Chapter 4

It is cold.

I can't see because of the cloth tied over my eyes, but I know we're outside. I smell the crisp scent of pine and hear my captor's footsteps crunch the snow.

My hands are bound. He's tied my feet together, too, boots and all. I'm wearing my new dress—it's brown velveteen and copper silk with pretty bows on the bodice and at the cuffs of the wide sleeves. I'd been wearing the matching hat. Its band is lined with copper silk roses.

I don't know what happened to it. My hair is loose and unpinned.

He must've done that.

After he hit me.

The blow to my jaw knocked me out. I awoke in his arms, blindfolded, my extremities tied. The left half of my face throbs with pain.

He puts me down.

I feel so weak. I am weighed down by the dress, and

by guilt. It didn't have to be this way. But I made my choice. Perhaps I deserve my fate.

He stretches me out, and, beneath me, I feel the snow all around. I smell the fresh earth, and I know his terrible purpose.

"Don't do this," I whisper.

He leans close, like he used to when he wanted to whisper sweet nothings, and says, "You did this . . . when you betrayed me."

I cry. The tears fall down my cheeks, drip into my ears.

He puts his hands around my throat and squeezes.

The pain and the pressure burst in my head, crowd my throat. I cannot cry anymore, or scream. Panic screeches through me. I kick my bound feet, writhe, and, in my mind, beg and beg for my life.

It's all useless. There is no escape.

He squeezes and squeezes until I cannot draw another breath. The pain fades, and I feel so light, so free. I drift up among the tall pines, and I see him undress the woman, stripping away the pretty dress.

Then I hear the rasp of the shovel and the thud of dirt. I feel caught by something, snagged by purpose. I cannot leave. Not yet. Sensations are fleeting . . . all, but one.

It is cold.

Chapter 5

"C'mon, princess, time to wake up."
In the murky dark, the calm voice offered me a rope of light, so I grabbed onto it and clung.

My eyes fluttered open. I was lying on the kitchen floor, propped in Tez's arms.

My head hurt.

"What are we doing down here?" I asked hoarsely.

"You can't handle your tequila," said Tez. The relief skittering across his face surprised me. Was he just a good cop, easily empathetic? Or did he feel like he had a genuine connection to me?

"Do let me up, Tez."

"No."

I stared at him. There was something hard in his eyes, and I recognized that brand of determination. I'd seen it in the mirror often enough. "Please. I can't continue this conversation prostrate on the floor."

"Fine." He scooped me up and stood swiftly—without so much as a grunt of effort. "I think we should call your wolf friend and get a security detail on your house. And you're gonna tell me who's trying to kill you."

"I have no idea." I gazed at him, realizing that I was shaking. I couldn't recall the last time I'd been so frightened. "It was the ghost. Only this time, I saw a . . . shadow."

"You're okay, Ellie Bee." He took me into the parlor and gently placed me in a toile wingback chair. He knelt next to me and showed me his cell phone. For a moment, I couldn't comprehend the image on the tiny screen.

Oh, my God.

It was me, unconscious, leaning lopsided against my pantry door. The obvious bruising around my neck startled me. I put my hand on my throat, which still felt tender. *I'll make you remember, Elizabeth.*

And he had. But I knew those were not my memories. I knew they belonged to the dead woman I'd found. I didn't understand my own connection to what was happening. It had all started with that damned ring box.

"If you were human, you'd be dead." He examined my neck. "You're already healing. This is the same, er, spirit that attacked you before? The thing you told Damian about?"

I nodded. "That box is from Patsy's home—the mansion that once belonged to my family. I have to believe that it has something to do with the past, with another Elizabeth, and this ghost is just . . . confused."

He kissed my forehead. I found the gesture oddly touching. It seemed that Tez was as capable of showing tenderness as he was of making sexual overtures. "We'll figure this out." He tucked his cell phone away.

"Why don't we go see Queen Patsy as planned, and discuss this situation with her?"

"Damian first," he said. "You're not gonna be stubborn about getting some protection 'round here, are you?"

"Of course not. But I don't think a few extra lycanthropes prowling around will help."

His expression was concern edged with suspicion. "You sure you don't know who this guy is?"

I shook my head, fear sliding through me once more. "But he seems to know me."

I told Tez I needed a minute to freshen up, and went downstairs to my room. I sat on my bed, clutching a throw pillow to my chest, trying to gather my wits. If I was able to use my lungs, I might have a hard time catching my breath. And if I had a heartbeat, it would be racing. I didn't have the physical reactions anymore, which was good, because they would have made what I was feeling much worse.

Someone, some*thing*, was trying to kill me. Or rather, trying to kill her, the other Elizabeth.

Again.

I pushed away the horror gathering like spiders in my stomach and allowed my thoughts drift to Tez. He was acting very protective, and I attributed such posturing to his law-enforcement background. At least, that would be the logical conclusion. I couldn't dismiss his gentle demeanor, or the sincere concern he displayed for me. Was it possible he truly cared for me? Or was this another case like those he must've solved in Tampa? He was an intelligent man, and one of the most stubborn I'd ever met.

I liked him very much.

After making sure I was truly all right, Tez had pocketed the box and started prowling around the kitchen, looking for clues. I'd noticed him flaring his nostrils, and realized he was trying to scent my attacker. Did ghosts have scents? I wasn't sure what to do about Tez's worry, or about his rather large and strange assumption that he somehow had the right to protect me. What also struck me as a little . . . well, desperate, was how much I liked how he treated me, even the rawness of his words and actions. I felt incredibly like a woman adored.

Maybe I was just unused to the concept of someone caring about me in a wholehearted way. I very much wanted to experience what other couples, especially the ones who'd fallen in love in Broken Heart, felt for each other. I don't know if it was part and parcel of immortal connections, or just incredible luck, but I'd never seen such solidarity between lovers. What would it be like to feel absolute trust? To know your best friend was also the person who drove you sexually wild? To never doubt for even a nanosecond that your husband would fight for you, rescue you, love you no matter what?

Maybe I'd read too many romance novels. It was probably coloring my perceptions of my friends' relationships. And it was certainly contributing to my rose-colored thoughts about Tez and our potential as a couple.

Well, then. First things first. I went into the bathroom and brushed my hair, fixed my makeup. Then I changed into black capris and a red sleeveless top. I also changed into a pair of black stilettos—which immediately made me feel better. Who needed prescription drugs when there were shoe stores?

When I got back upstairs, I found Tez waiting for me in the kitchen. He led me into the parlor and had me sit at the table. Then he sat down across from me and pointed to the cup of tea, jasmine by the scent.

"You were pretty shook up. Thought some tea might soothe your nerves."

"You're not having any?"

"Coffee's more my style."

I could almost hear the "not sissy tea" tacked on to the end of his sentence. I doubted a cuppa could do much to alleviate my fears. But it was a nice gesture all the same. A jar of honey sat nearby. I picked up the teaspoon sitting inside it and stirred the sweet substance into the tea.

"This was very kind of you," I said, "but Queen Patricia is waiting for our arrival." I hated to be late to any appointment, and was especially respectful of the queen's time. She was a very busy woman—ruling two different species and raising triplets.

"Oh, don't worry about her. She's comin' here."

Startled, I dropped the spoon on the table. The honey splattered on the white tablecloth. I stared at the glistening gold drops, then lifted my gaze to Tez. "Why?"

"Your iPhone accidentally slipped out of your purse and dialed her number."

He said it so casually that I didn't quite register the words for a moment. I closed my eyes and tried to pretend I could take a long, deep inhalation. I missed not being able to inflate my lungs to create some inner calm.

"Let's be clear. You took my cell from my purse, snooped through my contact list, called Queen Patricia, and invited her for a visit?"

"Icicles are hanging from your words."

The whisper of humor in his tone angered me.

"You had no right."

"No, I didn't."

His admission stalled my response. So did his steadfast gaze; I supposed this might be his "cop" stare. Or maybe I'd just seen too many episodes of *Law & Order*.

"Better to beg forgiveness than ask permission, I suppose." I finished sweetening my tea and sipped on it.

"Bullshit. I violated your privacy to do what I thought was best for you."

Carefully, I put down the china cup. The ritual of tea wasn't calming me any better than pretend breathing. He'd done it again—made my control vanish. "Ah. You know what's best for me," I repeated.

"Rewind, princess. I said 'thought,' not 'knew'."

He took my hand and turned it over, then traced the lines on my palm. The light touches sent shivers right up my arm. He stared at my hand for so long that I cleared my throat and whispered, "What?"

"Everything in me wants to claim you. Protect you. *Take* you." He snared my gaze again. I saw his vulnerability and confusion. He believed in what he was saying, and, my goodness, I believed it, too. My undead heart went *ba-da-bump*.

"I don't mistake your sympathy, or your perception of me as a victim, as anything other than kindness. To suggest that we somehow have an emotional connection, mysterious and uncontrollable, is ludicrous."

Tez let go of my hand, but his gaze roved my face. I had no doubt he was very good at determining the validity of someone's statements through their facial expressions. I didn't quite like the idea that he was examining my words with the same microscope used to determine the veracity of a perpetrator's confession. Especially since some untruth might be clinging to my words. We had a connection—I just wasn't sure what to do about it. I'd never been so emotionally walloped before.

Tez tensed, and looked over his shoulder.

Knock, knock, knock.

Obviously, Tez's senses were far more honed than mine. Only after I saw him glance at the door did my hearing pick up the shuffling of feet, the low murmur of voices, and, if I wasn't mistaken, the irritated sigh of Queen Patricia Marchand.

I rose from the table, and Tez did, too. He reached the door before I did, drawing his gun and peering out the peephole.

"Is queenie a blonde?"

"Yes," I said crisply. "Please don't call her that to her face. She's Queen Patricia."

"You called her Patsy."

"Well, she's my friend, not yours. Open the door."

He sent me a hard look, but did as I asked. Patsy stood with her fist raised to knock again. Her hand dropped, and blue eyes targeted mine. Within her annoyed gaze lurked worry. I wondered what Tez had told her. Or maybe the concern was related to what she'd wanted to tell me. I wasn't the only one with information to convey.

"You gonna let us in? I'm fucking freezing." She

swept past me, and behind her came her husband, Gabriel, then Damian. Lorcan and Eva had also made the trip.

Everyone crowded into my foyer. Tez slipped to my side, sheathing his gun in the shoulder holster.

"Well." I smiled brightly and clutched Tez's arm. His muscles tensed under my fingertips. "Shall we go sit down?"

I steered him into the formal living room. Everyone else followed. With two couches and four wingbacks, I had plenty of seating for guests.

"Would anyone like something to drink?" I asked.

"Don't hover, Elizabeth," said Patsy. Gabriel sat next to her, but I noticed there was some space between them. Usually they were quite affectionate with each other; however, they weren't even holding hands much less exchanging the usual tender glances. It didn't take a psychic to sense their emotional distance.

I sat on the couch and Tez joined me, squeezing between me and Damian. I looked at him with eyebrows arched, but he merely smiled and turned his attention to the queen. He pulled the silver box and his cell phone out of his pocket.

"Here's what the asshole did to her," he said as he worked the phone's tiny buttons to bring up the photo of my injured neck. He handed over the cell and then gave Patsy the silver container. "We think it's related to whatever the hell this is."

Patsy grimaced as she looked at my photo. I felt on display, even though full disclosure seemed the best recourse. I did not like being thought of as a victim. She tossed the phone to Damian so he could see the dreadful photo, too. Then she studied the box, turning it over in her hands.

"Is there a ghost?" I asked.

Patsy looked around, and shook her head. "Nothing here now," she said, "and I don't feel any spirit imprints on the box. Maybe we're dealing with something demonic."

I'd feared that might be the case. If Patsy, who was the most powerful ghost whisperer in Broken Heart—if not the entire paranormal world—couldn't sense a spirit, then it wasn't in the vicinity.

"Demonic or not, this entity was not in my house before Rand delivered the jewelry box. There has to be a connection."

"And with the skull?" asked Damian.

I nodded. I told the whole story again, from the first attack to finding the grave to meeting Tez in his jaguar form. Tez took the story from there, explaining how he'd chased off the person who'd struck me from behind and helped me get home before the sun rose.

"You did not see the intruder in the woods?"

Tez glanced at Damian. "I don't know how it is for you, but I don't process information the same way when I'm in my other form. I may not be able to pick out the bastard in a lineup, but once I catch his scent, he's toast." He grimaced. "But the rain washed everything away. Nothing registered." He tapped the side of his nose.

"I'm sure the storm washed away any tracks he might've left." Damian scowled. "Was it the phantom who tried to strangle Elizabeth?"

Tez sidled a glance at me. "I sank my claws into flesh."

"Two different people, one human and one not, both after me on the same night?" I shook my head. "That doesn't make any sense."

"I hate to keep saying it," said Patsy, "but this feels demonic. We might need to get Phoebe in for a consult." She looked at me. "What happened during today's attack?"

"I was holding that infernal box. Tez went upstairs, and I heard this man's voice yell my name. Then I saw a big black shadow. It pushed me with so much force that I hit the wall. He—it tried to choke me again. I passed out."

I told them about the vision I experienced—about the death of the woman in the brown dress. I saw Patsy and Eva share a significant look. Eva had chosen to sit in one of the wingbacks and Lorcan was stationed behind her. For some reason I couldn't discern, woman's intuition maybe, I deducted they were being rather cool toward each other. I frowned. In all the time I'd lived in Broken Heart, I'd never known my friends to be mad at each other for any length of time. No relationship was perfect—of course, I knew this. Perhaps I was putting too much stock into the coincidence of both couples having tiffs right before visiting me. I think this entire situation with the violent spirit and the murdered woman, and Tez, had me rattled.

"Where's the skull?" asked Patsy. "Maybe the ghost switched vessels."

"They can do that?" Tez frowned.

"They can do just about anything they damned near want." Patsy rolled her eyes. "Mostly, they're a pain in the ass."

"It's in the kitchen." I scooted forward, but Tez put his hand on my arm.

"I'll get it."

After he left, Patsy's gaze met mine. "Why the hell was he out in the woods?"

Damian explained that Tez had infiltrated the magical and technological protections surrounding the town due to the temporary tattoo—apparently issued by the alpha Calphon.

"He requested a few for visiting family," said Patsy. "He failed to tell me he was inviting strangers on in."

"I get the impression that the were-cats are interested in Tez for assimilation into their community," I said.

"What? Like the Borg?" Patsy snorted a laugh.

Damian seemed less than thrilled with the idea of Tez becoming a permanent part of Broken Heart. "You certain you trust him? What if he attacked you and convinced you it was someone else? It was raining, *Leibling*, and you weren't yourself."

"I saw the jaguar on the path," I insisted. "In *front* of me. Then something hit me from behind and he jumped over me to intervene."

"He says he was the jaguar," said Damian. "That does not mean that he was."

I looked at Damian. Maybe he was just exercising caution or maybe he was just being stubborn. "He discarded his clothes, woke me up, carried me through the rain, and tucked me into bed because he meant me harm? Why not finish the job and leave me for the sun?"

Damian couldn't argue with my logic. He glanced at Patsy.

"We don't know his purpose," she said. "I'd feel better if we saw him shift. At least we'd know for sure he was parakind."

"You think Calphon didn't check him out before he sent Tez the tattoo?" I asked. "C'mon. Obviously they wanted him to come here. Maybe we should be worried about the alpha's motivations."

"Motivations for what?" asked Damian. He sounded both confused and annoyed about my suggestion that Calphon had ulterior motives. Well, what did we really know about the were-cats? They rarely interacted with other people in town. In fact, meeting Tawny and Serri today was the first time I'd ever met any of them. Maybe Tez should be worried about why they wanted him to hang around. I wasn't sure how I felt about my own cir-cuitous thought processes. Why was I so determined to defend Tez? I didn't know. But I was firmly in his corner, and that was that.

Tez chose that moment to enter the room, carrying the hatbox. Oh, I knew the reason he'd left. He'd been eavesdropping. What better way to get information than to leave the room and see who talks behind your back? It wasn't even a tactic confined to policemen. Gossips at cocktail parties did the same thing. We hadn't been cir-cumspect at all in our dissection of his motives or char-acter, which was exactly what he was hoping for.

He put the hatbox on the coffee table and resumed his seat between me and Damian. He looked at me, and winked.

It seemed he was unconcerned about what anyone thought about him, and despite all our ruminations, he had yet to confirm why he'd taken Calphon up on the invitation to visit, or if he planned to petition for residency.

Gabriel leaned forward and plucked off the lid. He carefully removed the skull and looked it over. I wasn't sure what information he was gleaning from it, if anything at all. He glanced at his wife. She flicked an annoyed look at him and gave a somewhat imperious gesture that I translated as *Give it to Damian, you peon.*

I was shocked at her behavior. I'd never seen her treat Gabriel in such a manner. I peeked at Eva, who was staring at Patsy much the same way I was. Suddenly, Eva stood and went to Lorcan. He immediately put his arm around her shoulders and she clung to him, pressing her face against his shoulder. The tension between the two of them eased, although Patsy didn't notice the silent makeup between Eva and Lorcan.

Damian's examination of the skull was cursory. He handed it to Patsy and she stared at the sockets. "I got nothing. Can you show us where you found the grave? Maybe I'll pick up something there."

We all stood up and trooped out of the living room.

"Do you want your coat, Elizabeth?" asked Tez. He grabbed his leather jacket hanging from the newel post on the staircase and slipped it on.

"No, thank you. I'm fine."

He nodded, and we followed the others through the front door. I led the gang around the house and into the woods. The storm had left the path muddy and littered with debris. I watched Gabriel try to help Patsy over a tangle of felled branches, but his wife jerked away from his touch. Something was terribly wrong between the two of them—and my stomach hurt to think they might be having marital woes.

Lorcan and Eva were at the rear of the group, so I couldn't draw my friends aside and inquire about Patsy's obvious ire with Gabriel. For now, I had to focus on finding the grave and discovering why I was having visions of murder. Obviously, we'd stirred something up—and it had started with the little box that Patsy had uncovered at the Silverstone mansion.

I think it was the small whispering voice of the other Elizabeth that led me once again to the spot where I uncovered her. We gathered around the mucky hole. I was amazed at how much I managed to dig with just my hands, determination, and a little vampire strength.

We all examined the protruding bones.

"You're sure she was murdered?" Patsy asked.

"Yes." I felt an overwhelming sadness. "We should rebury her."

"We should find her killer," added Tez.

"Patsy, tell Elizabeth about the secret room," said Eva. She shared a look with her husband and grabbed his hand. Lorcan's silver eyes held trepidation.

Patsy rounded the grave and stood next to me. "It's what I wanted to show you," she said. "You know we finished up all the renovations last year. We didn't mess around much with the attic."

"I suggested we create a playroom for the kids," said Gabriel. He'd joined us, careful to stay away from Patsy, as if he were used to her being prickly. "I wish I hadn't."

"Well, if wishes were horses, then beggars would ride for free," said Patsy. She tossed a look of hurt in Gabriel's direction and then spun around and marched toward the path.

"What happened, Gabriel?" I asked.

He shook his head and then turned to follow his wife. A few seconds later, we heard their raised voices.

"Do you feel up to visiting the mansion?" asked Eva. She looked uncomfortable. "You really should see what they found. Patsy and Gabriel have spent the last four days in that awful place. Yesterday, she asked Lorcan and me to come by and catalog the items."

I was curious about this room and its obviously disturbing contents.

"I'll stay," said Damian, "and get a crew out here to remove the rest of our mystery woman. We'll take her to Dr. Michaels. Maybe he can tell us a few things."

"Thank you, Damian," I said, smiling. "We'll head over to the mansion."

Patsy and Gabriel's bickering continued, fading as they followed the path out of the forest. What had broken their once-solid faith in each other's love?

I looked at Tez, my self-appointed bodyguard, and he nodded. "Let's go check out the secrets in the attic, Ellie."

Chapter 6

I invited Eva and Lorcan to ride with us to the mansion. Tez didn't offer to drive, so much as assume that he would. I let him take the lead because I understood he felt the need to control something about the situation. I think it had occurred to him that he couldn't truly protect me, not from an unseen entity. I couldn't protect myself. I couldn't run away, couldn't fight this thing off. I was scared, but determined to figure out a way to save myself.

As for what Tez planned to do, or what he might think about what was happening . . . oh, I just didn't know. I certainly didn't understand his somewhat possessive behavior. It wasn't his responsibility to take care of me. And if a very, very small part of myself reveled in someone wanting to take care of me . . . well, I would simply have to remember that I could take care of myself.

Lorcan had the ability to magically transport himself and his wife. By "transport," I mean he could dissemble their atoms, and reassemble wherever he liked. Most ancient vampires had this power. However, neither he nor Eva protested the less convenient method of travel. It was a good thing, too, since they'd driven in with Gabriel and Patsy. The Mercedes, as well as its two arguing occupants, was gone when we came up the path.

I was grateful when Tez offered to procure the skull and the jewelry box. I hated not being comfortable in my own home, and I certainly didn't appreciate the grime of fear clinging to me.

We piled into Tez's Honda. He followed my directions to the main road. It wasn't as though it was particularly complicated to get to the Silverstone mansion, but I plugged Patsy's address into his GPS anyway. I wanted to talk to my friends and not worry about giving directions to Tez. After we were on our way, I turned in my seat and looked at Eva.

"What on earth is going on with Gabriel and Patsy?"

Eva slanted a look at Lorcan, who held his wife's hand tightly.

"I don't know," she said. "They've been fighting nonstop."

"About what? I've never seen Patsy so . . . vitriolic. Especially not toward her husband."

Eva bit her lower lip and shook her head. "It's strange. Lorcan and I had a fight on the way over here. I felt so angry. And now, I can't remember why."

"I can't, either, Eva." He kissed his wife's knuckles. "We've been cataloging the items in the secret room," offered Lorcan in his soft Irish brogue. "There's a darkness there, sure enough. An' I think it's affectin' the queen and her consort. Not that she'll listen to us."

"She thinks Gabriel cheated on her," said Eva.

Shock ricocheted through me. I gaped at her. "He would never do that, even if it were possible."

"Whaddaya mean?" asked Tez.

"I told you, remember? Bound vampire mates literally can't be with anyone else," I said.

"Turn left at Main Street, you delicious man. Mmm. Nice hands. I loooove how you grip that big . . . strong . . . steering wheel."

"That's the voice of your GPS?" I asked Tez. "She sounds like a porn star."

"Jenna Jameson," he admitted. He glanced at me, grinning. Did nothing embarrass the man?

"Jenna *who*?" I asked primly.

"Jameson," offered Eva from the backseat.

I switched my gaze to her. Had she the ability, I suspected she would blush. She cleared her throat. "What?" she asked. "She writes books, too. Hey, as a librarian I don't judge. First amendment and all that."

"Of course, a *stóirín*." Lorcan had a manly grin on his face, which matched Tez's.

I rolled my eyes.

"A friend of mine uploaded her voice as a joke," said Tez.

"An' how many accidents have you been in since Jenna's been givin' the directions?" asked Lorcan.

"Just some near misses."

"Your turn is coming, and if you keep driving like this, I will be, too. Go left, baby. Yeah, just like that. Oh . . . oh . . . oooooh."

I reached toward the dash and pressed the OFF button. The GPS powered down, and I glared at Tez. "Just follow this road. It leads straight to the driveway of the mansion. You can't miss it."

"Spoilsport."

For the first time since I was age eleven, I had the insane urge to stick out my tongue. Tez looked far too satisfied with himself, and that damnable humor lurked in his hazel eyes. Most disturbing of all, I found myself . . . um, turned on by the wicked possibilities. My sexual experiences had been rather limited, and I'd had none at all since my Turning. *Oh, dear.* I really was sexually repressed.

"Shall we get back to the subject at hand?" I asked. "Why would Patsy believe Gabriel cheated on her?"

"We don't know. Patsy and reason parted company," said Lorcan, grimacing. "She's certain he's been sleepin' with other women."

"He's been relegated to a guest room." Eva glanced at her husband. "Every day, Patsy seems to get angrier."

"And Gabriel?" I asked.

"Completely at his wit's end."

Unnerved, I turned back around and looked out the passenger window. The idea of Patsy being out of control was a scary concept. She held seven out of eight vampire Family powers, along with the ability to shape-shift into a wolf. What if her anger went beyond Gabriel? She was capable of leveling the entire town and everyone in it.

I wasn't looking forward to seeing the secret room—not if something within it held the power to poison the minds of whoever got close. Still, we didn't really know what was going on. Patsy's odd behavior might be related to any number of things.

Yet, I couldn't dismiss the obvious explanation, not when I'd had such terrible experiences with the silver box. Something had tried to kill me—and until we figured out what was going on, I wasn't safe.

No one was.

The Mercedes was parked askew in front of the mansion, and the door was wide open. Tez was the first out of the car, gun drawn. Lorcan was right behind him; Eva and I followed. We paused by the door and peered inside. The foyer was empty. It was quiet, too, and I found the lack of noise disturbing. The mansion was usually a beehive of activity. Patsy had workers for the house and the yard; housekeepers, babysitters, and assistants were always on hand. There were nearly always Consortium and Council members about, too, usually bothering the queen with some all-fire-important situations that needed queenly attention. I did not envy Patsy's life. I wasn't sure how much fun following the dictates of prophecy and destiny would be. No one liked to believe they didn't have control of their own lives.

"Where is everyone?" I asked.

"Patsy told the help to go on vacation for the week. The only people she allows in the mansion are Mary-Beth and the children."

So, Patsy had been isolating herself and her family. Just another symptom of her strange and disturbing behavior.

"You're not going to say something stupid like, *Wait here*—are you?" I asked Tez.

He glanced over his shoulder. "Hell, no, princess."

"I'll go first," said Lorcan.

Tez nodded. I liked that Tez didn't feel the need to assert his authority. It said something about a man willing to assess a situation and do what was best, rather than letting a testosterone-fueled ego get in the way of good judgment.

Lorcan darted inside, and Tez followed. Eva and I crept through the doorway. Lorcan and Tez swept through the area, assessing everything in sight. I paused by the stairs; Eva stayed with me, her gaze echoing the worry I felt. The hair on the back of my neck stood up. I looked at Eva and whispered, "You feel that?"

She nodded. "The air feels electrified."

We heard a crash, then a scream.

"Upstairs," I said.

Lorcan disappeared in a flurry of gold sparkles. The rest of us had to make do with climbing the stairs. At the far end of the hallway were the double doors that led to Patsy and Gabriel's bedroom. They were slightly open; it was obvious the ruckus was coming from their room.

We all ran. As a shifter, Tez easily kept up with our vampire speed. We all burst through the door.

"Oh, my God!" I cried.

Lorcan stood between the bloodied, prone body of Gabriel on the floor and a raging, dagger-wielding Patsy pacing nearby.

"He tried to kill me!" she screamed. Blood spattered her clothing. Hands shaking, she tossed the dagger to the floor. It fell end over end, landing near Lorcan's shoe. He picked it up by the bejeweled handle and grimaced.

Patsy was muttering now and pulling at her hair, which was streaked with something sticky and black.

"That cheating bastard tried to kill me. But I got him first. Got him real good."

Lorcan and Eva looked at each other and I realized they were using their vampire-mate telepathy. Tez joined me, stepping slightly in front, his gun readied. I doubted his bullets would do much to stop the queen if she decided to attack us.

While Patsy settled into frantic mutters, Eva glided across the room. Apparently, she and Lorcan had come up with a plan. At least I hoped that was the case. Tension knotted my belly. I didn't know what to do or how I could help. I hated to feel so helpless.

"Calm down, Patsy." Eva's voice was low and tranquil; the glamour's power hummed through me.

Patsy immediately stilled and raised her confused gaze to Eva. I hadn't been sure Eva's powers would work on our friend. Patsy was the most powerful vampire-lycanthrope in the world; before now, she'd been too levelheaded and down-to-earth for anyone to worry about her going mad with power. Or just going mad. I wondered what kind of universe, or god or goddess, would hand over so much responsibility and sovereignty to just one person. What was the purpose? It must be tremendously difficult to carry such a huge burden alone.

Maybe Patsy's behavior had nothing to do with the odd room or its nefarious contents. Perhaps the queen had just snapped.

"I want you to stand here, take a deep breath, and clear your mind. You're safe and comfortable. In fact, you feel tired . . . don't you, Patsy?"

The queen nodded, her gaze straying toward the huge four-poster bed that dominated the space.

I leaned next to Tez, and whispered, "Eva is from the Family Koschei, which are vampires with incredible glamour skills. She's particularly good with animals and can even communicate telepathically with shifters."

"Good to know," he murmured.

"You're tired, Patsy," said Eva, so understanding, in a voice as soothing as ocean waves lapping at warm sand. "You need to sleep now."

"Sleep," said the queen. She walked to the bed and flopped onto it. Her eyes closed and her body went limp.

"How's Gabriel?" I asked.

Lorcan knelt beside the fallen man. "He's alive, but she damned near killed him. He'll heal, but I'm takin' him to the hospital."

"Might want to put a detail on him," said Tez. "We don't know for sure what happened here; maybe the danger includes more than his crazy wife."

Lorcan nodded. He picked up Gabriel, holding the big man like an oversized baby.

"Elizabeth." Lorcan nodded toward the bedside table. I saw the glittering gold of a chunky necklace. My Family powers allowed me to determine types of metal, along with the knowledge of how to manipulate them. Granted, I'd spent a lot of time learning how to use my power and honing my craft. I had been the assistant to Zela, the Ancient who founded our vampire sect. She split her time between Broken Heart and Africa. In fact, she was there now, tending to some business for the Consortium. She taught me much about my abilities, and had become a friend as well as a mentor.

"Fairy gold." I crossed the room and picked up the necklace. "Where did she get this?"

"It's some of my grandmother's jewelry," said Lorcan, referring to Brigid, a Celtic goddess with incredible metal-working skills of her own. Aside from Dr. Clark, our current human doctor, she was the best healer in town. "She gifted some pieces to Patsy after the birth of the triplets."

"Where are the triplets?" I asked.

"MaryBeth took them on a playdate at the park," said Eva. "Patsy told me before we headed over to your house."

"Shackle her," said Lorcan.

Surprised, I stared at him. "You want me to bind her?"

"We must take her to the holding facility," said Eva. "We don't know what she'll be like when she wakes up."

"Furious," I said. Still, as much as I hated the decision, I saw the value in their caution. Patsy was dangerous to everyone so long as she was mentally unstable. We would have to call Damian and an emergency Council meeting. Someone would have to take over the day-to-day running of the town until we figured out what was going on, and found some suitable way to fix Patsy.

"All right. I'll do it," I told Lorcan.

He nodded, grim faced, then sparkled away with the unconscious Gabriel.

"Why isn't she affected by Gabriel's injuries?" I asked. "The minute she hurt him, she hurt herself."

"I have a feeling I'm going to ask this question a lot," said Tez as he walked around, his gaze cataloging everything. I realized he was in cop mode, examining the crime scene. I also saw his nostrils flare. He was scenting, too. His shifter abilities probably helped him be a terrific detective. "But . . . what does that mean?"

"Mates are connected," said Eva. She sat on the bed next to Patsy and pushed ratty strands of hair away from her face. "What happens to one, happens to the other. If you get sick, mortally wounded, die . . . then so does your spouse."

"That's one helluva bond," said Tez.

"It's part of the ancient magic that the first seven . . . that is, eight vampires used to create the binding magic. It was supposed to protect the humans from vampires misusing their powers. Taking blood is a very intimate act, rife with temptation," said Eva. "It gives pleasure to both parties. It's very easy to see why it would entice both participants to have sexual relations."

"Really?" Tez shot me a look, and I shrugged. He quirked an eyebrow; his gaze said, *We'll just see whose neck you suck on next, sweetheart.*

Little did he know that vampires were forbidden to drink the blood of shifters. It had something to do with the power exchange. A pint of human blood was plenty to live on, but a pint of shifter blood would be like having a dozen Red Bulls. Power could be addictive.

"Well, certainly not with the binding magic," continued Eva, who'd missed our little exchange. "With a hundred-year-marriage contract looming over you every time you sup, you tend to maintain more self-control."

"Too bad," muttered Tez. He squatted down and examined the spot where Gabriel had lain.

I tended to the gold necklace. Working with a metallic substance was a little like asking it to perform tricks. With some metals, that was actually more akin to begging—and fairy gold certainly ranked among the more difficult metals to work with. It was almost organic because it held magic, and magic had its own kind of life. Plus, I was trying to coax the thing to imprison its owner. It didn't help that Brigid's very strong stamp was on its creation. *Why,* it seemed to ask, *would it bend to the will of a mere vampire when it had once served a* Sidhe *goddess?*

I was nothing if not patient, especially when it came to my craft. Finally, the metal began to unwind from its intricate design. The precious gems embedded in it dropped to the floor as it slowly morphed from beautiful necklace into thicker, less pretty and far more practical cuffs.

After I sealed the magic, the metal solidified enough for Eva to slip on the bracelets. A chain looped between them. They clicked shut, and our queen was effectively imprisoned. Since I had created the manacles, I was the only one who could take them off. Well, me or Brigid. But she hadn't been around lately. She didn't live in town, though she visited frequently.

"That was amazing," said Tez. He looked at me, his gaze full of wonder. "I've never seen anything like it."

I stopped short of preening. Instead, I shrugged nonchalantly. "We all have gifts."

Eva stood up. "Tez, can you transport our queen?"

Eva and I were both strong enough to haul Patsy

downstairs, but so was Tez. Though I despised gender stereotyping . . . sometimes, it came in handy. The big strong he-man should take the frail, ill woman. I admit to some cowardice here. I didn't want to be the one holding Patsy if she suddenly shook off Eva's glamour.

"You should be careful," I said, feeling guilty about throwing Tez into potential harm's way.

"Don't worry, princess." Ever so gently, he picked up Patsy from the bed. "I can handle her."

"Downstairs," said Eva. "Go left. There's a door that leads to the basement. That's where the containment facility is."

"She means the paranormal-proof prison."

Tez strode through the room and I moved to follow. Eva grabbed my arm and stalled me. As soon as we heard Tez's footsteps fade down the hallway, Eva fiercely whispered, "You have a thing for him."

"I like him." It would be the only sentiment I admitted to; after all, I had no idea how I really felt about Tez. Other than those embarrassingly frequent attacks of lust, I hadn't known him long enough to get a true sense of his character. Or so I would tell myself until I figured out a better rationalization for my unreasonable reactions to the man.

"You *like* like him."

"What are we—in eighth grade? He saved my life. Twice, I might add. He's strong and handsome and . . ." I trailed off, stunned. *Good heavens*. I did *like* like him. "We've only just met. I certainly can't form an opinion about a man I know so little about."

"Right. We'll see how that works out for you." She

patted my shoulder. "Just remember that shifter-vampire matches can be difficult."

"You're a shifter," I said. It was true. Lorcan was one of the few vampires who could also shift into werewolf form, the others being the *loup de sang*. It was a side effect of being cured of the Taint by royal lycan blood transfusion. Feeding off her mate's blood had also given Eva the ability.

"I hardly ever go wolf," she said. "The transition is rather . . . um, icky. And it hurts."

"Do you think that's another reason why vampires are forbidden to drink shifter blood? Because we might absorb their abilities?"

"Maybe," she said.

"Yo! Ladies!" Tez yelled. "I need some help."

We hurried down to the first floor. The door to the basement was locked; I'd forgotten about all the security. Dr. Michaels had long since moved his lab to the compound, and the prison was rarely used. Why had Gabriel and Patsy reengaged the system? The only thing that came to mind was to keep the triplets out. They were only four years old, but very mischievous.

Eva punched in a code and the metal door snicked open. She led the way down the stairs and flipped on the lights. The area where the laboratory had once been was a big, empty white room.

Our steps echoed as we approached the prison. Once again, Eva put in a code, to another security door, and flipped on the lights. We entered a narrow hallway.

"What the—?" The first cell on the right had several objects sitting on a single bed: an old typewriter, a pair of men's shoes, a yellowed pair of evening gloves, a box full of lace scraps, and a bouquet of dried flowers. Black smears were on the walls and floor.

"That looks like the same substance Patsy has on her hair," I said. "Why would they put a bunch of random items into one of the cells?"

"You said it's paranormal proof," said Tez. "Obviously they suspected something was strange about this stuff and they were trying to nullify it."

Eva nodded. "I recognize the gloves and the lace scraps. We cataloged those yesterday." She frowned. "But why these things? They seem rather benign."

So did the ring box, and look what it had unleashed.

We continued to the end of the hallway and put Patsy in the last cell on the left. Tez carefully placed her on the narrow bed, and Eva covered her with a thin white blanket. We exited and she coded the cell lock.

"I'll call Damian," said Eva, "and make sure he, or one of his brothers, watches over her."

"When she wakes, she's going to be very angry," I said.

"We'll deal with that when the time comes," said Eva. "Let's figure out what's happening first."

We paused outside the prison and Eva once again locked in the security codes. Then we headed up the staircase.

"Let's start with the secret room," said Tez.

"I'm not sure anyone should go up there until we figure out the cause of Patsy's mania. I would've never imagined Patsy would hurt Gabriel. Or vice versa. They love each other too much." Eva shook her head. "It has to be an outside factor—that dark goo, or poison, or something."

She opened the door to the first floor and stepped through; I went next, then Tez.

I nearly ran into Eva, who'd stopped short. Tez grabbed me as I stumbled, and we both moved around my friend.

I saw immediately what caused her to still so suddenly.

"What the hell?" Tez stepped in front of us, once again drawing his gun.

I put my hand on his arm, but he didn't stop aiming the weapon.

A pair of concerned golden eyes met mine, and I nearly swallowed my tongue. The man Lorcan had just spirited away to the hospital, bloodied and near death, stood three feet from us in the foyer.

Gabriel.

Chapter 7

Gabriel wasn't bloody, unconscious, near death, or even wearing the same clothes. His moon-white hair was drawn back into a ponytail. Behind him was an overnight case and shopping bags.

His gaze flicked to Tez. "I suggest you put away the gun."

"I suggest you start explaining why you're not in the hospital." Tez's arm didn't move even a centimeter.

"Quickest recovery ever," murmured Eva. "Unless he's not Gabriel."

"Who is in the hospital?" he asked. "Is Patsy okay? Our children?" He frowned. "What do you mean if I'm not me? Of course, I'm me!"

"Everyone's fine," offered Eva, skipping over his ire about identity, "relatively speaking. You just got back from a trip, Gabriel?"

"I've been at the hotel," he said. "Connor asked me to drop by to see the progress on renovations."

On the recommendations of Phoebe and Connor

Ballard, the Consortium had purchased the decrepit Knights Inn in Tulsa. Worried its use by a cult had weakened the veil between hell and earth, it had been decided to purchase, psychically cleanse, and invest in restoration. The plan was to create a haven for traveling paranormal beings. It was to be open to humans as well, to keep up the illusion of a typical, if not kitschy, hotel. Broken Heart had one bed-and-breakfast, which was used for visiting relatives of the residents. With all the trouble the town had endured over the last five years, the Broken Heart Council was being particularly picky about new residents.

Phoebe and Connor had been put in charge of the Knights Inn. They live in a penthouse suite on the property. In fact, Phoebe's ex-husband, Jackson Tate, and their son, Danny, had also moved to the hotel and lived in another suite, just across the hall. Connor's sister, Jennifer, lived in the hotel as well. It might all seem an odd arrangement, but Phoebe was a unique vampire—the last female of the Family Durga, whose power was to control demonkind. She was also the talisman, given the ability to bind (or unbind) magic. She was the only known person in the world who could break a vampire marriage. Sorta. It seemed that the inherent power of the talisman was to choose who could or could not be bound. So far, in the year since Phoebe had gained the power, only one couple had been released from their accidental nuptials. Other attempts had failed. Her husband was half demon and her sister-in-law, a full demon (one of the few with an actual soul), and most parakind were uncomfortable around Pit dwellers. I wasn't too surprised when they offered to take on the project. And it did seem as though the entire town issued a sigh of relief once they had gone. Personally, I adored Phoebe and her family, and I planned to visit them soon.

"I will not be held hostage in my own home," said Gabriel. A growl entered his tone. "Tell me what's going on. *Now.*"

The saying "saved by the bell" never held more true than when Eva's cell phone rang. No one wanted to tell Gabriel his wife was locked in the downstairs prison, much less that someone had been impersonating him. While Eva moved away and had a hushed a conversation, I tried to cross the divide of silence.

"How long have you been in Tulsa?" I asked.

"Three days."

"Were you with Patsy when she found the room?" asked Tez.

Gabriel's expression went from irritated to confused. "I found the room. There was a wall, which hadn't been in the original blueprints. I realized there was empty space behind it, or so I thought, until I broke through it. Patsy and I agreed not to do anything about the place until I returned from Tulsa. I'm not a psychic, but the vibe in there is . . . dark."

I shared a look with Tez.

Eva finished her call and shut the cell phone. "That was Lorcan. He said he took Gabriel into the emergency ward, then went to confer with Dr. Carter. When they returned so the doctor could examine him, he was gone."

"Except that I'm standing here." His gold gaze burned into us. "Let's go into the living room. Tell me everything from the beginning."

"No offense," said Eva. "But we can't be sure you are . . . you."

Gabriel's gaze roved our faces. "You'll have to take the chance," he said. "Now, someone better tell me what's going on, where my family is, and why you're in my house."

"Sounds good to me," said Tez. He sheathed his gun, and tugged me toward the opened double doors that led to one of the main living areas.

Eva followed us, and then Gabriel. The air was thick with tension. We couldn't be sure this was Gabriel. And what had happened to Lorcan? Why hadn't he returned? Magical transportation took only seconds. Surely Eva had conveyed we were still in the house, but with another Gabriel.

Tez chose to sit me on the red velvet couch, sitting as close as was possible without him actually being on my lap. Eva, even though she was obviously worried about this new situation, took a moment to smirk at me as she took the wingback. I shot her a *shut-up* glance.

Gabriel took the couch across from us and focused on Tez.

"Who are you?" he asked.

"Tez Jones."

Gabriel was obviously dissatisfied with that answer, but Eva launched into the explanation, starting with when Patsy had asked her and Lorcan to come help catalog the mystery room. She left nothing out—though she was clearly uncomfortable with explaining how he'd been fighting with his wife, accused of adultery, and then nearly killed by Patsy's own hand.

Nor did Eva seem to relish admitting that we had stashed his wife in the prison underneath the house.

After she finished, I took over the thread of the story and told him about my experiences, from the time Rand gave me the silver jewelry box to the moment Patsy arrived in my home.

We all sat in the resulting somewhat uncomfortable silence, trying not to stare at Gabriel as he processed the information.

"It seems you did what was best," he finally said. His gaze flicked to Tez. "You're a shifter."

"You, too."

"Loup de sang," offered Gabriel.

"Jaguar."

Gabriel's eyebrows went up, but, unlike Damian, he didn't seem to dispute Tez's claim. Before Gabriel came to Broken Heart and married Patsy, he'd been part of a group of outcasts. He knew, more than any of us, what it was like to be the only one of a species, not to mention ostracized because of it. Last year, Gabriel found out he was one of triplets; now his sister, Anise, and his brother, Ren, lived in town with their charge, Astria Vedere. Astria had been known as the prophet, but after suffering mortal wounds, she'd been Turned. Once she became undead, her powerful visions disappeared. The three of them ran the Old Sass Café now, and seemed to enjoy being part of the community. I idly wondered what Tez planned to do, now that he'd confirmed Broken Heart was a parakind sanctuary. Would he stay . . . or return to Tampa?

"Elizabeth?"

I looked at Tez. "What?"

One eyebrow quirked. "Gabriel asked us to examine the attic room."

"Of course," I said, embarrassed I'd drifted so deeply into my thoughts that I'd ignored what was being discussed by the others. "Although I don't know what I can do. I'm not a detective."

"The Silverstone mansion was built by your family," said Gabriel. "You might have some insight to offer." He glanced at Eva. "You're satisfied that I am the real Gabriel?"

She nodded, though it seemed to me that her gaze still held suspicion. "We should call in Phoebe and Connor," I said. "Patsy seemed to think we might be dealing with a demon, and they're the experts." I paused. "Maybe we should ask Lenette to drop by, too."

"She into demons, too?" asked Tez.

For a shifter fairly new to the paranormal world, he was taking all of this in stride. Of course, what other choice did he have? Well, other than simply leaving.

"Not exactly. Lenette is Wiccan," said Eva. "She's a very powerful white witch who runs the bed-and-breakfast with her two sisters." She nodded. "She would be able to sense the use of magic or seals."

Gabriel looked surprised. "That makes sense. Whoever boarded up the room might've magically sealed it as well. I can't usually sense such things, but Patsy should've. And she said nothing about demonic energy."

Patsy had the same demon powers as Phoebe, so it made sense that she would be able to determine if the room had the stink of sulfur to it. I was disappointed by this realization. Were we really dealing with a ghost released when Gabriel opened up the room? Could this whole situation be as simple as a vengeful spirit who believed I was the woman he killed—and wanted to kill again?

Maybe Gabriel was right. I didn't know much about my ancestor Jeremiah Silverstone, or about the history of the house. We never visited Broken Heart. In fact, the first time I had ever been in the house was the same day I had died.

Now I wondered if Great-uncle Josiah knew something about that room. Maybe he was the one who had closed it up. Had he been affected by a paranormal happenstance? Or had he just gone mad in his old age?

I glanced at Eva. "I was hoping you might know something about the place. You've been collecting information about the town."

Eva shook her head. "I've been archiving what I can find, but there's not much paperwork left from the early days. I have a few property deeds, and that's about it. It's strange because, I imagine, people kept diaries, recipes, receipts, even newspapers. But as far as I know, nothing of the sort has been uncovered. Not even in the library. And the LeRoys have been caretakers of it since the town was founded."

"Did you find *any* papers, Gabriel?" I asked.

"We've barely delved into this. Given that Patsy has been going through everything without me, I have no idea what's been found." He rubbed his temples. "I'm going to check on my wife. We need to figure out what's going on. I don't like Patsy being confined."

"Gabriel."

We were all startled by the appearance of . . . Drake, I

believe. He was one of the werewolf triplets, brother to Damian and Darrius. I was fairly certain this was Drake; I knew his hair was a lighter brown and that he was about an inch or two shorter than either of his brothers.

"I see we are taking every precaution against me being a doppelganger," said Gabriel as he studied Drake's stoic expression.

"I'm here to guard Patsy," said Drake. "Teams are stationed around the house."

"And my children?"

"Taken care of," said the werewolf. "We need to verify your identity."

Gabriel stood up, nostrils flaring and jaw muscles ticking. I could see now that he'd been keeping a very tight rein on his emotions. It must've been very difficult to choose statesmanship when he probably just wanted to go to his wife and take care of her. I knew about duty versus love; it was a difficult path, choosing to do what was right even if it meant sacrificing a little of your heart. "Get Dr. Michaels here, or call upon whomever you wish, so that we can determine that I am the real Gabriel Marchand."

"The doctor is on his way," said Drake. Sympathy seeped into his gaze. "I'll go with you to check on Patsy."

Gabriel nodded. "Very well."

"Shouldn't we go to the hospital so you can examine the scene, Tez?" I asked.

"That's not my job, princess. Besides, I bet all we find is some black goo."

Eva's gaze widened. "That's right. Lorcan said it was all over the bedsheets."

Tez's eyebrows went up. "When the hell did you talk to him?

She smiled and tapped her temple. "Meeting of the minds."

"Oh, right. Mates can do that telepathy thing."

"Eva, can you make sure someone at the hospital is getting a goo sample to Dr. Michaels for testing?"

"Of course," she said.

Gabriel nodded to us, plucked out his cell phone, and strode toward the security door as he made a call. I heard him say MaryBeth's name and realized he'd called her to check on his kids. Obviously, they were not safe in the house. It was reassuring that Damian had already put them in protective custody.

I hoped Gabriel got his identity confirmed soon. I felt badly for him. It was surely a terrible thing to come home to find your wife insane and imprisoned, and your children out of your reach.

"Let me show you how to get to the attic," said Eva. "Lorcan is already at the archives trying to find more information about the town. We'll widen the search, and maybe we'll find some outside sources."

"You're still doing that mind-meld thing?"

"Same as breathing," said Eva, smiling, "if I breathed."

Ah. At least that explained why Lorcan had not returned. It appeared he didn't doubt Gabriel's identity, or he trusted that his wife was safe enough. Eva was obviously eager to reunite with her husband.

"I remember where the stairs are," I said. Even though I had only visited the place once as a human, as a vampire, I'd been in the mansion many times. "You go on."

Eva gave me a quick hug, waved at Tez, and then hurried out the front door. Tez looked at me, frowning. "How is she going to get there?"

"Probably steal your car."

"Seriously?"

I laughed as we headed down the wide hallway to the kitchen. "I guess you'll find out when we try to leave."

"Very funny." He pinched my bottom.

I stopped and shot a look of annoyance over my shoulder. "I find such actions inappropriate."

One brown eyebrow rose. "I expect you to try a little harder with vocab," he said. "Especially if you want me to kiss you."

"I wasn't trying—"

"Exactly."

"You're infuriating."

He grinned, unapologetic as usual. "It's one of my better qualities."

I sniffed and turned back around, mostly to hide my smile. I really shouldn't encourage such behavior.

In the large pantry, I walked to the back shelf and pressed on the end. It swung forward and we squeezed into the gap.

"The house has several hidden hallways and secret rooms," I said as we walked down the very narrow space. "Jessica and Patrick lived here for a while, and their kids became quite adept at finding all the nooks and crannies."

"You gave this whole place up?" he asked in amazement.

"It was never really mine." I explained to Tez about my great-uncle's will, the reason I had come to town, and how I met my end. "I woke up a vampire and very happy to be alive. Or rather, undead."

"Lorcan's okay? He hasn't turned back into that thing?"

"Completely cured. However, he can shift into a wolf. The ability appears to be a side effect of the cure. And since Eva mated with him and started sharing his blood, she has the ability now, too."

"Interesting."

"How so?"

"That vampires can become shifters."

"Oh, but they can't," I said. "It worked the opposite way—Lorcan was a vampire first who gained the ability to shift from a full transfusion. Eva doesn't drink from donors anymore, so she gets the full effect of the transfused blood."

"How's that any different from a vampire sucking on the neck of a shifter?"

"Vampire to vampire," I said, although I was beginning to doubt my own logic. "Not vampire to shifter. See the difference?"

"Nope."

At the end of the teeny hallway was a wrought iron spiral staircase. When I stepped onto the first stair, it squealed ominously. I hurried upward and Tez followed closely, the iron steps protesting the whole way.

We entered the huge open space and I hit the light switch on the wall nearest to me. Lights flickered on and revealed the vastness of the attic.

"Wow. I think you can fit an ocean liner in here," said Tez.

"Maybe half of one." Gabriel and Patsy had managed

to clear out much of the moldering furniture and collapsing boxes. I pointed to the right. "There."

We approached the mysterious hidden room. I felt trepidation creep through me. Maybe no one had been able to sense magic or demon energy, but even a nonpsychic had mentioned the "dark" feeling. It was like a suffocating blanket. The air felt wrong—and we hadn't even entered the room yet. Debris littered the sides of the doorway. And once, there had been a door—though it was long gone. It was obvious the entrance had been boarded up for a great while.

We peered inside. Temporary lighting had been connected to the existing wiring. The room was much larger than I had imagined. In fact, it seemed to be several rooms.

"It looks like a bunch of junk," said Tez as he stepped through and wandered between two long tables piled with objects. Shelves lined the walls, filled with items I couldn't believe had any meaning except to previous owners: rusted tins, glass bottles, moth-eaten clothes, gold-rimmed dishes, wooden trains, bolts of fabric . . . The amount of items was endless. And inane. It smelled musty, and, of course, dust coated everything. Unfortunately, there were no windows to open to clear out the stale air.

"Maybe they stored items from the general store here," I mused. "Jeremiah Silverstone owned it, after all."

"You'd think he'd put supplies in a more convenient location." Tez had found a box filled with marbles. He put it down again and sniffed the air. "Something's really wrong here."

I had to admit I felt the hair standing up on the back of my neck. I couldn't put my finger on the source of my uneasiness. Even with the lights on, the place felt somehow murky. It was almost like it shouldn't exist at all. I had the overwhelming feeling someone, probably my own ancestor, had invited evil into this house. Evil that had been trapped until Gabriel and Patsy's zest for remodeling opened it all up again.

"Elizabeth."

I didn't like the awful tone of Tez's voice, or the fact he'd used my full name. I'd gotten quite used to his playful nicknames. I felt much like the misbehaving child whose irritated parent had called out my full name in reproach. Truly, there was no reproach in his tone, just a terrible dread.

Tez stood at the far end of the main room, staring through another doorway. I knew I wouldn't like what he wanted to show me. All the same, I joined him. The door had been propped open with a barrel that smelled like sour pickles. For all I knew those were the exact contents. It wasn't as well lit as the main room, but that was a blessing.

"It looks like a museum." I didn't want to go inside. I didn't even want to breathe its fetid air. Somehow I knew the silver box had come from in there.

"This smells like . . ." Tez took another whiff and frowned. "I don't get it. The guy who attacked you in the forest—he smelled like this. He came from here. I don't know how, but he did. Or spent a lot of time in this room."

"But . . . you said you didn't catch his scent."

"It wasn't enough of an imprint to track him. But I

got up close and personal, and his flesh had this same smell."

I felt my knees buckle. "Oh, my God. Gabriel."

Tez's arm went around my shoulder and he pulled me close. "You mean the dude pretending to be Gabriel." He nodded. "Yeah. That makes sense."

"This ghost or shadow or bogeyman can take someone's form." The idea was terrifying. How would anyone know who was really who? "Gabriel was right. We're dealing with a doppelganger."

"Seems so."

"Why would it encourage Patsy to come up here and go through everything?" I asked. "Surely his main goal had been freedom."

"Obviously not," said Tez. "We don't know his motivations. Maybe he's pissed off about being trapped." He frowned. "He's gotta be looking for something. Why else would he keep returning?"

The questions were piling up. "Why did he convince Patsy that Gabriel was cheating on her?" I asked. "Why did he push her to go crazy?"

"Did he?" asked Tez. "Maybe she was already unstable. Maybe some part of her knew the doppelganger wasn't her husband and she finally took action. She said he was trying to kill her—maybe he was. I bet it surprised the shit out of him when she stabbed him with her fancy blade."

I stared at Tez, foreboding twisting my belly. "He took another form."

"Slow down there, Sherlock," he said. "This is all supposition. We don't have any evidence, and there's no

reason to panic until we actually know what we're dealing with. He could've slithered out of the hospital and
holed up somewhere to recover. No matter what kind
of freak he is, he would still have to heal from griev-
ous wounds." Tez gave me a reassuring squeeze and said,
"I got shot a few years ago. I normally heal very fast,
but I damned near died so it took me a while to get my
strength back. I couldn't shift. I guess it was my body's
defense mechanism. What I'm saying is that maybe the
same thing applies to our bogeyman. Maybe getting
knifed slowed him down."

"More supposition," I said. "He wasn't so injured that
he couldn't leave the hospital."

"But he also left some of his muck behind. Maybe it's
his version of blood."

"Or another bodily fluid."

"True. Who knows what's really oozing outta that
guy." He grasped my hand. "C'mon. Let's go explore the
little shop of horrors."

"Joy of joys."

He grinned at me, then slipped through the doorway, and I followed, clutching his hand harder than
necessary.

Unlike the clutter of the previous space, everything
in here was in order. Except for the dust and the terrible smell permeating the air, it was clean and tidy. Five
shelves made from rough-hewn wood were arranged
against the wall to our left. Only the middle shelving
unit held any objects. On the opposite wall was a work-
space. A table bolted to the wall ran the entire length
of it; above the empty table various tools and other im-

plements were fastidiously arranged. Five trunks were pushed against the wall facing us. All were locked and none had been pried open.

"Whatever sick asshole used this place had an obsession with the number five," said Tez. He pointed to the shelves, the trunks, and even the insidious tools. "Each unit has five shelves, and look at the one in the middle— each shelf used to hold five items on each one."

The objects seemed randomly placed, nothing grouped in a way that made sense to me. Tez was right. Each shelf was missing an item, which was obvious from the impression left in the thick dust.

"Five trunks," said Tez. "And the tools are split into five sections—with five tools in each section. This is fucking creepy."

Something niggled at me. The idea of "five" was familiar, but as was the case when trying to remember an important fact, it immediately escaped me. I stopped concentrating so hard. I knew that if I let go now, whatever it was would become clear at an unexpected moment.

Tez plucked the jewelry box from his pocket and walked to the first one. "Look." He placed the box on the second narrow ledge down; it fit perfectly atop a square marked in the dust layer.

"All these items are small," I said. "None of those things locked in the prison belong here."

"Maybe Patsy figured out something was up before she lost her marbles and was trying to figure out what needed to be nullified."

"Or the shadow man did it. Maybe those things affect him in some negative way."

Tez looked at me, concern lighting his gaze. "Good call, Ellie Bee. I hadn't thought about it that way."

Even after looking everything over and puzzling over the dust imprints, neither Tez nor I could figure out what might be missing.

"How did you get the box?" asked Tez.

"Rand brought it to me. He's dating MaryBeth, the nanny, so he's over here all the time. He said Patsy wanted me to have it."

"More like our unseen nemesis. Maybe he wanted other people to have some presents, too," said Tez. "Four others, I bet. But who?"

I shook my head. "It'll be easy enough to figure out if anyone who received one of these . . . um, gifts, has had the same kind of trouble I'm having. I've never seen a ghost before, much less been attacked by one. Or been directed to find a grave, either.

"If only we had some information about the town. I know it's been more than a century, but you would think a newspaper or diary would turn up somewhere."

"Maybe it was deliberate," said Tez. "How's this for supposition, princess? Something big and bad happened in town and the people who lived here at the time went through a lot of trouble to cover it up."

It seemed a logical conclusion—as logical as was possible given how much we didn't know about this room, the ghost, or the doppelganger. Was the spirit able to create human forms? I'd never heard of such a thing. And the person who might know was passed out cold in her prison cell. But what if it was a demon? And if so, why would it care a whit about me, or the other Elizabeth?

Maybe we were dealing with two different problems that had converged from different points. Or even
worse, we were dealing with two different entities with
the same purpose. And I was right in the middle of it.

Had my family, and the other founding families of
Broken Heart, done something so awful it had created
paranormal repercussions all these years later? Was
that why my great-grandfather bought a manse in south
Tulsa—the same home my parents lived in now—to
escape what had happened here so long ago? And was
that why Uncle Josiah had finally fled to Alaska? Had
he lived and died alone because he'd been tormented by
whatever lived in the attic?

"We should go to my parents' house," I said. "When
my great-grandfather moved to Tulsa, he took a lot
of heirlooms. It could be that valuable information is
tucked away in some antique bureau or in his old papers. My family keeps everything." I knew for certain
that my grandfather's room had been kept intact and
was rarely used by my parents.

"Good idea," said Tez.

My mind was already racing ahead, past the research
I knew must be done at my parents' home. Luckily, they
had gone to Europe, again, and no one would be home
to bother me with questions. I did so hate Mother's
queries—and she would certainly have a thing or two
to say about Tez. I loved my parents, but they could be
such snobs.

I was thinking now about the story Jessica had told
me about how the town had gotten its name. Before the
town had incorporated, Mary McCree, despairing because her husband had been unfaithful, drowned herself

in the creek. Jessica said that before Mary had completed the terrible act, she cursed the place, saying that anyone who dared to live and love here would know her heartbreak.

Her daughter demanded the place be called Broken Heart, as penance for her mother's death.

I didn't know if the story was true; oral histories weren't always accurate. Without newspapers or other confirmation, we couldn't know for sure. However, when the Consortium had swept into Broken Heart and rescued those of us killed by Lorcan, Broken Heart had the highest rate of divorces and unwed mothers in the state. I couldn't help but throw those facts into the mix and wonder about their implications.

Coincidence?

Or the curse?

Chapter 8

"What are you thinking, Ellie?" asked Tez.
At least he'd left off the "Bee" part.

"About the Broken Heart curse." I told him about Mary McCree and how, as everyone generally believed, the town had been named.

"You think the bones you found were hers?"

"No," I said. "I think I found Elizabeth."

"And she is . . ."

I shook my head. "You know how they say many myths start with a seed of truth?"

"You mean like all those legends about werewolves and vampires?"

"Ha, ha. But, yes, that's what I mean. Maybe the Broken Heart curse is real. Maybe it was trapped in this room, and when Patsy and Gabriel broke inside here, they released it."

"That's a helluva leap. Now it's not a ghost or a demon, but a . . . a living curse? I liked it better when we decided you've got a ghost after you."

"Or a really annoying demon," said a female voice from the doorway.

We turned. Neither Tez nor I had heard the approach of others. "Phoebe! Connor!" I hurried to my friends and gave them both a hug. "You certainly got here fast."

"Connor's got the transport mojo," said Phoebe. "And it sounded urgent. Especially since Patsy is cuckoo for Cocoa Puffs."

"Hey, I like her," said Tez.

Connor's brows rose and a proprietary hand snaked around his wife's waist. Wasn't testosterone delightful? *Humph.*

I made the introductions, and then Tez and I stepped aside while Connor and Phoebe examined the room.

"Five of everything," said Connor, his Scottish accent thick. "Ach. Not good."

"Really weird vibe here," added Phoebe.

I felt like a hot brick slid from my chest into my stomach. "Demonic?"

"Sorta," said Phoebe. "I've never felt this kind of energy before."

" 'Cause it's ancient," said Connor, "an' rare." He glanced at me, and the look in his eyes frightened me. "The obsession with five makes me think we're dealin' with Mammon."

"What's a Mammon?" asked Tez. He put his arm around my shoulders and pulled me in close, but I wasn't sure if he meant to comfort me, or himself.

"He's a prince of the underworld, like my father, but much, much older. Most of the demons that have been around as long as Mammon are . . . Well, I guess *asleep* is the word. Demon offspring aren't born like humans.

They're created from the energy of the ancients deep in the Pit. Then many of 'em spend centuries climbin' into the upper levels, and some break through on the earthly plane." He gestured around the room. "But someone invoked Mammon's power."

"You mean there's an ancient demon walking around Broken Heart?" I was horrified. About a year ago, the entire town had been attacked by a demon named Lilith and a legion of her demons. Thanks to Phoebe and Connor, as well as help from the goddess Morrigu, Lilith had been defeated.

Connor shook his head. "Mammon wouldna leave the Pit. The ancient demons are Hell, if that makes any sense. Their energy creates an' sustains other demons. Ancients . . . I suppose you'd say they specialize in darker qualities, and those traits create the purpose of their children."

"And Mammon's purpose?"

"The original demon of greed," said Connor. "In all its forms. Greed has many facets—money, love, ownership."

"So greed could turn into lust or into jealousy?" I asked.

Connor nodded.

"If this demon is as badass as you say," said Tez, "then what would entice him to give away some of his power? A human called on Mammon, right?"

My thoughts aligned with Tez's. Someone who lived in Broken Heart more than a hundred years ago—someone who thought they needed help to get what they wanted—had invoked a demon.

Like Jeremiah Silverstone.

Dear God. Had my ancestor brought down the wrath of a demon on himself and this town? I couldn't wrap my brain around the concept. I was the one who'd suggested the curse had been released, but I hadn't realized how close my supposition might be to the truth.

"Sacrifice interests Mammon," said Connor. "Nothing less than a blood offerin' woulda made him take notice. After that . . . I dinnae know."

"Well, if Mammon's not really here, then what's walking around Broken Heart?" asked Tez.

"He probably sent a shadow." Connor examined the shelves, frowning. "Shadows are reflections of their creator. Same qualities. Same desires. They tend to be obsessive."

"Like collecting the same number of objects over and over?" asked Tez.

"Exactly," answered Connor. "And Mammon's shadows are particularly obsessed with the number five."

"Think of shadows as demon lite," said Phoebe. She was near the trunks, disgust worming across her features as she stared at them. "They're not as strong or as smart, but they are relentless. They'll fulfill the purpose they were called for, no matter what."

"They're temporary, though," said Connor.

"What's temporary mean for demon lite?" asked Tez.

"Couple of centuries, maybe." Connor pointed to the knickknacks. "These are tokens. They were stolen from the people chosen as sacrifices. Havin' these gave the shadow control over 'em. Keep an object long enough and it's imbued with your essence. Even the tiniest bit can give a demon power over you."

"Seriously," Tez whispered to me. "This town is *really* fucked-up."

"Let's find out for sure what we're dealin' with," said Connor. He joined his wife and they turned toward the center of the room. Phoebe looked at us and made shooing motions. "Move back."

Tez and I did as she asked, plastering ourselves against the far wall.

Using hand gestures and uttering words in a language I didn't know, Phoebe and Connor created sparkly black ropes of light that weaved into intricate patterns above the center of the floor.

"Holy damn," murmured Tez.

Their magic thickened the air with the scent of sulfur. I felt electrified by whatever they were doing. The back of my neck tingled, and I found myself squishing against Tez. He held on to me, and I clutched his forearm. I could feel the goose bumps formed there.

Then the interwoven ropes drifted to the floor and then . . . *bam!* The magic blasted onto the wood planks. The spell revealed a circle etched into the floor. Within the circle were drawn five symbols I didn't recognize along with odd squiggles and crossed lines in between. Connor seemed particularly interested in the middle symbol.

Then the black sparkles completely dissipated, and everything that had been visible on the floor disappeared.

"Mammon," said Connor. He turned his gaze to the doorway, which made the rest of us do so as well.

Lenette Stinson stood there. She was a lovely woman with loosely curled red hair and moss green eyes. She wore a long black dress cinched with a wide green belt and underneath the swirled skirt, a pair of black ankle boots. Several strands of necklaces in various colors and lengths hung off her neck; and she wore two rings: on her left, a large emerald set in gold; and on her right, a pure silver band that covered her forefinger from bend to knuckle.

"What kind of moron locks a demon in an attic?" she asked. She pointed from the top of the doorjamb to the floor. "It was amateurish at best, but it did the job."

"It's bespelled?" asked Phoebe.

"It was. The seal was easily broken by Patsy. It couldn't have resisted her innate power. She's too strong. No doubt she opened the door and walked through it without any resistance."

Fear feathered through me, but I was tired of feeling scared. I couldn't control the demon, but I could control myself. And what I did next.

"So," I said, as I moved away from Tez and gazed around the room. "We are dealing with an ancient demon's shadow, one that apparently didn't fulfill its purpose before it was caught."

"And that's what it must be doing now," said Tez. "But what does that have to do with your attacking ghost?"

"You don't think it's the same thing?" asked Phoebe.

"No, I don't. The ghost shows up and tries to choke her to death. Then, when she goes to find the grave, she's attacked by a real person," continued Tez. "I'm betting on the Gabriel doppelganger."

"That's true," I said. "Why would the demon use a ghostly form to scare me when he was already pretending to be Gabriel?"

"He knew where she was buried," said Tez. "He was going to the grave, too, but you found it first."

"Why would he need to find Elizabeth's grave?"

"Just another question we gotta answer, princess."

Lenette stepped inside the room. "Ugh. This place is awful. I can feel my aura shriveling." She looked at Connor and Phoebe. "Perhaps a cleansing is in order?"

"Not yet," said Phoebe. "We need to look at everything carefully and make sure there are no traps or spells we're unaware of."

"Getting rid of the shadow won't be that easy," said Connor. "It would help to know what it's trying to accomplish so we could figure out the reversal spells."

"Well, I can add protections to the house," said Lenette. "Maybe that will slow it down."

"I think it's time to leave and let them work," I said. I dragged Tez toward the exit. I didn't want to spend another second in the room. I'd had enough of feeling choked, whether by invisible hands or the cloying ick of this location. I felt like the longer we stayed here, the bigger the chance something bad would happen. It was an irrational feeling, one fueled by my fears, but I couldn't help it. I wanted to get as far from the mansion as possible.

Besides, I had a plan to implement.

"You're right. Everything's tied to the past," I said as we made our way out of the deplorable space. "We find that link and we might be able to stop whatever the shadow is trying to do."

"Think we'll wrap up in a day, do you?" asked Tez.

I smiled to hide my trepidation. "Of course."

When we returned to the kitchen, Gabriel was there

along with Patrick, Jessica, and Damian. Startled, I stopped suddenly, and Tez plowed into my backside. His hands went around my waist. "Whoa, princess."

"I'm me," said Gabriel, his gaze bouncing between me and Tez. One blond eyebrow winged upward, but I ignored his curious look. "Dr. Michaels confirmed my DNA and Lenette did an identity spell."

"Well, I'm relieved you're you," I said. "How's Patsy?"

He shook his head. "She's still sleeping. She looks like hell." His voice was ragged with pain. The poor man looked as though he'd aged a decade or two . . . and shifters didn't really age. They weren't immortals per se, but they did live hundreds of years. Empathy welled, and I wished I could help him.

"Well?" asked Jessica impatiently. "What's going on up there?"

Tez and I took turns revealing what we'd found out from Connor, Phoebe, and Lenette. I finished up the explanation with, "Connor thinks we shouldn't do anything magicwise until we figure out what the shadow's doing. But Lenette is going to add some protection spells."

"And I'll put a security detail in the attic," said Damian. "We already have patrols around the house and garden."

"Eva and Lorcan are combing through the archives and library again," I said. "Tez and I are going to my parents' house in Tulsa to do some research of our own. It's possible my great-grandfather saved items, maybe even papers, from the time period we're looking for."

"Why all the hubbub about old paperwork?" asked Jessica.

"We need to start somewhere. The room is definitely original to the house," I said. "I have to assume Jeremiah Silverstone built it, and I can't imagine it served a good purpose. Tez and I have a theory." I looked at him. I don't know when I had started thinking of us as a team, but I couldn't deny that's exactly how I felt.

He took the conversational ball and ran with it. "Something really shitty happened. And it was so awful everyone who lived here got rid of the evidence and did everything possible to cover it up. Elizabeth told me about Mary McCree. Maybe her death wasn't a suicide. Or maybe it was, but not for the reason everyone thinks. It may have something to do with the body Ellie found in the woods. And it damn sure has something to do with that demon's shadow."

"Dr. Michaels is examining the bones now," said Damian. He was leaning against the center island, his arms crossed. He seemed a little less hostile toward Tez, but, if I knew Damian, he wouldn't be satisfied about Tez's identity or purpose until he'd proven it for himself. "All he can tell me so far is that you were right about the gender—definitely a woman. And the bones are old. He's running tests now to figure out how old. We uncovered some scraps of clothing, too." His lips quirked. "He asked about the skull."

"Oh!" I felt like an idiot. I should've handed it over sooner, but, honestly, it hadn't occurred to me. How strange I felt so attached to some dead woman's skull. It was rather macabre. "It's in the car. We'll drop it off to Stan."

"So, you don't know if she was murdered?" asked Gabriel.

"Not yet," said Damian.

"She was strangled," I said. "And her name was Elizabeth, too."

"You sound sure," said Jessica.

"I am."

Since we were all paranormal beings living in a paranormal town, no one doubted my surety about this—even though I had no proof. If you learned one thing living in Broken Heart, it was to take a leap of faith. Not much was impossible for us.

"We're calling a Council meeting," said Gabriel. "While we figure out what's going on and Patsy recovers, we must, as she has told me so often, keep on keeping on. Everyone stay in touch. Hopefully, we will resolve our problems quickly."

"Daddy!" Three blond whirlwinds shot into the kitchen and gathered around their father, all talking and trying to claim his attention. The triplets were angelic in features, if not temper. Patsy wasn't the type of mother to dress her triplets in look-alike clothes, but the girls tended to choose the same type of dresses and colors. The boy wore a graphic tee and jeans. MaryBeth leaned against the doorway to the kitchen; she had that same happy, but exhausted, expression I'd seen so often on mothers' faces. Like me, MaryBeth would not have children of her own; I'd made my choice early in life, but hers had been taken from her. She crossed the kitchen and poured a cup of coffee for herself. She glanced at me and mouthed, "Patsy?" I shook my head. She nodded, obviously concerned about her employer and friend.

Gabriel crouched down so he could hug his children. He spent time talking to each one, and then he shushed them. "How would you like to stay with Jessica and Patrick for a while?"

This suggestion was met with great enthusiasm. At least it explained why Jessica and Patrick were here. Patrick was a member of the Council, but Jessica was too blunt to do well in any political forum. Patsy was blunt, too, but she had learned a lot about decorum and navigating the minefields of politics. Jessica—ah, not so much.

"Where's Mommy?"

"Napping. You'll see her soon."

The voices started again, and Gabriel's attempts to calm them went unnoticed. Finally, Patrick scooped up the girls and Jessica, the boy. They squealed in delight and then started talking again, asking questions so quickly that neither Jessica nor Patrick had time to formulate answers.

"I'll pack their clothes and toys and get their car seats ready," said MaryBeth. She took a moment to place a comforting hand on Gabriel's shoulder, then followed Patrick and Jessica out of the kitchen.

"Gabriel, is there anything more we can do for you?" I asked. I was feeling inadequate and, vaguely, as if everything unfolding was somehow my fault. I could certainly lay the blame at my ancestor's door, so in a way, it was my fault.

Gabriel shook his head. "I've left messages for Brigid. If anyone can help my wife, she can."

"Well, if you need anything . . ."

"You're doing plenty to help," said Gabriel. "Thank you."

There was really not much else to say, so I gave him

a quick hug, said good-bye to Damian, and then Tez and I left.

When we got outside, I stopped on the flower-lined sidewalk and took a moment to enjoy the crisp air and the beauty of the night. So much had happened, and there was so much to do yet. I knew the philosophy well enough: The journey of a thousand miles begins with a single step. I had a feeling it would take all of us working together to defeat whatever terrible thing was unfolding. It wasn't like we didn't know how to handle trouble. Over the years, we'd defeated rogue vampires, Ancients gone bad, a secret military group, and, as I've mentioned, demon attacks. However, this new threat was more insidious because it came from the inside. We didn't know our enemy—and worse, our enemy could wear our faces, and that would make it difficult to fight.

"What's going on in that head of yours?" asked Tez. He took my hand and led me to the Honda.

"Just thinking about how to solve this mystery."

"Okay, Velma."

I looked at him. "As in, Scooby-Doo?" Even I was familiar with the cartoon. I blinked. "You think I'm the smart one?"

"I always figured Fred had it all wrong," he said, grinning. "I like girls with really big . . . brains."

"I look terrible in orange," I said, giving him the snooty-bitch look.

"Will you at least wear the knee-length socks and Mary Janes?"

"Tez!" I lightly slapped his shoulder while he guffawed. "I'm not sure how I feel about you fantasizing about a cartoon character."

"Don't get your panties in a twist, princess. Completely naked is okay, too." He was still smiling, his hazel eyes twinkling, and I realized he was doing a good job of alleviating my tension. "You like it, don't you?"

"Like what?"

"Puzzling out all the pieces, seeing how they fit together."

Tez's perception surprised me yet again. I did like to work my way through problems. It was always very satisfying to figure out the appropriate solutions. I'd never thought of myself of the Scooby-Doo and the Gang sort of mystery solver, though.

"You'd make a good cop," said Tez.

"I'm not fond of firearms."

He leaned against the trunk of his car and drew me into his embrace. Until I met Tez, I didn't realize how much excitement my life had lacked. I'd been content to fulfill the role of matron, hostess, and wise old woman. If I felt the creeping tendrils of boredom, I looked to my jewelry making or meeting a friend for lunch or logging on to eBay to see what treasures I could find. It was only at that moment that I realized I had been "living" my unlife the same way had lived my human life. I couldn't have what I wanted, so I made do with what I had.

What a terribly sad way to spend eternity.

And so, when Tez held me close, his hazel eyes glittering with sensual intent, I didn't pull away or protest. He was the sexiest man I'd ever met, and I'd once hosted a party that included among its guests Brad Pitt, Johnny Depp, and Gerard Butler.

"You got a thing against all guns?" he asked, his tone smoky.

I swear, I felt my womb clench. It had been a really long time since I'd flirted; I was much more a woman of action. I never really enjoyed the dance of courtship, which may have been another reason I so easily acquiesced to my parents' choice of husband.

Tez tugged my arms up and slipped them around his neck. I happily accepted this hint, and snuggled closer. Excitement pulsed through me. How was it that Tez could make me feel as though I was the only woman in the world?

Tez pressed his warm, soft lips against my mouth.

The shock of the gentle contact froze me for a second. It had been such a very long time since I'd been kissed. I needn't have worried about my slow response. Tez seemed to understand I needed wooing.

He did not demand, but coaxed. With every sweet parting and return of his mouth, a fire built within me. I wasn't ashamed to admit that I clung to him, accepting his gift with selfish indulgence, greedy—so greedy—for his touch.

I had not realized that I'd missed being wanted. When was the last time I'd been thought of as a woman with needs, desires? I hadn't dated, but no one had asked me out, either. How easily I fell into the trap of fulfilling the role that was needed by others rather than exploring what I might need for myself—and from those who shared my life. I allowed myself to feel what I had denied for so long: the need to be loved and cherished.

"Elizabeth." Tez pulled back, just a little. I saw in his eyes all that I'd ever wanted—if not forever, then for the moment. Here was a man who wanted me, whose desire for me made my undead heart want to beat again.

Tez pressed his mouth at the hollow of my throat.

"Oh," I managed. "Oh, my."

My neck was very sensitive, rather an irony for a vampire. Tez nipped kisses, flicking his tongue against my skin. Every light touch drove me crazy; tingles traveled to my breasts, to my belly. Desire twisted inside me, heat and need that threatened my self-control.

One of Tez's hands cupped the back of my skull, and then, once again, he lowered his head toward mine.

He stopped a breath away. His mouth curved into a half smile—and I knew as much as he that, as much as he tortured me, he was doing worse to himself.

His tongue flicked out: first to taste each corner of my mouth, and then to trace the inner curve of my lower lip.

Longing pierced me to the core. Oh, how I wanted him to plunder, to take. But he chose to torment me with mere flashes of wicked sensation.

And then . . . finally, *finally* he claimed my mouth fully. He deepened the kiss, pulled me closer still, and slipped his tongue through the seam of my lips.

I felt as though I might be melting away. From the heat. From the passion. I met each delicious stroke of his tongue with my own and couldn't resist sifting my fingers through his hair. I was pressed so tightly against him, I was sure he could feel the taut beads of my nipples against his chest; I could certainly feel the hard length of shaft against my belly.

Had I not been a vampire with a hundred-year-marriage curse, I would happily indulge in my first sexual quickie. Followed by a very long night of lovemaking.

Tez pulled away. He was breathing hard, his eyes

glazed with passion. For me. It gave me such a thrill to know I inspired such lust. He was a handsome man who'd no doubt had his share of women. And he wanted *me*.

"Elizabeth," he said in a jagged voice. He cupped my face and feathered kisses along my jaw. Relentless, he again took my lips in a fierce possession, showing me with his mouth what he wanted to do with my body. "God, I want you."

"I want you, too," I managed. "But we can't act like irresponsible hormonal teenagers."

"Why the hell not?"

"Tez. We've known each other not quite two days. I hardly think that enough time to determine one hundred years of marriage."

"I'm not the one with the issue."

"That makes no sense."

"I know what I know," he said.

"Well, I know what I know," I said as I unglued myself from his very fine, muscled form. "Lust is not love."

Tez frowned. "You don't think I have feelings for you?"

I wasn't sure how to respond to his question. I knew that I had feelings for him—something that certainly went beyond the obvious physical need. I liked him. He was funny, irreverent, sexy, protective; he understood me, and what I wanted. I couldn't accuse him of not caring about me when I knew I already cared about him.

And yet, I still found it hard to believe.

"I want you," he said. "Not just with my body, but with my heart. You make me laugh, you make me think, you make me crazy. My world feels brighter because you're in it. I'm not giving you up because of vampire rules.

Or shifter rules. I'll take you however I can have you."
Tez caught my hand to prevent me from completely
moving away. "Whatever you want to give me, princess.
Whatever you want from me." He pressed my knuckles
against his lips.

His words just made me want him more. He was sincere, and I'd already figured out he was persistent. Okay,
stubborn. Still. Was there a chance for us? Could we
have love?

"I'll have to think about this," I said.

"Okay." He rubbed my knuckles with his thumb, and
then he let my hand go. He grasped my shoulders and
planted a kiss on my forehead. "C'mon, princess. We
have a mystery to solve."

I think I was more shaken by his tender regard than
his lusty advances. I had no idea what to do about Tez.
However, I had very clear ideas about what I wanted to
do *to* him.

I supposed that would be a start.

It was only after we drove through the gates to the Consortium's compound that I thought to ask Tez about the
jewelry box.

"I left it in the evil room," he said. "I figure doing the
opposite of what our creep wants is a good way to start
fighting back. With your friends working all that mojo,
it's probably the safest place for it. All we have to do
is find the other four objects. I don't like knowing the
shadow has those tokens—or worse, that he's actually
already given them to his new victims."

"We should have a bonfire," I said. "If none of those

things existed, then maybe the shadow would burn away, too."

"I keep wanting to intone 'only the shadow knows,'" said Tez.

"What?"

"You know, that movie with Alec Baldwin? Only the shadow knows the darkness in men's hearts?"

"What does that have to do with a demon?"

Tez sighed. "Don't tell me. You love watching movies like *The English Patient* and *Sense and Sensibility*."

"I adored both those movies."

"Crap." He glanced at me. "We'll have to work on bridging the gap between our film preferences."

"Hmm. Oh, go right here. The lab is on the left side of the road." I had refused to let Tez turn on the porno GPS. I just couldn't take listening to that breathy female make even innocuous phrases into sexual innuendo. Tez accused me of being jealous of an inanimate object. Being the lady I was, I declined to answer such a ridiculous supposition.

Tez pulled the car into a front parking space, and we exited the car. He retrieved the skull from the trunk, and we headed into the building.

"Why is everything here white?"

I laughed. "I don't know. But it's a theme carried on through every construction project the Consortium has completed."

"I'd settle for some beige," said Tez as we crossed the lobby. The chairs were white and chrome; the wall decor included only paintings of black lines and splashes. Tez paused by one and said, "That's art?"

"In the eye of some beholder," I said. "C'mon. Stan's office is down the hallway."

Lucky for us, Dr. Stan Michaels, the premiere scientist for the Consortium, was at his desk scribbling copious notes. The office walls were the expected white, with floor-to-ceiling shelves overflowing with books and papers. His large desk held the same kind of chaos. Even the two chairs positioned in front of the desk had files and books piled on them.

I rapped gently against the frosted glass of the opened door. "Stan?"

He looked up; his fingers reached up for glasses he no longer wore. About three years ago, Dr. Michaels had been human. After a ceiling collapsed (from a dragon attack) on him and mortally wounded him, he was Turned by none other than his now wife, Linda Beauchamp. She was one of the original victims of Lorcan, too. Her daughter was MaryBeth, who'd been killed by Wraiths—nasty vampires with world-domination issues. Linda had begged for her daughter's life. Lorcan, who'd been cured by then, took the responsibility of Turning MaryBeth. After watching that experience, Linda had sworn she would never Turn a soul.

There's a reason the saying "never say never" had merit. Linda was the only Broken Heart Turn-blood to ever make another vampire. She'd broken her own vow to save the man she loved.

We'd been told that only the Masters had the magic and energy necessary to do a Turning. Even then, only one in ten humans survived the process. It always struck everyone as strange that all eleven of Lorcan's victims had survived the process. If the statistics had been correct, then only one of us should've made it.

The theory had been that Lorcan's warped DNA had somehow contributed to the success of our Turnings. I wondered now, though, if it had been the paranormal elements that had obviously existed in Broken Heart before the vampires ever arrived.

"You brought the skull?" asked Stan. His gaze moved to the hatbox in Tez's hands. "Excellent."

"This is Tez Jones," I said as we crossed to the doctor's desk and Tez put down the cargo. "And this is Elizabeth."

Stan blinked. "You named the bones after yourself?"

"I feel certain that they belong to another woman named Elizabeth."

"I see." He stood up and leaned over to lift off the lid. He peered down. "It's in decent condition. That's good. Very good."

"Damian told us you'd confirmed the bones were female, and old," I said.

Stan nodded. "Female. In her twenties. And she'd borne children. And the bones appear to be about a hundred and ten years old."

"That's accurate?" Tez asked. "I thought tests for bone age were iffy."

"We have much better equipment," said Stan, only sounding slightly arrogant. The man really was unaware of how he sometimes came across as pompous. Stan removed the skull and studied it. "Some of our technology is years beyond what's currently available to the human world."

"That's great. So you can tell us the cause of death," said Tez.

"The hyoid bone was fractured."

"Strangulation."

The doctor jerked his gaze away from the cranium and stared at Tez. "Who are you again?"

"A cop on sabbatical."

"And a were-jaguar," I added.

Stan's expression brightened. "I thought jag shifters were extinct. I'd love to examine you sometime."

"Sure," said Tez. "Just as soon as hell freezes over."

"Don't say that," I said. "We know the kind of demons that could make it happen." I turned toward Stan. "She was strangled?"

"Possibly." He returned the skull to the box. He seemed unconcerned by Tez's sarcasm. Of course, Stan was used to it. After all he was friends with Jessica, and she was the queen of sarcasm. "The hyoid bone doesn't fuse until about the age of thirty. The fact that this woman's was not is another indication she was in her twenties. She had some rib fractures, too."

"It's like you said, Ellie Bee. Her assailant sat on her and choked the life out of her," said Tez.

"It's the most likely scenario."

"Murder in Broken Heart," I said.

Tez nodded. "The question now is, was it the only one committed?"

Chapter 9

By the time we returned to my house, I realized that in a few short hours, it would be time for vampire sleep. I was itching to get to my parents' house so I could dig through my great-grandfather's treasures. Too bad leaving tonight wasn't the wisest course of action. It would be better to stay here the rest of the evening and leave first thing after I awoke.

I discussed this with Tez as we pulled up to the Victorian, and he agreed.

I have to admit to feeling uncomfortable about returning to my home. I had no intention of allowing the demon or the ghost to scare me out of my own house. However, I was glad that Tez would be staying with me for a while. It was such a girly reaction, and here I was, a big, bad vampire. But I'd been ineffective protecting myself. How did one fight a phantasm? Not to mention an ancient demon's shadow. I shivered. Ugh.

"Crap."

Tez's outburst startled me out of my thoughts. I glanced at him. "What?"

"My fan club," he muttered.

We got out of the car, and that's when I noticed that a sporty little red car had pulled up behind us. The doors opened and out spilled Tawny and Serri.

"Tez!" Tawny waved so hard, her substantial assets shook like palm trees in a hurricane.

Tez gave a halfhearted wave back; I was relieved to note he'd managed not to glue his gaze to her chest, a commendable act. Instead, he looked irritated. I, on the other hand, was fine. Certainly not jealous of Tez receiving the attention of these two nubile young were-cats. Not. At. All.

"I'll just go inside," I said.

"The hell," Tez said under his breath. "You stay right here."

"Scared?" I murmured.

"Terrified. Don't leave me alone with them."

Tawny and Serri had retrieved packages from the trunk of the car and were headed in our direction. Serri's friendly smile encompassed both of us; Tawny's calculating gaze and curved lips were only for Tez.

"What a surprise," I said. "I haven't checked for messages. Did you call to say you were dropping by?"

Insinuating rude behavior was the first weapon in a good hostess's arsenal. I laid a proprietary hand on Tez's arm. "Did you know they were going to visit?"

Tez's gaze glinted with amusement and, if I wasn't mistaken, a smidge of admiration.

"Nope," he drawled.

Serri flushed. "We apologize," she said. "The entire

pride is excited about Tez's arrival. Several members have offerings for you."

"And the alpha wished for us to bring them right way," said Tawny. Her narrowed gaze flicked to mine, and I got the distinct impression that she felt her alpha trumped my idea about good manners any day of the week.

Tez seemed taken aback. "Offerings?"

Serri shared a look with Tawny, and then smiled tentatively. "It's an old-fashioned word, I guess."

"Well," I said, "let's get everything inside, shall we?" I looked at the boxes and bags. "Do you need help?"

"Oh, I do," said Tawny. She handed a stack of Tupperware to Tez, which put him in close proximity to her breasts. She was a master at wielding those melons. I took a distinct satisfaction in the panic that flashed across Tez's features.

"Lead the way, Elizabeth," said Serri. "And thank you for inviting us into your home."

I appreciated that Serri was at least trying to make up for an etiquette faux pas. I opened the door for everyone, and they trooped inside. Tez led them to the kitchen, and I followed.

"You have a lovely home," said Serri. "So many beautiful things."

I heard longing in her voice, and I turned from the pantry to look at her. Serri's expression was wistful as she unloaded one of the bags. I knew dissatisfaction when I saw it; heaven knows I'd felt the emotion often enough. She caught me staring, and sidled a glance at Tawny. The redhead was too busy flirting with Tez to notice either me or her companion. Serri very slightly shook her head, a warning that I had no idea what to do with, and resumed unloading the "offerings."

"Mostly it's food," said Tawny. "I made the cookies. You seemed like a chocolate chip kind of man."

"Oatmeal raisin," said Tez, slipping away from her to check out the items Serri had put onto the counters. "Your pride is very generous." He slipped a yellow Post-it off the top of a covered dish. "'Hope you enjoy my famous Sex in a Pan dessert,'" he read. "'And if you want something else sweet, just call me.'"

"That bitch!" Tawny reached for the paper, then realized what she was doing. She looked down, away from Tez's surprised gaze, and curled her hands into fists.

"Do you mind if I see the note?" asked Serri.

Tez handed it over. Tawny's fury was so palpable I wouldn't have been surprised to see her ignite the floor with her glare. I wisely stayed on my side of the kitchen.

"Who?" hissed Tawny.

Serri sighed, and placed the note back on the foil. "Merrian."

"What the hell is going on?" asked Tez. "It's just a damned note."

"No one is supposed to contact you. Not until . . ." Serri trailed off, her gaze flicking toward Tawny.

"The party," finished the redhead weakly. She smiled, but the attempt did not soften her angry expression. "Tomorrow evening."

I'd been so caught up in my own situation, I'd forgotten that Tez had arrived for a specific purpose: to meet the pride and decide if he wanted to be part of it. I would be happy for Tez to settle in Broken Heart, but not thrilled with him living near so many available, and willing, were-cats.

Still. It was his choice.

It looked like I would be headed to Tulsa by myself. I pushed down the disappointment. I'd looked forward to spending more time with Tez. He'd been right. Despite the more terrifying elements, I very much enjoyed trying to figure out the puzzle. We were missing so many pieces.

Tez's gaze met mine, a question in his eyes, and I shrugged. Obviously there was some undercurrent here that neither of us understood. The were-cats mostly stayed to themselves. I knew very little about their culture or their societal mores. However, it didn't take an anthropologist to figure out this Merrian had broken a rule. What made me worry was that Tez was at the heart of an unknown situation. They wanted something from him, and now I was worried. Something felt desperate about Tawny and Serri, but what did I know? I just wanted Tez to be safe . . . and these were-cats were dangerous. Oh, I knew Tez could take care of himself. But that knowledge didn't stop the foreboding clutching at my stomach.

"I'm going to make tea," I said. "Serri, can you help me? And, Tez? Be a dear, and show Tawny the garden. It's much prettier in the spring, but it still has some lovely foliage."

Tez's eyebrows nearly hit his hairline. I knew he'd probably prefer being dumped into a pit of scorpions than being alone with Tawny, but I was afraid he'd just have to take one for the team. I needed to talk to Serri alone, and there was no way she'd say a word to me with Tawny in earshot.

Tawny, of course, was all on board for a little alone time with Tez. She brightened. "I love gardens," she said. "Through the back door there?"

"Yes." I jerked my head toward the door, and gave Tez a *Get going* stare. He lobbed back a *You owe me big* glare, and then guided Tawny outside.

"What kind of tea do you like?" I asked. I crossed the room and opened the cabinet where I stocked all the tins. "I have many varieties."

"Ah, yes. *Tea.*" She laughed and I knew that Serri hadn't been fooled for a minute. "I can't go against her, you know. Tawny is the alpha's first mate."

I stopped examining the tins, and looked at her. "First mate?"

"Most prides are small. The variety of cat isn't as important as keeping the structure intact. Most of us are blends with dominant features. I'm leopard. Tawny is tiger. Our alpha is lion. Traditionally, there are more females than males. Our pride leaders have a coalition. That means we have two male leaders, the alpha and his second." She began unwrapping treats, probably trying to keep busy because the conversation was making her uncomfortable. She was sharing information that was not mine to know.

"The alpha has more than one mate?" I asked.

Serri sighed. "Revealing the secrets of the pride is a punishable offense." Her gaze flicked to mine, and I saw her unhappiness. "Screw it. What more can they do to me?"

She leaned against the counter, and I grabbed a tin from the shelf, then started the kettle to boiling.

"Two males in each pride, and they each have three

mates," said Serri. "Those not deemed mates are still expected to share the beds of the males. Procreation is important."

I tried to wrap my brain around what she was saying. The conclusion I reached put a sour taste in my mouth. "Oh, Serri."

"I know what you're thinking, but that's not the case. Not these days. In ancient times, the shifters were incestuous and were-cats stayed with their own breeds. A vicious cycle, if you will. All were-cat species were weakened, and some went extinct. That's when elders got together and decided interbreeding would save us—as would not mating with our direct blood relatives."

I was relieved to hear it. I knew many ancient cultures, from the Egyptians to medieval royalty, indulged in incestuous relationships to keep the bloodlines pure. I tried not to be judgmental, but the idea of people sleeping with their siblings or their children made me nauseous.

"At the most, two or three females within the pride will have a child. It's why the males spread the love around. They never know who's fertile. Usually the first female to have a child becomes the alpha's first mate."

"So Tawny had a baby?"

Serri shook her head. "She was the alpha's second mate. She got pregnant, but miscarried. The alpha's first mate passed away a couple of years ago—before we relocated to Broken Heart. Tawny basically got a promotion."

"And where are you in the social strata?"

"First mate to the second," she said softly. "His name is Trak. We have a son. Dayton. He turned a year old last month."

"You must love your family very much." The kettle started to whistle, and I hurried to the stove and removed it from the heat. Then I prepared a pot of green tea. It seemed just the thing we needed. As I waited for the leaves to steep, I glanced at Serri. "It must be difficult to share your husband."

"It is. He loves me," she said. "Only me." She sounded fierce, and underneath the possessive tone was sorrow. "He angered the alpha when he refused to take on another two mates. But he cannot deny his duties to the pride. He must take another lover at least once a month."

I poured the tea and handed her a cup. "Would you like honey to sweeten it?"

"No, thank you." She blew on the water and then sipped. "This is quite good."

"The trick is not to let green leaves steep for more than a minute or two; otherwise the tea tastes bitter." I poured my own cup, and stirred honey into the fragrant liquid. "So, if incest is banned, how do you get new blood into the pride?"

"Exchange programs with other prides. Once our children reach the age of eighteen, they are required to leave our pride and go to another. Every child gets a college education, but they must return to the pride and accept their place within it. The alphas use the children as bargaining chips. Boys have more value than girls, especially sons of alphas." Serri sighed and put down her teacup. "I would give almost anything to live as others do. How wonderful would it be to have a house like yours, Elizabeth. My mate and I could live and love each other in such a place, and raise our son free from the constraints of the pride."

"You could make that choice," I said. "I know how it feels to be trapped by duty. It suffocates your happiness."

"Yes, that's how I feel," said Serri, nodding. "Leaving isn't really an option. We would be outcasts and lose the protection of the pride. Sometimes outcasts are hunted and killed. Dissension means death."

"That's terrible!"

"It's the way of the world," said Serri.

"Not in Broken Heart," I insisted. "You could go to Queen Patsy and ask for sanctuary."

Serri looked at me in surprise. "She would grant such a thing?"

"I don't see why not. You shouldn't be stuck in a life you don't want."

"Maybe." She seemed to absorb the idea with a tiny, hopeful smile. Then she hesitated. "Tez likes you very much."

"I like him, too."

"That makes things . . . difficult. Were-cat females are vicious competitors, especially before mates are named."

I laughed. "Don't be ridiculous. I'm not in any sort of competition for Tez."

"I'm afraid you are." She looked over her shoulder, probably to make sure Tawny wasn't stepping through the door. Both of us would probably hear Tez and Tawny before they even reached the door, but I didn't blame her for using caution. Tawny was not a person I wanted to cross, either. "Our alpha is dying."

"Dying?" Shifters were long-lived and most were immune to human disease and illness. Of course, that didn't mean they never dealt with any ailments.

"He suffers a rare, aggressive form of cancer," said Serri. She looked away, nibbling her lip. "Calphon is the last male child of a very old pride that ignored the new laws of the elders. Even though 'new' in this case means hundreds of years."

"You mean . . . incest?"

"I hate to admit it after trying to reassure you that were-cats, as a whole, no longer practice the old ways, but some prides are stubborn. But they are very few. Calphon's lineage was weakened by the intermarriage of siblings and parents. He's not as strong as most shifters."

"But he's alpha?"

"It's one of the reasons he sought refuge in Broken Heart. He didn't want to face challenges, or endure territorial battles. He's nearly six hundred years old. I think, too, that he's just weary. Tawny is . . . um, high maintenance."

I had no doubt Serri was being kind in that description. But I could see why Tawny was angling so hard for Tez. She didn't want to give up her status as alpha's mate.

"Calphon has weeks, maybe days, to live. In most cases, his successor would be his second and the new second would be chosen from eligible men from a different pride. Except Trak doesn't want the status. And the alpha is being cautious about letting others know about the pride's vulnerabilities."

"So, he managed to track down a complete outsider who has no knowledge of were-cat rules and regs?" It had been a clever thing to do, and I respected Calphon's foresight. It seemed he cared about what happened to the pride. I might not agree with the were-cat lifestyle, but I had no right to judge it.

"How did he find Tez?" I asked.

Serri shrugged. "I have no idea. But Tez is handsome, virile, and strong. He's the rarest of our species. If other prides find out he's without a home, we won't be the only ones competing for him. You can imagine our urgency to snare him, if you will."

Something cold and awful squirmed in the pit of my stomach. "You want Tez to be the new alpha."

She nodded. Pity flashed in her eyes, and it made me wonder just how much my feelings for him had shown. For a long moment, I couldn't even speak. The teacup trembled in my hand, and I put it down before I dropped it. "He's perfectly free to make his own choices. If he wants to lead your pride, I'm sure he'll be quite good at it." Inside, I was seven kinds of jealous and worry. I couldn't stop thinking about that bone-melting kiss I'd shared with Tez, and how I'd very much like to share more. A lot more. "Tawny's jockeying for position."

"Exactly," said Serri. She eyed me. "You look ready to explode."

"I'm incapable of taking a breath to calm down!" I felt wretched. Even as I was trying to decide whether or not Tez and I could possibly have anything together, I'd been walloped by knowledge that, no, no, we would not have a relationship. How could we? He was the last of his species, and it only made sense that he should procreate with another of his kind. I couldn't deny him children. I knew all too well the regret incurred by not having children. It was too late to dream of the life I might've had if I'd only had the courage to find a man who loved and cherished me.

Perhaps, it wasn't too late. I might not be able to have Tez, but I didn't have to be alone for all of eternity, either.

"I know you must be upset." Serri reached out and patted my shoulder. "But what future does Tez truly have with you, Elizabeth? Even if you were alive, you couldn't bear his children. None of us claim pure bloodlines. None but Tez. Would you deny him?"

"I would deny him nothing," I whispered. In my heart of hearts, I knew it was true.

"Then let him go. Let him have a life with his own kind. Let him be a father." She squeezed my shoulder one last time before she let me go. "I'm trying to protect you. If Tawny or any of the other females realize you might be a threat, they will come after you."

"This isn't the savanna," I said. "It's Broken Heart. They have an accord with the town. I seriously doubt Queen Patricia would put up with were-cats trying to harm me, or any vampire." Of course, they didn't need to know Patsy was incapacitated, and quite mad.

Good Lord. This had been a helluva bad day.

I heard Tez and Tawny's voices and realized my vampire hearing had picked them up while they were still several feet from entering the house. Serri had heard them, too, with her cat ears, and she immediately got busy arranging things on the counter.

I didn't think I could behave pleasantly with Tawny, and I knew that Tez would realize right away something was wrong. He had that silly Elizabeth radar. Why was it that the only man I couldn't have, that I shouldn't want, had me figured out?

"I'm not feeling well," I said. I was being a poor hostess as well as a poor sport. "Would you make my excuses?"

"Of course," said Serri. She looked at me, her gaze filled with empathy. "I'm sorry, Elizabeth."

I nodded, and then I hurried to my bedroom. I locked the door behind me and leaned against it, trying to find my center. I did so miss breathing.

I heard Serri make my apologies, and offer to pour tea. I assumed that Tez would try to get rid of the girls as soon as possible. At which point, he'd want to talk to me.

Damn.

I clambered down the stairs, and flipped on the lights. All I needed was a minute or two to gather my wits. Then I could face Tez, and do what needed to be done. Probably. Elizabeth Bretton: she who understands duty, and its deplorable price.

To rein in my agitation, I brushed my hair and redid my makeup. Then I straightened my room. I put the stack of romance novels I'd finished this past week into a bag to donate to the library. I realized my bed was still crusted with mud from my woodland trek, so I stripped the bedding and remade the bed with fresh sheets and a clean comforter. Then I plumped the pillows.

I supposed I could have gone through my closet to collect the clothing I didn't wear anymore. I had some shoes and bags that were still in good condition, too. When we—that is, *I*—went to Tulsa tomorrow, I could drop it all off at my favorite charity.

I flopped backward onto the bed.

What I really wanted to do was kiss Tez. I wanted to talk to him and laugh with him. I wanted to take the chance he'd offered. Why was he so sure about our potential? It was flattering and frustrating. When had I ever been that certain of anything? I was tragically not one who took leaps of faith. I tended to think situations to death, just as I was doing now.

Argh!

I rolled onto my side, tucking a pillow under my head, and lamented my inability to, as Patsy might say, put on my big-girl panties and deal with it. With Tez. With the shadow. With my own insecurities.

I focused on the lamp situated on my nightstand. Maybe I should replace it. It was pretty enough, I supposed, but I was envisioning a redesign of my bedroom. I was feeling the call of blues and silvers, and certainly I could—

I rose up, my gaze on the shade. Draped on the side facing the bed was a gold pendant necklace.

It wasn't mine.

But I knew who it belonged to. I remembered it from the vision of Elizabeth. She'd been wearing it as her killer carried her out to the woods.

The hairs rose on the back of my neck, and I slowly sat up. How had it gotten here? I clutched the pillow to my stomach, feeling a little sick.

Had the shadow brought it to me?

Another token. But this had not been on the shelf in the attic.

Was that why he'd gone to the grave? To find the

necklace as a backup connection? It didn't make sense to give *me* the objects imbued with *her* essence.

I shook off my fears, and tried to call upon some reason. Why on the earth would the dark entity leave me another gift? If Tez and I were right in our supposition, then I was only one of five victims. And if I was supposed to be the recipient of all the stolen objects, then why just send over the silver box? And now, this necklace?

I studied the pendant. It was a lovely sapphire, about the size of a quarter, inlaid in gold and surrounded by diamonds.

It occurred to me then that perhaps the gift was from Tez.

Knock, knock, knock.

Silly, wishful thinking. I glanced at the staircase. I shouldn't touch it until I knew for sure how it had gotten here, and who had put it in my room. I didn't want to issue another invitation to the brutal phantom. He'd only shown up, and managed to strangle me, when I was holding the silver box. So, he needed a conduit— something from the past in order to touch the present.

I hated feeling vulnerable in my own home. Until we were able to figure out the shadow's purpose, and what my role was in the whole debacle, I couldn't assume anything was innocuous. Not even very lovely jewelry.

Knock, knock, knock.

"Elizabeth. Can I come in?"

I stood up, tossed the pillow onto the bed, and made my way up the staircase. I opened the door. "Did our guests leave?"

"Yeah."

His gaze flicked over me, and he frowned. "Why did you disappear?"

"I have other things to do than entertain your potential girlfriends. If you'll excuse me, I have some chores to finish."

I tried to shut the door, but he grabbed the edge and held it open.

"I expect better from you," he said. The disappointment in his tone raked me like a shard of glass. "You know I'm not interested in them. I've made it clear I want you. Only you."

"Hah! How egotistical of you to assume I will simply swoon at your feet."

"No, you don't, princess." He pushed open the door and grabbed my wrist, yanking me through the door. He spun me around in his arms and kissed me.

I tried to protest such a he-man move. *Honestly!* Did he think I would just melt under the assault of his wonderful mouth? I had pride. I had strength of will. So what if his arms felt good around me? And the hot press of his body against mine made my shiver?

"I really must protest," I managed, pulling away just enough to attempt to glare up at him.

"Okay," he said. He held me tight, giving me no room to wiggle free. He leaned down and nibbled my bottom lip. Then he looked at me, challenge glittering in his eyes. "Go on, princess. Protest."

Chapter 10

"We shouldn't get involved," I said, though my voice held little resolve. "You should date your own kind. And m-marry and have children. You would be an excellent alpha for the Broken Heart were-cats."

"Alpha," he stated flatly.

"Oh. Um, yes. Serri told me that Calphon is dying. They need a new alpha. They want you." I tried for a smile and failed. "Didn't you know?"

His gaze flicked away, and hurt ghosted through me. "You did know."

"I came to check it out," he said. "I was tired of being alone. I could never get close to anyone. Being a shifter isn't a secret you can share with your pals." He captured my gaze. "I haven't agreed to anything."

"But you're considering it."

"I didn't know I'd meet you, okay?" A muscle ticked in his jaw. "You . . . you . . . goddamnit!" He kissed me so hard my lips felt bruised and swollen when he came up for air. His breath feathered my mouth, and I noticed that the irises of his eyes were diamond shaped. The jaguar was stirring. "I have never wanted anyone like you, Elizabeth. I want to be near you all the time. I love the way you smell. I get a jolt at the sound of your voice, your laugh. I know it sounds crazy."

He was doing it again—using his words to show tenderness. Yet, there was a raw quality to his tone, as though he were not used to saying such things. Of course, that could also be the perception of my romance-starved imagination. His honesty carved through my jealousy, my doubts, my self-control.

"You deserve a life with a wife, or two, and children, Tez. I can't give you a family. I can't lock you into my marital curse, either."

"Uh-huh." He stared at me, his expression inscrutable. "You through with all your protesting?"

He sounded angry. I was just trying to be practical! For both our sakes. "I believe so, yes."

"Sure?" he asked impatiently. "*All* done?"

I nodded.

"Good." He kissed me again—administering a full-on sensual attack with teeth and tongue, and his hands stroked from my hips to my rib cage, and dared to touch the undersides of my breasts. My body tingled with need, and all points south were experiencing quite the reawakening. I heard a moan, and was shocked to realize the low sound had come from me.

Tez stepped back, his hands settling on my hips. "I'm not interested in any other woman, human, undead or were-cat."

"Tez, it's premature to make any decisions about your future."

"Our future. Fine. Let's focus on the right now, princess." He rubbed his knuckles under my jaw. "I want you. You want me."

"Yes." Why deny what was so obvious?

To my astonishment, he dropped to his knees. His fingers dipped under my shirt and undid my pants.

"Tez!"

"Don't give me the 'sex is marriage' lecture again, all right?" He peeled back my trousers and wiggled them down my hips. I felt exposed . . . and expectant. The impromptu eroticism shushed my common sense.

He pressed his mouth to the vee of my thighs. *Oh. My. God.* His accuracy was uncanny. The wet warmth of his lips penetrated the thin lace of my panties. His breath fluttered through the barriers and ghosted over my labia.

Shock and pleasure reverberated in my core as I tried to form words of protest. *No, enough of protests.* Yet, I couldn't even form words of encouragement.

"The black ones are nice," he said. His fingertips dipped under the band. "I can't wait to see you in red."

I didn't even bother to deny he would see me in red. I already knew we'd be getting naked soon enough. I just didn't know how we were going to effectively manage this affair.

I grasped his shoulders to steady myself, and to readjust a tiny bit to the left.

He took the hint. He pulled my panties down, and took precious seconds to strip off shoes, socks, pants, and undies. I was completely exposed, and vulnerable—physically and emotionally.

Tez pushed my legs apart and studied the thin strip of blond curls between my legs.

"Brazilian waxing," I stated unnecessarily. I was nervous. He was being too quiet—channeling that jaguar stillness of his. "One of the last beauty treatments I did before dying. I had no idea I'd never need to suffer through it again."

"Beautiful," he murmured. Then, because he obviously took torture lessons from the CIA, he blew on my exposed clitoris . . . and *then* he sucked it between his lips. His tongue flickered over the sensitive nub, and the floor tilted. Or maybe my knees just gave way.

I couldn't believe I was standing in my kitchen while a man I'd know forty-eight hours pleasured me with his very talented mouth. And tongue. *Dear God.* Did I mention his tongue?

He spread me apart and slowly licked the titillated flesh. Honestly, I didn't know how I managed to remain standing. My thighs quaked and my knees kept threatening to buckle. I had never known this kind of wicked pleasure, not even with my husband. I wasn't naïve about the ways to make love; I'd just never had much of a chance to explore the possibilities.

He rained kisses everywhere, his lips soft and warm and persistent.

His tongue swiped me, deeply, and I grabbed his hair. I'm afraid I pulled rather hard, but Tez didn't seem to mind at all.

He cupped my buttocks and pulled me to his mouth . . . kissing . . . licking . . . sucking. Then he pushed his tongue inside me, and thrust over and over, until I was soaked and panting (Breath? Who needs breath?) and squirming.

He pulled back and looked up at me, breathing hard, his eyes glazed with passion. "Come for me, Elizabeth."

His words were as powerful an aphrodisiac as his actions. His fingers dug into my buttocks as he returned to suckling my clit, alternating the tender assault with sweeps of his tongue.

"Oh!" I tipped over the edge, falling into white-hot bliss. The intensity of the orgasm was nothing like I'd ever experienced. It was a free fall into electric pleasure, and I wanted it to last forever.

Alas, it did not.

When I was finally able to form a coherent thought, I looked down at Tez. I was still shaking, but he held me upright. He was lazily licking away the evidence of my enjoyment.

"Tez." It's all I could get out. I wasn't exactly sure what I wanted to say, except maybe, thank you.

There was something to be said for he-man behavior.

He helped me to redress, all the way to putting back on my shoes; then he climbed to his feet and gathered me into his arms. "You are delicious."

His hard-on was very obvious. I lightly touched the ridge of his shaft through his jeans.

He took my hand and brought it up to his lips. "Don't worry about me, princess. We'll have time later to play." He smiled. "Unless you've thought of more protests."

"Me? Protest? Don't be ridiculous."

" 'Atta girl." He smoothed away my hair, and looked

deeply into my eyes. I could see he was still feeling rather lusty, and I was more than willing to reciprocate the pleasure he'd given me. Granted, I wasn't well-versed in fellatio, but I was certainly willing enough. Tez put a finger to my lips. "Don't even offer. I wanted to give something to you, Elizabeth. You don't owe me."

"I don't feel as though I would be repaying a debt."

"Good to know. I have every intention of exploring that luscious body of yours, and allowing you to take whatever liberties you want with mine." He stepped back a little, but kept his hands on my waist. "When you said I was sure about us, you were right. I am. My mother was a human, but she raised me the best she could in the shifter ways. My father told her a lot about our kind, and she used that knowledge to help me."

"She sounds like a marvelous woman."

"She was." He swallowed hard. "She died last year."

"I'm so sorry." I laid my hand against his cheek and turned his face to kiss my palm. I realized now that for so long as Tez had his mother, he probably didn't have the desire to seek out others like him. How lonely he must now be without the only person who'd known, and accepted, his true nature. My heart ached for him. He probably needed the connections with other parakind, and that's why he traveled to Broken Heart.

"She told me that when I met my mate, I would know and the knowledge was absolute—two pieces clicking together perfectly. Mom said I would always feel like half a person, until I met the woman who made me feel whole."

"Well," I said, somewhat dismayed by this news, "I will be happy to be yours until that happens."

Tez looked at me as if I were crazy. "It already has, Ellie Bee. That night on the path, even in the rain, I could smell you. Feel you. *Mine.* It beat in my heart, pulsed in my veins. I saw you, and I knew." He cupped my face. "You are my mate."

I gaped at him. "I'm not a were-cat."

"We've established that."

I pointed to my stomach. "I can't have your babies."

"Again, facts in evidence."

"Why would a vampire be your mate?" I asked, still grappling with the idea Tez thought I was his by virtue of an absolute *feeling* wherein he suddenly felt *whole.* Talk about a leap of faith! (Not to mention a really screwed-up version of the birds-and-bees talk.) No wonder he'd been unconcerned about the hundred-year-marriage contract. The delusional man thought I was his destiny.

"I don't know how to feel about this," I said. "It's . . . it's a little . . ."

"Crazy?"

"Overwhelming."

He nodded. "I understand. But I'm not going anywhere." He kissed my forehead, and then let me go. "Couple hours before dawn. You wanna watch a movie and make out?"

I laughed. "You sure know how to change a subject. Yes, I'd love to do both of those things."

"All right. You got popcorn?"

"And an air popper." We separated to gather the needed supplies, and that's when I remembered the pendant in my room. I didn't want to ruin the moment. The idea of spending my last awake hours snuggling with Tez was a temptation I couldn't resist. Almost. I had to tell him about seeing that stupid necklace; we had to deal with it. Once we'd solved the problem of the demon shadow, I'd have plenty of time to spend with Tez. At least, I hoped so.

"Tez, I found a pendant in my room, just hanging on my lampshade. I don't suppose you left me a present."

He stopped poking through my cabinets, and turned to face me. "What pendant?"

The hope for a cozy evening with Tez evaporated. "It's in my bedroom."

We went downstairs and I led him to the nightstand. "If it is from that thing, I don't know how he got in here. Last time, he used Rand as a delivery boy."

"Maybe he's trying a more direct approach. Where is it?"

"There," I said, pointing to the shade. "It's on the—" I stopped abruptly as I saw exactly what Tez saw.

Nothing.

No pendant necklace.

"I swear it was there. It was a gold chain with a large sapphire."

"I believe you," said Tez. "But it's not here now."

We searched the nightstand, looking behind it, and then inside the lamp itself. A perusal of the floor revealed nothing more than a need to vacuum up dust bunnies. I couldn't believe it had just disappeared. Had I imagined it? Was it some sort of ominous gift from the shadow, or a ghostly vision from Elizabeth? I doubted she was still around. What I didn't understand was why Patsy so clearly hadn't seen any ghosts around me.

"He put Patsy out of commission on purpose," I said, suddenly sure. "She's the biggest threat. She can see ghosts and she can raise the dead. If she could see him, she could bind him with her powers. He drove her crazy enough to attempt murder."

"Why not just kill her?" asked Tez.

"She has another purpose to serve. Or maybe he knows that killing Patsy means the end of all vampires—and he wants that pleasure himself."

"Whoa. Wait a freaking minute. If Patsy dies, you all die?"

"Well, she is really hard to kill," I said. "But, yes. The vampires lost one-eighth of their population thousands of years ago because a demon killed an Ancient named Shamhat." I waved my hand. "That's a long story, one for another time. Before Patsy became our queen, the vampires were ruled by seven Ancients. Two were banned—sent into paranormal limbo—and a third named Lia was killed. If Patsy had not assumed all the powers, then a lot of vampires would've died with Lia. At least, that's the working theory."

"It seems kinda stupid to put all your eggs in one basket," said Tez. "That has gotta be hell on her. She's gotta be a wife, a mother to triplets, and ruler of an entire species?"

"The lycans, too," I said. "They follow her edicts as well."

"I can't believe she didn't go crazy way before now."

He was right. Hadn't I thought the same thing? I worried about Patsy. I very much sympathized with anyone trapped by duty, as I had so often felt trapped by my own circumstances and choices made to benefit others. Women were predisposed, most of the time, to take care of others, but not themselves. Patsy had Gabriel, of

course, which surely helped—but she bore the full responsibility of leadership.

I shook off thoughts of Patsy, and returned to the
issue at hand. Chased by a vengeful . . . something. Spirit.
Shadow. Bogeyman. I sat on the edge of my bed, feeling
miserable. "He can get in and out of here anytime he
wants. I don't think I'm ever going to feel safe again. Not
until we catch him."

"I could sleep with you down here," offered Tez. He
put up his hands. "Just sleep. Promise."

I hugged myself, feeling unaccountably chilled. "It's
this house," I said. "I don't want to be here. I hate feeling afraid."

"Let's get out of here for the night. You got somewhere we can go?"

I considered all my friends, and one by one discarded
them as potential spots to spend the day. Jessica had
her hands full with her own children plus the triplets,
Phoebe and Connor had returned to Tulsa, Patsy was
mad as a hatter, and Eva and Lorcan really didn't have
the extra space. Then I thought of the perfect place.

"We can go to the Three Sisters," I said. "It's the bed-
and-breakfast that Lenette and her sisters run. They
have special rooms for vampires."

"Call 'em up, princess. Get a room for two." He wag-
gled his eyebrows, and leered outrageously. I laughed. I
had to admit staying the night at the Three Sisters with
Tez made me feel much better.

I resented not feeling at ease in my own home. It was
disturbing to realize the shadow could come and go as
he pleased, although he seemed to wait until I was alone
to attack me.

If he had left the necklace . . . why take it away again?

There was so much I didn't understand about the situation.

"Hey, Velma," said Tez. He took my hand and squeezed it. "Let it go. We'll sort fact from fiction tomorrow, okay? Everything's gonna be all right."

You know what? I believed him.

Lenette, and her sisters, Dorica and Nell, welcomed us warmly. Even with a mere hour before dawn, the pull of vampire sleep already upon me, Tez and I took up their invitation to enjoy tea and scones. The sisters were very well known for their excellent baked goods. I often purchased their mango-lemon muffins to enjoy with my afternoon tea.

As I mentioned earlier, Lenette and her sisters practiced Wicca, and wielded quite powerful magick. They often added little enchantments to their aromatherapy products, which they sold in the gift shop.

We went into the cozy kitchen. The table occupying the breakfast nook was already set. Lenette was tall, her hair a stunning red, and, as Tez might say, stacked. She nodded toward her sister.

"Nell told us you'd be arriving soon," she said. "And that you might be feeling unsettled."

Nell was blond, thin, and quiet. She offered us a smile. "We're glad you're here," she said in a whispery voice. "You are always welcome."

"Thank you," I said.

"Yeah," said Tez. "Thanks."

Each sister held a particular gift: Lenette's was, as she

called it, necromancy lite; Nell could see into the future, but only by hours; and Dorica read auras. Her hair was brown, and freckles splashed across her dainty nose like cinnamon. She was the middle sister, and fit the designation well: shorter and thinner than Lenette, but taller and plumper than Nell.

Dorica studied both me and Tez, and frowned slightly. *Oh, this can't be good.* Tez didn't seem to notice the scrutiny. He chose the chair next to mine, and waited for the sisters to join us. We made small talk while I sipped their excellent jasmine tea, and Tez tried for a world record in how many scones he could eat in five minutes.

"How did it go at the mansion?" I asked.

"I'm afraid I don't have much more information to share. Connor and Phoebe said the symbols of Mammon's shadow were knotted. It might take a while to remove the circle. I added some protection spells in the attic and some around the house, too. But that demon magic . . . it's not something I've ever felt before."

Tez ate yet another scone, and I turned to look at him.

"These are awesome," he said.

"Thanks," said Lenette. "I'll make some for you to take with you on your trip tomorrow."

"You know about us going to Tulsa?" I asked. I snared a scone and split it so I could add some clotted cream. Except I didn't think Tez would be accompanying me. Not with the were-cat party to attend. I really needed to stop worrying so much about it.

If only I *could* stop, though.

"Gabriel told me about you and Tez doing some extra research into Broken Heart's past." Lenette seemed content to sip on her own cup of tea. "We love this town, but we only arrived a few years ago. Unfortunately, we have no history in it. Not like you, Elizabeth, or Jessica or even Eva."

"History." My teacup clinked loudly as I clumsily dropped it on its saucer. I don't know why Lenette's comment sparked the information, but now I knew why "five" had been so important. "Five families."

I turned to Tez. "During the Oklahoma land run, five families staked out claims around this area. The Silverstones, the LeRoys, the McCrees, the Clarks, and the Allens."

"You're the Silverstone," said Tez.

"Jessica is a McCree. Phoebe is an Allen. Eva is a LeRoy." My excitement turned to ashes. "Darlene was a Clark, but she was killed."

"Aren't you all technically dead?" asked Tez.

"Darlene was vampire, too," I said, "but we had some problems with a military group named ETAC. One of the soldiers killed her. All we found was her ashes."

"Harsh," said Tez.

"Her daughter, Marissa, lives here," said Lenette. "She's eleven now—she was six when she almost died from drowning, if I remember right. Her father is Dr. Clark. He moved back to town after he realized he needed help with his daughter's special needs."

"Special needs?" I asked. I didn't know Dr. Clark or Marissa very well. Actually, I hadn't particularly liked Darlene Clark. She was a decent mother, I supposed, but much too concerned with appearances. And she didn't seem to have a lot of common sense.

"Marissa crossed the veil when she drowned," said

Dorica in her whiskey voice. "She was touched by death."

Lenette nodded. "We're helping her deal with her powers."

"Which are what?" asked Tez. He eyed my scone, and I pushed my plate toward him. He happily devoured both halves.

"It's difficult to explain," said Lenette. "She has a connection to death. Her gift manifests in different ways. We're still trying to figure it out." She turned to me. "You think the entity that attacked you is somehow related to an old secret."

It wasn't a question. "Yes, I do." I explained about my vision, finding the bones of the other Elizabeth, and the two strangulation incidents.

"You're on the right track," said Nell. "You'll find more answers in Tulsa."

"Be careful," said Dorica. "Danger is all around you." Her gaze snagged mine. "You'll have a decision to make soon, Elizabeth. You might find neither choice will be palatable."

"Dire warnings from witches," said Lenette. She sent an admonishing look to her sister, who shrugged it off. "Don't let it bend your brain, okay?"

Tez reached under the table and squeezed my hand. "We'll be all right."

His reassurance eased back the fear creeping through me. How in the world had I come to rely on him so thoroughly in such a short amount of time? If I were to believe Tez's story, then I was his mate and felt exactly as I should. Or, more likely, I had hidden from myself how desperately I missed male companionship and I eagerly accepted every ounce of affection and comfort he gave. I wasn't sure which scenario was worse.

"I'm afraid I'll fall asleep in my tea." I wanted to dismiss the talk about unfair decisions, and all thoughts of mating with Tez. All right. Maybe not *all* thoughts.

"I'll show you to your room," said Lenette.

Tez and I said our good-nights to the sisters, and then followed Lenette down a set of stairs into what had once been the basement of the house. She walked us down the hallway.

"How's Meyer?" I asked.

"Still loves numbers. The more complicated the equation, the happier he is."

Meyer P. Dennison was Lenette's fiancé. He'd arrived in Broken Heart as an IRS agent under the mistaken impression he was going to audit Jessica, and had no idea she was a vampire. He'd been accidently bitten by a zombie; Lenette's necromagick saved him. He wasn't dead, but he wasn't quite alive, either. He stopped aging, ate rarely, and required little sleep. He was, I supposed, a half-zombie. He'd taken an accounting position with the Consortium, and he and Lenette seemed very much in love.

She opened a door at the end of the hall and turned on the light. She swept inside, turning down the covers on the four-poster bed, and doing a general inspection to make sure all was in order.

"Please don't worry so much about Dorica's warning," she said. "My sister can be dramatic."

Tez put his arm around me. "We'll take it as it comes," said Tez. "Thanks for the room."

"You're welcome. While you're here, you're safe. No evil can penetrate our magick," she said. "Sleep well."

She left, quietly shutting the door behind her.

My suitcase and Tez's duffel bag had already been put on luggage racks in the opened closet. I took the bathroom first, brushing my teeth, washing my face, and putting on my nightgown.

Tez whistled when I stepped out of the bathroom. "Nice nightie, princess." He grinned wickedly. "Hope you don't mind. I like to sleep in the buff."

I wrapped my arms around his neck, and kissed him softly. "Mmm. I don't mind a bit. Too bad I will be, quite literally, dead to the world."

"Yeah." He sighed. "That is a problem."

He went into the bathroom, and I got tucked into bed, plumping the pillows. I waited for him to join me; I hoped for snuggling. It had been a long time since I'd shared a bed with someone else.

Tez crawled into bed and gathered me into his arms as if it was the most natural action in the world. Despite his earlier teasing, he was wearing boxer shorts, which I admit I was disappointed to see.

Pressed against Tez's delectable chest, listening to the comforting sound of his heartbeat, I surrendered to vampire slumber.

Chapter 11

In the attic, in the secret room, he accuses me of greed.
I have never asked for trinkets. His petty words wound me, and I want to hurt him back. I hold my tongue, though, because I owe him, and he knows it. It's why he can be so cruel, and why I do nothing.

Candlelight flickers across his handsome face. Here was a man I had thought I might love. Why does he want to torment me? He stares at me, and the look in his eyes is so strange, I feel my heart skip a fearful beat.

"You're mine," he whispers. "Mine."

Desperation tinges his words, that and some other emotion I cannot define.

I shouldn't have followed him upstairs to this terrible room. I shouldn't have kept his secret. It was wrong.

It seems I am doomed to make the wrong choices.

I look at the floor, at the odd symbols that float like coal dust above the wood planks. It smells like rotten eggs, and I hold my gloved hand up to my nose. "What have you done?"

His eyes are wild, and I'm frightened.

Downstairs in my beautiful home, the party is in full swing, and I am the hostess. I am wearing my pretty brown velveteen dress, the one with the copper roses. I have removed my hat. It, too, has copper roses. I'm very pleased with my outfit, but I suppose he would accuse me of vanity should I say so.

"We should go," I say, and I back up a step. "The guests."

"You were with him."

I shake my head because I cannot trust my voice. I try to be brave. I think of my children, and I know that no matter what harm I might've caused, they were worth the price. The choice.

"You betrayed me!"

Panic wells. I don't like the way he's looking at me, and I know he wants to hurt me.

"I have done everything right," he says. "You're mine. I won't share you." He rips the hat out of my hand and tosses it to the floor. "You think I don't know where you got that necklace? Give it to me."

I put my hand on the sapphire that dangles from my neck. "No."

He grabs the chain and pulls so hard, it cuts into my neck. It does not break, and that infuriates him. I cry out, and back away, but he's worked up now. His rage is palpable.

He cocks his fist—and hits me.

The pain is immediate and intense. I slam into the wall and hit my head. Then I fall, fall, fall into darkness.

Chapter 12

When I woke up, I found Tez already out of bed and awake. He was pacing, shoving his fingers through his already ruffled hair. His worried expression had me sitting up and tossing off the covers.

"What's happened?"

"Elizabeth." He pulled me out of bed and wrapped his arms around me. "I'm sorry, princess. I'm so sorry."

"Sorry for what?"

He pulled back and stared down at me. "I've been waiting for you to wake up. Lenette came down about an hour ago. Your friend Eva tried to commit suicide."

I went cold.

"No. Never."

"I'm only telling you what Lenette said. With everything else going on in this place, I don't really believe it, either."

"Where is she?"

"The hospital."

"And Lorcan?"

Tez hesitated. "He's disappeared."

"He would never abandon Eva. So, either he's hurt or stuck somewhere." Horror slicked through me. "The shadow."

Tez's expression confirmed my fears. "No one's said so, but, yeah, I think he took Lorcan's form and did the same thing to Eva that he did to Patsy."

"Why?" I cried. Frustration and fury wound through me. "What purpose does it have? To destroy love?"

Shocked by my own revelation, I sank to the bed and fisted my hands in the covers. "Is that what he's doing? Replaying the scenario over and over?"

"What scenario?"

I explained about my most recent vision and, in it, the confirmation that I had seen the necklace around Elizabeth's neck. "She betrayed him by taking a lover. He killed her." I frowned. "But he'd only called on Mammon's shadow. I saw the symbols on the floor."

"It's a good theory," said Tez. "But I feel like there's a deeper purpose. We don't know what the end game is yet."

"We better figure it out quickly," I said. "Let's go see Eva."

I hurried into the bathroom and quickly completed my ablutions. As soon as I dressed and packed, Tez grabbed my suitcase and his duffel.

Lenette was waiting for us in the kitchen. She looked worried as she directed Tez toward the coffeepot. I declined a cup.

"I can't believe Eva would intentionally harm herself," said Lenette. "Mammon's shadow must've affected her, the same he affected Patsy."

"That was our thought, too," said Tez.

Lenette sighed. "Dr. Clark seems to think she walked into the dawn of her own volition."

"Oh, my God. She tried to go into the sunlight?" I asked, horrified. "Who found her?"

"Tamara hadn't gone to bed yet," said Lenette. "Thank the Goddess she was there. Tamara's been out in the field, training with Durriken. She just got home yesterday."

"Training?" asked Tez.

"Durriken is a Roma—a werewolf who only shifts during the full moon. He and his family are vampire hunters. He's been training Tamara to fight and to hunt."

"You live in a town with vampire hunters?"

"They have a pact with the Consortium," clarified Lenette. "Anyway, Tamara heard her mom go outside. She said Eva was upset and telling her she couldn't live with the heartache of Lorcan's unfaithfulness."

I wasn't surprised that Lenette already knew most of the story. This was Broken Heart, after all, and small-town secrets were hard to keep—except the long-ago travesty that had set all we were experiencing now into tragic motion. That had been kept secret from all of us.

"How'd she manage to get her mom back inside?" asked Tez.

Lenette piled scones into a bakery box and closed the lid. "The Roma hunters are very good at what they do. She dropped Eva with some kind of crazy move and dragged her smoking body back into the house. Then she called Patrick and Jessica."

"Where's Lorcan?" I asked.

"Nobody knows."

"If Eva was harmed, so was he. That's how the mate bond works."

"Well, he's alive," said Lenette practically. She eyed Tez, who'd already dipped into the scones she'd just packed, and started putting together another box. "Otherwise, Eva would be gone."

"Let's assume the shadow took Lorcan's form," said Tez. "Somewhere between the emergency room and finding Dr. Clark, the Gabriel doppelganger disappears. We think he's crawled under a rock to heal."

"But he took on a new form," I said. "Lorcan."

"Eva goes home and they start digging around in the archives. Maybe they find something, and he's trying to hide it. He starts pulling the same crap with Eva that he did with Patsy."

"He took three days to make Patsy nuts."

Tez nodded. "She's stronger, maybe harder to push toward a breakdown. Or maybe he needed access to the house and that room, and when he was done doing whatever, he pushed her buttons."

"I can't believe he meant for her to stab him to death." I took the bakery boxes from Lenette; otherwise Tez would empty them before we even got to the car.

"Probably not." Tez popped the last bit of his stolen scone into his mouth, and finished off his coffee. He looked longingly at the boxes in my hand and I scooted out of his reach. He sent me a doleful look, but I would not be swayed. Besides, I wanted one, too.

"If the shadow knows that killing a vampire means killing his mate, maybe he held off on hurting Lorcan until he figured out what Eva knew," said Tez. "Or maybe he just didn't have time to kill Lorcan. Could be he's unconscious and locked up somewhere."

"Somewhere a vampire couldn't escape?" I asked. "Lorcan's practically an Ancient, and he has shifter abilities. The only thing that could hold him is fairy gold or . . . or I don't know what else."

"Let's get to the hospital," said Tez. "Talk to Eva. If I know that security chief of yours, he's already looking for Lorcan."

"Is that grudging admiration I hear in your voice?" I teased.

"He's good," said Tez with a shrug. "I bet dollars to scones he's turning the hospital upside down right now."

"Then the best thing we can do is continue Eva's research work."

"I agree. Soon as we're done visiting Eva, we'll head to Tulsa."

"I'll head to Tulsa," I said. "You're going to the werecat party."

"Shit." He looked at me, frowning. "Wait. You're not going with me?"

"You didn't invite me."

"I didn't . . ." He trailed off, obviously annoyed. "Are you kidding me?"

"You assumed I was going with you? Hmm. Interesting." I might've gotten some satisfaction from Tez's flummoxed expression, but I was also doing a little girly happy dance that he'd expected me to be his date. Still, he should've asked me.

The priority, however, was to get to Tulsa—although I did have that lovely red wrap dress I hadn't worn yet.

No, Elizabeth. Focus. We needed information more than ever, and it seemed like my great-grandfather's heir-looms might hold the keys we needed to unlock the mystery and the motive of the shadow man.

"Good luck," said Lenette. "I'll pray that the God and the Goddess keep you protected during your journey."

When we got outside, Tez loaded our bags into the Honda's trunk. He slammed it shut. Then he rounded the car and looked pleadingly at me. "Please go to the party with me. We won't stay long, I promise."

"Well," I sniffed. "I suppose. But only for a little while."

"Cruel, cruel woman," he muttered. Then he kissed me soundly. "Where's the hospital?"

Tez managed to finish off half of one box of scones by the time we got to the hospital. He parked close to the main entrance, and shoved a final bite into his mouth. He looked at me, his expression tinged with guilt. "What? I have a high metabolism. Shifters eat a lot."

"Mm-hmm."

Just as Tez predicted, Damian was in the hospital lobby coordinating the search for Lorcan. He'd come to the same conclusion we had about the shadow taking Lorcan's identity, and made the same assumption that the vampire was still alive somewhere.

"Is there anything we can do?" I asked.

"No, *Liebling*. Until we figure out how to stop him, no one is safe. We're attempting to take precautions, but there's not much we can do. We don't know how he takes the form, or whom he might attack next."

I told Damian about our theory, explaining how

Tez and I believed that the founding families of Broken Heart might be involved with a conspiracy to cover up something terrible that happened—something that started with the murder of Elizabeth Silverstone.

"Started?" asked Damian. "You think there's more than one victim?"

"I don't know," I said. "Tez is right. This doesn't feel finished. If the demon shadow is trying to fulfill some sort of purpose prevented more than a hundred years ago . . . there may be no stopping him."

"If you're right, Elizabeth, then we have much to fear."

Damian's admission ramped up my own worries about what was unfolding in Broken Heart. I only hoped we could stop it—*him*—before someone died.

"How's Patsy doing?" asked Tez.

"Not well. When she awoke, she was immediately enraged. She's not herself. Dr. Michaels issued a sedative—a knockout gas, if you will. Unfortunately, we must keep her unconscious for now." Damian's phone buzzed, and he turned away to answer it.

"Let's go see Eva," I said to Tez. We got the room number from the receptionist and took the elevator to the second floor.

When we arrived at Eva's room, I saw Darrius, who was one of the royal lycan triplets and brother to Damian, standing guard outside the door. Usually he and his other brother, Drake, were the cutups, but his demeanor was all business. His jade green eyes didn't even hold a glint of his usual humor.

"How is she?" I asked.

"Alive," he said. "But not in her right mind."

Trepidation filled me as I pushed through the door and into the dimly lit room. Tez followed me, his hand resting on the small of my back. I stopped near the bed and gazed down at Eva. Her eyes were closed; her wrists and ankles were strapped to the bed. I sensed the fairy gold interwoven through the restraints.

"Eva?"

Her eyes opened and within their brown depths I saw pain so deep, so jagged, I felt cut open by it. Surely no human was meant to suffer like this. Had Patsy felt the same way? Did it torment her still, and that was why she was enraged?

"Let me die," she whispered. "Without him, I'm nothing. He broke my heart, Elizabeth. And I cannot bear it."

"Lorcan would never hurt you. He lives for you."

She squeezed her eyes shut, pressed her lips together, and turned her head. Her shoulders started to shake. Vampires could not cry, but that didn't mean the urge to shed tears left us.

"He doesn't love me," she said in a wounded voice.

"Eva, shhh." I reached out to touch her, to offer some small comfort, but Tez stilled my hand. He was right, of course. If she was as volatile as Patsy, she could well rip off my hand with just her fangs.

"Darling, can you tell us what you found out about Broken Heart?" I asked softly. "Do you know what happened a hundred years ago?"

She looked at me once again, her expression filled with anguish. "What?"

"You and— Well, you were looking in the archives for old newspapers, diaries, anything that could help us figure out how Elizabeth died."

Eva frowned, and her gaze flickered. It was almost as if the need to mourn the loss of love wasn't her emotion but someone else's forced upon her. If the shadow had somehow *injected* grief into my friends, then Eva and Patsy had been emotionally poisoned. I had no idea what the cure might be, if my theory was correct.

"I don't remember . . . Wait." She frowned as though she were sifting through the murk of her memories. "We found something in the archives—a suicide note tucked into a book of poetry. Lorcan found it."

"Was it written by Mary McCree?" I asked.

She shook her head. "Catherine Allen. She hung herself in a big oak tree outside her home. Her note said that her husband's infidelity had broken her heart, and she couldn't bear to live another day." She looked at me, and behind that terrible sorrow in her gaze, I could see the flicker of Eva's true self. "That was when Lorcan told me I should take a hint. That he didn't love me, either. That he'd been with other women—women who loved him better. He . . . he . . ." Her mouth quivered.

"It wasn't Lorcan," I said. "He would never say such terrible things to you."

I could tell I was losing her to the miasma that had seeped into her soul and tainted her love for her husband. "Eva, you must try to contact Lorcan with your telepathy. He's hurt and he needs your help. We need to find him."

"He keeps trying to get inside my mind," she said, her mouth thinning. Her gaze went flat. "He's killed me," she said in an ugly voice. "Let him die, too."

"That's our cue to leave, Ellie." Tez guided me out of the room.

"She any better?" asked Darrius. The tone of his voice suggested he already knew the sad answer.

"She's heartbroken," I said. "And it appears Lorcan's been trying to contact her." I tapped my temple. "He must be alive someplace he can't escape. He's probably very confused and worried about not being able to reach his wife."

Darrius's phone rang, and he plucked it from the holder on his hip. *"Ja?"* He listened for a moment and then hung up. "Lorcan gave up on trying to convince Eva to talk to him, and used his mind connection to Jessica. He's been trapped down in the morgue freezer. Whoever knocked him out took everything, including his clothes, then used one of Patsy's fairy-gold necklaces to chain the handle."

Relief flooded me. "I'm so glad he's okay." I looked over my shoulder at the closed door of Eva's room. "I hope he can get through to his wife."

"If he cannot," said Darrius, "we will escort her to the prison and drug her, as we did Queen Patsy."

I hated the thought that another friend would be imprisoned—all because of the shadow. What had happened to the ghost? Had I been wrong thinking we were dealing with two entities?

We said our good-byes and headed out of the hospital. As we got into the car, Tez said, "How come Jessica can hear Lorcan? I thought that telepathy was just between vampire mates."

"For some reason, Jessica had a connection with Lorcan, too. Maybe it was because she was the first person he killed, or maybe it's because he's the twin of her mate. She's the only of one of us, other than those of the

Family Koschei, who has a telepathic connection with someone other than her husband."

"Huh." Tez reached toward the GPS and I slapped his hand away.

"I'll give you directions," I said starchily.

"Can you do it in a breathy voice and make sexual innuendos?" he asked. "Because that's really what I'm looking for in a navigator."

"You can have another scone," I said.

"That's porn enough for me," he said, and laughed.

"Wow," said Tez.

I did a little spin, smiling. The red wrap fit perfectly, and, naturally, I had the perfect pair of stiletto heels to match. I had taken some care with my makeup and hair, sweeping it into a simple updo. I wanted to look nice . . . and wasn't about to arrive at the were-cat colony without appropriate battle armor. If Serri was right, showing up on the arm of the potential alpha would make me a threat to the were-cat females hoping to woo the alpha.

"I'm gonna smear your lipstick, princess," said Tez. He kissed me, pressing me fully against him—and, I swear, I saw stars. When he finally let go, he'd made good on his promise. I repaired the mess, and we left.

Unfortunately, we had to let GPS Jenna guide us to the destination. I had never been to the community, so Tez plugged in the address to the unit, and we listened to the breathy voice direct Tez to the location.

I was nervous. I didn't really want a showdown with the were-cats. I wasn't sure how they would feel about having a vampire in their midst.

The were-cats had settled outside the town, choos-

ing to build their houses on a vacant lot of land. I'd
never bothered to find it before because, as I've mentioned, they kept to themselves. They never participated
in town events, not even the public-welcome Broken
Heart Council meetings, and they didn't encourage visitors. Given what I had learned from Serri, I could see
why they wouldn't invite outsiders.

The gravel road leading to the were-cat living quarters
wasn't well defined or paved, and had a lot of potholes.
Thank goodness the bumpy journey didn't last long.

There were no streetlights and, without a full moon,
darkness blanketed everything.

After a few minutes, the headlights illuminated a
single long building painted white with a black shingled
roof. It looked austere and unwelcoming, especially without any windows or other aesthetic touches. We parked
behind this building and got out of the car.

"Looks like soldier housing," said Tez.

I wondered if the females all stayed in one place. I
couldn't imagine living in a crowded space with women
who shared the same men, and had no other purpose
than to breed. I thought it was a terrible way to live. And,
I wondered, if Tez decided to become alpha . . . would he
take on the traditions of the pride?

Tez took my hand, and together we walked past the
bunker, following the sounds of music and laughter.
I could also hear the crackling of a fire. We rounded
the corner, and I could see immediately that I was
overdressed.

Directly across from it was a small white building
with a steeple; it looked like a church. On either side of
the clearing were two houses. The one on the left was

bigger; and although it, too, was white, it was obviously the most luxurious accommodations. The other house was smaller, less showy, and struck me as a home rather than an example of power.

So, the bigger house was certainly the alpha's, and the other must be the second's, where Serri and her family lived. That left the bunker to house the other females and their children, although according to Serri, there were very few kids here. I wondered what deity they worshipped at the church—it looked very traditional, especially with its stained glass windows.

In the middle of all these buildings, in the huge clearing, a bonfire raged. People milled around the blaze, most holding either beer bottles or plastic cups. To the left were several tables set up buffet-style and laden with food.

"This is my kind of party," said Tez. He glanced at me.

"I know," I muttered. "I'm overdressed."

"Take off your high heels," he suggested.

"Over my cold, dead body."

"Looks like most of the ladies are barefoot," he pointed out.

I sent him a withering look.

"Or you could keep 'em on."

"Tez!" Tawny, wearing a pair of tight faded jeans and a halter top, bounded toward us. She wasn't wearing shoes. She stopped in front of us, and eyed me. "You dropping Tez off before you go to the opera?"

"She's my date," said Tez. He wrapped an arm around my waist. "Unfortunately, we can't stay long, so . . . where's Calphon?"

The double whammy of claiming me and asking to see the alpha made Tawny's eyes narrow. *What?* Had she planned to liquor up Tez and have her way with him? I really didn't like this woman.

"He's over there," she said, jerking her thumb over her shoulder. "I'll take you." She gave me a strange look before turning away. Apparently, we were supposed to follow her. The wide-hipped, buttock-twitching sashay was no doubt for Tez's benefit.

"Princess, your fangs are showing."

I rubbed my tongue along my teeth. I'd never felt compelled to show my fangs before. I used them only for feeding. My anger at Tawny had had a visceral, physical response.

"You hungry?" asked Tez

"Starved," I said. "Do you mind swinging by the donor's home before we head to Tulsa?"

"Hell, yeah, I mind. But I'll do it anyway."

He held on tightly to my hand, and we followed Tawny across the clearing, past the bonfire, to a large man sitting on a lawn chair. He looked pale, his eyes shadowed with pain. When he stood up to shake Tez's hand, it obviously took a lot of effort to get to his feet.

"Glad you're here," said Calphon. He sat back down heavily, the chair squealing in protest. He lifted a beer bottle to his lips. His hand trembled, and I looked away. I was embarrassed for him. "You mind if we talk alone?" He slanted a gaze at me, and I realized he wasn't happy that I was here.

Well, that made two of us. Actually, it probably made a dozen of us. I doubted anyone else at the party was thrilled I was here, either.

"I'll check out the buffet," I said before Tez could respond. He needed to chat with the alpha, and I needed
to eat something with fat and carbs and sugar. I gave
him a little wave of my fingers and strolled toward the
tables.

"Elizabeth!" Serri was at the far table, holding a little
boy. A tall, lean man with gentle gray eyes stood next
her, his hand on her shoulder.

"Hello, Serri." I hurried to join them, glad to find
someone who didn't seem disappointed I was around.
"This is your mate? And your son?"

"Dayton," she said fondly.

I shook the little boy's hand. He giggled, and then
shyly laid his head against his mother, his big eyes on
me. "He's darling."

"And this is Trak," said Serri.

He shook my hand. "It's good to meet you," he said.
"Serri has nothing but good things to say about you."
He looked around, then leaned in. "Is it true that your
queen would grant us sanctuary?"

"Yes," I said.

He shared a look with Serri. "That's good news." Then
he gave her a kiss, and chucked his son under the chin.
"Nice to meet you, Elizabeth."

"And you, too, Trak."

Serri's gaze followed the loose gait of her husband as
he headed toward the beer coolers. It was obvious she
loved him very much. "He wants to wait until the new
alpha is named," she said. "If it's Tez, then maybe we
won't have to move. Maybe he'll create new traditions
for the pride."

"I have no doubts about that."

She looked startled, and then she tilted her head toward Tez and Calphon. "Doesn't seem like their talk is going too well."

I looked over my shoulder. Tez stood up abruptly, his face mottled with anger. Calphon's expression was pure stubborn. He gestured at Tez with the hand holding his beer bottle and then waved it toward me. Tez leaned in very, very close to the alpha's face and said something that made Calphon rear back.

Then he turned and marched toward me.

"You hear any of that?" I asked.

Serri shook her head. "Too far away."

"Yeah. For me, too."

Within seconds, Tez had arrived. "You ready?"

"Um . . . sure." I shot Serri a look, and she shrugged. But her gaze was worried.

"Good night," I threw over my shoulder as Tez took hold of my elbow and steered me away from the party. "What happened?"

"Calphon's an asshole. And I'm allergic to assholes."

"But what about being alpha of the pride?"

Tez opened my door, and I slid into the passenger seat. He got in the driver's side and started the car. "I don't know if I want to be part of this pride, Elizabeth, much less their leader." He reached over and squeezed my hand. "Let's go to Tulsa, okay? We have a mystery solve."

We arrived at my parents' home a few minutes before eleven p.m.

Tez followed the paved drive and stopped a few feet from the marble stairs. He looked at the house, and whistled. "You grew up here?"

"Yes," I said. I didn't bother trying to downplay the grandness of my childhood home—which was huge, with marble columns, red brick, arched windows, and surrounded by beautiful landscaping. I couldn't pretend I wasn't rich, or that I didn't enjoy the perks of wealth.

Martha, our longtime housekeeper, greeted us at the door, sharply dressed in black pants and a crisply ironed white oxford. Frankly, my mother would be lost without Martha: she ran the household, performed secretarial duties, mitigated the chaos of the kitchen, and generally kept everything in working order. I wasn't surprised she looked as fresh as a daisy this late at night—I swore the woman never slept. Oh, how I adored her.

"Miss Elizabeth!" She grinned broadly. Her once-raven black hair was now nearly gray, and wrinkles gathered at her eyes and mouth. But she still had the same twinkle in her brown eyes that let me know she'd baked cookies—just for me. Martha led us into the foyer and hugged me. She was small and compact, with just enough roundness to her form to give the best hugs ever. For a moment, I was transported back to my girlhood days, and I enjoyed the wisp of nostalgia.

"This is Tez Jones," I said. "He's a police detective from Tampa."

"Oh, my," said Martha, blinking up at him. "Is something wrong?"

"Nope," said Tez, grinning at her and offering a saucy wink. "I'm just the boyfriend."

"Well, then." She sized him up, and nodded. "It's about time Elizabeth found someone who deserved her."

"I worship at her dainty feet."

I skewered him with a glare, but he pretended not to notice.

Martha patted his cheek, her smile widening. "He's a keeper, all right." She looked at our overnight bags and then back at me. "How long will you be staying?"

"Just the until tomorrow evening," I said. "I need to go through some of Grandfather's things—papers or other items he brought with him from Broken Heart."

"Well, you know your father kept the library and study just as he left them. They're practically museums. I can't recall the last time anyone even went into them. I keep them clean, of course," she said, as though we might accuse her of not performing her duties, "but your parents claimed the east wing of the house. They rarely bother with rooms in the west wing. You know they're in Europe until the end of the month?"

I nodded. "It seems they spend more time out of the country than in it."

Martha waved away my concern. "They're just enjoying their lives, honey. They always thought the moon and the stars hung on each other. Do you want to stay in your old room, or would you prefer another? And where will Mr. Jones be sleeping?"

"With her," said Tez.

Martha tried for stern, but that twinkle in her eyes got in the way. Getting Martha's approval was not an easy thing; the fact that Tez had garnered it so easily took me aback. Did everyone think we were destined soul mates? *For goodness sake!*

"Put us in a room as close to the library and study as possible," I said. "Isn't there one with a four-poster with those curtains you can pull shut?" I vaguely recalled such a bed in the west wing. Like my parents, I had rarely ventured to the that side of the house. Most of my explorations had been when I was six or seven years old. In any case, I had to consider that since my family was unaware of my undead state, I would have to take precautions with my sleeping arrangements.

"Yes, yes," said Martha. "That's your grandfather's old room. It's right between the library and the study. In fact, I think they all connect. The linens go through a weekly washing, even though no one has slept in that bed in forever."

"So there are curtains still on the four-poster?" I asked.

"Just bought new red velvet ones," said Martha. "Your father insists we keep the rooms as close to the originals as possible.

"Sounds bawdy. I like it already," said Tez. He scooped up our bags before Martha could lay a finger on them. "Show us the way."

After Martha fussed about putting away our things and turning down the bed, she led us into the library. Floor-to-ceiling shelves covered every inch of the wall space, save for the huge marble fireplace. The furniture was big and dark and masculine. It had the faint odor of lemon polish. Two massive wingbacks sat before the fireplace, to the right of which was my grandfather's ornate desk. Everything was in order on it, including its inkwell and pen set, a globe on the corner, and a box that once held my grandfather's beloved cigars. It was as if my grandfather had stepped out of the room just for a moment, instead of being dead for more than two decades.

"We'll probably be up the whole night," I said. "Do you mind if we sleep in?"

Martha slanted a look at Tez, who winked at her. She smiled widely. Martha said that if we planned to stay up all night poking through the past (and her expression said she didn't believe that explanation for a minute), she would bring us a fresh pot of coffee. She also mentioned lemon cake—so you know Tez was interested.

Since I was no longer within Broken Heart's borders, I couldn't eat or drink human food. Then I realized I'd forgotten to do something very important before leaving town. I'd completely forgotten to drop by the donor's house.

"Oh, dear."

Tez stopped perusing the photos lined across the mantel of the fireplace. "There's a picture of Amelia Earhart," he said. "And Charlie Chaplin." He looked at me. *"What?"*

"I need my pint," I said. I showed my fangs.

"Shit. I forgot to take you by your donor." He tapped the side of his neck. "Take some of mine."

"You're a shifter," I said. "It's forbidden."

"Well, would you like to ask Martha?" he said. Sarcasm tinged his words. "Or maybe you prefer snacking on one of your neighbors?"

"Don't get snippy," I said. "We could always go to the Knights Inn. Phoebe and Connor keep donors on staff there."

"Or you could just drink from me," he said.

Vampires needed live, circulating blood from humans. We could live off animals when necessary, but it was only a temporary measure. Animal blood did not provide the same kind of sustenance. Drinking shifter blood was dangerous—no doubt why drinking it was forbidden. Still, I abhorred the idea of tracking down an innocent animal, which I'd never done, as much as drinking from some random human's neck and exercising my glamour, which I hardly ever use.

"We've only got a few hours left. You really wanna waste a couple of them driving across town to the Knights Inn to get a suitable snack? Five minutes," he said, tapping his neck again, "and we'll be able to spend our time more productively."

He had a point. And a pint.

"Look, Ellie Bee. You're my girl. I don't want you fanging some other guy's neck anyway. Don't mates gnaw on each other?"

"Almost exclusively," I said. "But all the mates I know are actual vampires. I've never known a vampire to marry a pure shifter. Most shifters have to stay with their own kind." I gave him a knowing look.

He rolled his eyes. "Me being a jaguar doesn't make me king of the cats, all right?" He glanced at the door. Like me, he heard Martha's steps coming down the hallway. She was humming a song I didn't recognize. Cups rattled on a tray. Tez pinned me with his stare. "You want me to hold her down while you take your pint?"

"Absolutely not!" No matter how hungry I was, I wouldn't betray Martha's trust by taking her blood. My glamour could remove the memory of the experience from her, but never from me. I wouldn't be able to look her in the eye again. Well, it looked like it was Tez or nothing. I supposed that indulging this one time would be all right. "Fine. I'll drink from you."

Martha opened the door and brought in a tray with a French press, two coffee cups, and an entire plate of lemon-cake slices. She arranged it on the table between the wingbacks.

"Do you need anything else?" she asked.

"This is perfect, Martha," I said. "Thank you so much."

She said her good-nights and left us to our work. Tez wasted no time scooping up a slice of cake. He munched it down in three bites and sighed contentedly. "No offense, princess, but I think I might have to marry Martha."

I laughed. "You'd have to fight my mother for her—and, frankly, I don't think you would win."

"Yeah, well. Probably not."

He crossed to the desk, where I was examining my grandfather's things, and took my hand. He led me to one of the wingbacks; then he sat down and pulled me onto his lap. "Okay, princess," he said. "Bite me."

Chapter 13

I was hungry, and decided that if Tez wanted to be my meal, who was I to complain? I sat sideways on his lap, loosely putting my arms around his shoulders. He obligingly tilted his neck, and I easily found the carotid artery.

I sank my fangs into his flesh, and began to drink.

He had an exotic taste, one that flowed into me like the finest champagne. He moaned, and I felt his hand creep under my shirt and cup my breast. His essence granted me the facade of life. I felt tingling warmth spread through me, and when he gently tweaked my nipple, pleasure arrowed straight to my core.

The act of feeding could be erotic, for me and for my donor. It was something I always thought I controlled. Yet, I had never felt this way—so responsive to each touch, so greedy for the pulsing life spilling into my mouth. For the first time, I understood the necessity of the hundred-year-binding magic.

I wanted Tez in the most primal way.

I knew I had gone past my pint and that, too, was a red flag that I was losing control. Vampires could certainly attempt to drain a body—and though they might not succeed, the rush of power and magic in the overindulgence could destroy morals. It was why the soulless of our kind, the *droch fola*, often killed their victims. Like I said, blood drinking could become an addiction. An uncontrolled vampire was a very, very dangerous one.

I managed to pry my fangs from Tez's neck. I felt the hard length of his shaft press against my thigh and I wiggled one of my hands between us so I could stroke it through his jeans. I licked my way up his neck, peppering kisses along his jaw.

He growled.

Literally.

I reared back and saw that his eyes had taken on an animalistic quality—the irises, diamond-shaped, and the color, a much richer gold. Here was the jaguar threatening me. But I wasn't afraid.

Tez grabbed my hair and brought me in for a punishing kiss. He didn't seem to care that his blood coated my tongue, or that I had little mastery of my impulse to take him. His hunger for me, his primal actions, brought forth within me something ancient and dark.

When he tumbled to the floor with me and ripped off my dress and bra in one fell swoop, I repaid the kindness. He nuzzled my breasts, sucking my nipples until they were hard, aching peaks. His hands were everywhere on my bared flesh, and eventually they found their way to my panties.

He shredded my lace thong.

Awareness rippled through me, a whisper of caution.

"Tez. Please." I didn't know if I was protesting or begging.

"I want to be inside you," he said, his voice husky. "I want to fuck you."

His coarse language unexpectedly inspired another shocking wave of lust. I couldn't believe I wanted him to speak that way to me, that it made me want to open my legs and let him take me.

"I can't." His fingers stroked my clitoris and I lost my ability to speak for a moment. "We can't."

"I know." He lightly bit my neck. "Goddamnit, I know."

I worked his jeans free, and he helped me unsheathe his large cock. I didn't know what I planned to do with it. I couldn't use it the way I truly wanted—not unless I wanted to bind Tez to me for a century. And no matter what he said, what he believed, it was not the right thing to do.

But Tez was undeterred by our consummation problem. I was so wet that it was easy for him to slide his cock between my labia. Every thrust rubbed my clit, causing a storm of sensation that clouded my mind, and my judgment. I wrapped my legs around him and dug my nails into his shoulders.

He scraped his teeth across my breast, all the way to my turgid nipple. His lips clamped over the peak and he sucked it, hard. The pleasure-pain spiraled through me, and I felt the wave of orgasm crest . . . and then I fell over into the sensations of light and heat and bliss.

Tez released my nipple and rose up, increasing his pace. "You feel so good, Elizabeth. Oh, God. You're gonna make me come." He groaned, his expression going tight, and then he stilled, his hot seed splashing onto my stomach.

He was breathing hard, and I too might have been had I the use of my lungs. I looked down and saw that his cock was still rock hard. I glanced up at him and saw that his expression was still predatory and his eyes still had their animal shape.

"It's a perk of being a shifter," he said. He bared his teeth at me. "How many ways do you think we can fuck without actually fucking?"

I swallowed the knot in my throat. I wasn't worried because I was afraid of this new Tez; I was worried because I liked the dangerous side of him. Because I wanted him to talk dirty to me and pleasure me in every way possible, and . . . *Oh, dear*—I was very much losing my mind.

His grin was razor sharp. "You like it when I say *fuck*."

"I most certainly do not. That would be . . . uncouth."

"Well, then. Let's test out my theory." He took his torn shirt and used it to clean off my stomach. Then he flipped me over. "Hands and knees, princess."

"I think we've pushed our luck enough," I said from the floor. "I don't think we should continue this . . . this sexual madness."

"Oh, we're not. This is a scientific experiment." He patted my buttocks. "Up and at 'em."

I really should've been more reluctant, but I'm afraid the adjective that applied here was "eager." I got to my hands and knees, and Tez took position behind me. He slid his cock between my thighs; his thick length once again teased apart my labia and settled hard and hot against my clitoris.

"*This* is scientific?" I scoffed.

"Yep. See, I'm gonna hold your hips, and keep my cock right where it is. No movement."

"Oh," I said, somewhat disappointed. "I see."

"I'm not going to touch you anywhere else, either. But I am gonna talk."

"And, do forgive me, the *point* of this endeavor is what?"

"Let's find out, princess." His hands tightened on my waist, and he made sure his length was pressed tightly against me. "Close your legs some. Keep me tucked against that tight little pussy."

I gasped. "Tez!"

He laughed and patted my bottom. "Oh, this is gonna be fun."

I closed my legs as much as I could until Tez was pulled snug against me, his cock cradled within the confines of my thighs. I had to admit, it felt rather good.

"You're a very beautiful woman," said Tez quietly. "Your skin is so soft. You smell like flowers. Your hair feels like silk. I love touching you, kissing you, being with you. I want to be gentle with you, but I'm too greedy for you, Elizabeth. I want to take you like the animal I am. I want to fuck you."

Shock zigzagged through me, a direct shot to my . . . well, you know.

"You're wet," he said. "Wet for me. One day, Elizabeth, I'm going to take you. I'm going to bend you over, just like this, and slide my cock deep inside you. I'm going to fuck you over and over, until you're coming on my cock, until you're screaming my name."

Every word created a rush of feeling straight to the spot where his cock was so deliciously pressed against me. I felt hot and tight and expectant.

"You want me to fuck you, don't you?"

"Y-yes."

"Tell me how you want it."

For a moment, the words wouldn't issue forth. Then I whispered, "Hard." I easily imagined Tez behind me, slipping his shaft deeply inside, so deep it stretched me and filled me, and then he would plunge his big cock into me over and over.

I moaned.

"Are you imagining me fucking you, Elizabeth?"

I swallowed the knot in my throat. "Please," I said. "Please."

"Princess." He leaned forward and kissed my spine. Then he began to move, rubbing his cock against me until I screamed with pleasure, pleasure he created just by saying those highly inappropriate but—oh, so deliciously—naughty words. My fingers clawed at the floor as my second orgasm exploded. It took me a minute, or five, to get my thoughts unscrambled.

How could I ever give up this man?

In that moment, I was sorely tempted to give in to my need, and to his. But did I really want to risk his future? Even for us, a shifter and a vampire, a hundred years was a very long time. I couldn't do it. I didn't think I'd be able to live with myself if I truly took away his choice.

Tez moved back, slipping away from me. I turned and

sat at his feet. He joined me on the floor, and cupped my face. "You're the one, Elizabeth."

"I know you think so."

"I've made my choice. You just have to make yours." He kissed me. "But I hope until you make up your mind, we can do a lot more of this." His finger reached down and swiped my clit. He was so bawdy.

And I loved it.

"Yes," I said. "I do believe we can accommodate each other."

"That vocabulary of yours," he said. "Maybe next time you can dress up as the English professor and I'll be her naughty student."

I smiled. "How do you feel about being . . . punished?"

"Seriously? I'm so gonna marry you."

We took fifteen minutes to clean up our clothing mess. I couldn't regret the loss of my wrap dress. I'd never had my clothes ripped off before. It had been exhilarating.

We took showers. Separately. Otherwise, we would've never accomplished what we set out to do. I donned my black nightie, which hit me at mid-thigh and had a plunging neckline—too distracting. I dug through Tez's duffel and grabbed a pair of his sweats and an old concert T-shirt. I rolled the waistband of the sweats up because they were too big; the shirt almost fell to my knees.

"'KISS'?" I asked, pointing to the painted faces of the seventies' phenom. "Really?"

"KISS rocks," said Tez. "You look good in my shirt. You don't really need the pants."

"If we're going to do any actual research, then yes, I do."

He was wearing a pair of sweats, too, but nothing else—and I was having a hard time looking away from his muscled chest. His skin was the color of caramel latte, and I wanted to lick him. He was probably walking around shirtless because he knew I would be tempted.

In fact, our sexual romp had moved us up a relationship level. Neither Tez nor I hesitated to show our affection, whether it was a touch as we walked past each other, a quick kiss, or just a tender look. Granted, Tez didn't exactly show restraint in holding my hand or putting his arm around me *before* we made love. I was the one who hesitated to display affection.

We settled down to poke and prod through the library.

I started with the desk, and Tez started at the far end of the library, working his way through the shelves.

"Most of these are first editions," he said. "And the subjects are eclectic as hell. Darwin is next to a book about spiritualism. And there's a biography of John Updike next to a hardback about early Hollywood."

"My grandfather had varied interests," I said. "He invested in Oklahoma oil fields, sponsored archaeological digs in Egypt, and gave scholarships to women to attend college—in the 1920s. He was a very progressive man."

"If we're lucky, he was also a man who hedged his bets. He seems likely to keep information, especially if he needed to protect his family."

"He wouldn't have been the one to commit the crime," I said, admitting what I had been trying not to think about. "His father, Jeremiah, built the Silverstone mansion. My grandfather lived there with his brother Josiah until their father passed away. Then my grandfather moved to Tulsa, got married, and built this house."

"And his brother stayed in Broken Heart."

I paused from digging through a desk drawer. "He was grandfather's younger brother, not particularly likeable. He neither married nor had children. When he died, the mansion was essentially abandoned."

"You mean Pops might've found the room, or discovered the big secret, and decided it was just as awful as we think it is. How long was the mansion empty?"

"Forty, fifty years."

"That long?" He whistled. He'd made his way to the fourth set of shelves, and I was on the last drawer of the desk. It was as empty as the rest. Why would my grandfather empty the drawers but leave everything else as it was? Or had my father cleaned them out?

Maybe Grandfather kept his important papers in his study, although "study" wasn't quite the word to describe the other room. It was the place my grandfather would go to relax. It had the same masculine feel as the library: big, dark furniture, paneled walls, dark green carpet, and an oversized stone fireplace. It also had a full bar and a billiard table. My grandfather had enjoyed old-fashioned comforts, and his study reflected the man. Simple. Solid. Unchangeable.

"Anything, Ellie Bee?" asked Tez. He'd worked his way through the bookshelves all the way to the fireplace. He stood near the mantel and stared up at the large painting above it. "Is that a Van Gogh?"

"I believe so." I sat down in the large leather chair and sighed. "There's nothing here."

"We're only half finished with the room, Velma."

"Thanks for the pep talk, Fred."

He grinned at me. Then he walked to the next bookshelf and peered at the upper shelves. "I don't know why I thought your gramps would be a secret-button kind of guy." Experimentally, he pulled a book from the shelf. "Damn. No door."

"Did you expect the house to have hidden passageways?" I asked.

"Well, yeah. This house was built in the twenties, wasn't it? Prohibition was a real bitch. Lots of rich dudes built secret rooms for their hooch and their hooch parties."

"Now you think you're in a History Channel special," I said. Still, the idea had some merit. My grandfather enjoyed fine liquors. He certainly wouldn't have let a mere law get in the way of his pleasures, especially not as a young man with his financial resources.

"Check under the desk," said Tez, obviously warming up to his secret-room theory. "Maybe there's a button or switch."

"I think my parents would've discovered such a place." I slipped underneath the desk and looked closely at the exterior. Nothing. Disappointed, I climbed to my feet. I have to admit Tez's idea of a hidden room had a certain romanticism.

"Martha said your parents stayed on their side of the house. And P.S.: This place is big enough to accommodate all the people in a Third World country."

"Why on earth keep something secret when there was no longer a need?"

"Let's say your grandfather's protecting this Broken

Heart problem—information passed along from *his* dad. Would he tell your father? Or take it to his grave?"

"I honestly don't know."

We finished examining all the bookshelves in the room, but it was quite obvious that all that lined the shelves were books. Nothing looked odd or out of place, and our random checking of the tomes didn't reveal hidden papers or notes or a map with a big X indicating "Broken Heart Secret Here."

"Don't give up," said Tez. He kissed me lightly. "We still have another room to check out."

He took my hand, and we left the library.

The study was just as I remembered it. Like the previous room, it smelled vaguely of lemon polish. I swore, I could detect a hint of cigar smoke, which reminded me of my grandfather. He died when I was twenty-two. He'd been a good man, solid through and through. At least that was what I had always believed.

I hoped it was true.

Tez prowled the room, scenting it, and I wandered over to the corner where the bar was located. Leather stools lined up in front of the elaborately carved cherrywood counter. It was polished to a high shine, and even the bottles and glasses, which hadn't been used in years, gleamed.

"This place is the best man-cave I've ever been in."

I looked at him. "Man-cave?"

"Yeah. You know, a dude space." He waved his hands around. "This is all testosterone, princess."

I wasn't sure how to respond to that, so I didn't. Tez didn't seem to notice. He was too busy fondling the billiard table. Even though I didn't buy into Tez's theory about a hooch room, secret or otherwise, I still checked underneath the bar for any buttons or switches.

And I found one.

"Tez!"

He put down the cue ball and hurried over to me. "What?"

I pushed the button, and a panel near the fireplace popped open.

"Holy shit." Tez leaned over the bar and kissed me. "Way to go, Ellie."

Giddy, from both the kiss and my unexpected find, I joined Tez by the narrow opening. We peered inside the dark passage, and then looked at each other.

"If Martha knew about this place, there wouldn't be cobwebs hanging from the ceiling or dirt on the concrete," I said. A small shelf at eye level held a row of tapered candles, some half melted, and a stack of boxed matches. "I'm fairly sure flashlights were available at some point, yet he continued to use candles to light his way. Old-fashioned to the end."

Tez lit one of the unused candles and slid past me through the doorway. I followed him. It was a tight space, especially for Tez, who was much larger and taller. Even I was squished; my shoulders kept scraping against the walls.

"There's a set of stairs here," said Tez. "They go up."

"The attic."

The staircase was just as narrow as the hallway, and spiraled up quite a distance. Finally, we reached the top, which revealed a trapdoor above us. Tez pushed it open and entered. After a moment, he reached down and offered his hand, which I grabbed, and he helped me up.

The flickering yellow light of our inadequate candle revealed a small, tidy room, dusty with disuse. On the far wall, there was a closed rolltop desk with a leather chair parked in front of it. On the opposite side, wooden crates were stacked neatly: two rows of two with the fifth box centered on top of them.

"Five," said Tez.

Foreboding sat heavily in my stomach. What had my grandfather known about our family's past in Broken Heart? Had he always known about his father's sins . . . or had he found out the truth and the knowledge had driven him out of town?

I wasn't sure I wanted to know. Here was the evidence of my own family's complicity in the murder of Elizabeth Silverstone.

"I feel sick." I walked to the chair and threw myself into it. "He knew. My grandfather knew."

"We don't know anything yet. Those crates could be filled with the finest Scotch this side of Scotland. We either need more light, or to haul this crap downstairs."

"No electricity up here," I said. I pointed to a shelf nearby that held supplies: boxes of pens and paper clips, sheaves of yellowed paper, and several kerosene lanterns.

We lit them all and placed them around the room. It wasn't the same as overhead fluorescent lighting, but I supposed it would do.

Tez grabbed the first crate and pulled off the lid.

We peered inside.

"Newspapers," I said. I gently picked up the first one. "*The Broken Heart Banner.* Look at the masthead—the managing editor was Jonathon LeRoy. And the publisher was Jeremiah Silverstone."

"Looks like your great-grandfather had his finger in all the pies."

"It appears so."

I carefully unfolded the newspaper. It was a single sheet printed double-sided and folded into quarters. "Not a big publication," I said. "Then again, how much news was there to report?"

"The Allens got another cow," said Tez, pointing to a front-page tidbit. "And Jeremiah Silverstone donated copies of the new Edith Wharton novel, *Madame de Treymes,* to the library. Hey, look. 'To be added to the Elizabeth Silverstone Memorial Collection.'"

"What's the date of the paper?"

"March 28, 1906."

"This one is June 13, 1907." I looked down at the other newspapers. "They don't seem to be in any particular order."

"Well, let's remedy that," said Tez.

It took us an hour to create a time line for the newspaper. It appeared that my grandfather had kept every issue of the weekly paper during a two-and-a-half-year period. Issue One of the *Broken Heart Banner* was published on June 14, 1905, as evidenced by the huge "FIRST ISSUE" that blared across the front page. Even though the five original families had settled the area in 1889, Broken Heart didn't become a town until Jeremiah Silverstone built the general store in 1894. We knew this because the paper did a huge story about my great-grandfather—a propaganda piece if I'd ever seen one. Jeremiah Silverstone either owned the buildings, or financed them. Even the bank owed its structure and its coffers to my great-grandfather.

The last issue we had was published on December 11, 1907.

"Do you think there were more papers?"

"Could be it only had a short run," said Tez. "It's obvious that Elizabeth died prior to the newspaper's start." He pointed to a November issue. "Hell, Oklahoma wasn't even a state until nearly the end of 1906."

"Why keep these papers if they're not important?" I said, frustrated. "And why hide them in here?"

"Maybe your grandfather didn't know their true significance. Maybe he took what he thought might be important."

"And never told anyone? He built a secret room so he could put these things in here. What he did just feels wrong to me."

"Don't judge your grandfather just yet, Ellie. We don't know his motivations. And we have yet to find any evidence linking your family to any crime." He put his arm around me and tipped my chin. "Let's go over everything again. We're probably missing something. Sometimes the smallest detail can crack open a case."

I eyed the other crates. "Let's open them," I said, "and see if Jeremiah Silverstone's sins are tucked inside."

Chapter 14

Tez and I opened the other crates. While I went through the contents, he studied the newspapers. He could be incredibly patient; as a homicide detective, it was a necessary trait. That, and pure stubbornness. He was sure the old papers held information that could help us, and I didn't doubt Tez's instincts.

I supposed that I just wanted a big blinking sign that said: *Read This. It Explains Everything.*

"Let's assume," said Tez, "Elizabeth died before 1894. Let's also assume the suicides of Mary McCree and Catherine Allen occurred before then, too."

"Why would we assume any of that?" I asked.

"Because if the legend of how the town was named is true, and the town didn't become official until 1894 . . ."

I picked up the thread of his thoughts. "Then we know for sure that the death of Mary McCree happened before then. But why the others?"

"I think Elizabeth was killed first." He glanced at

me. "I hate using your name and 'killed' in the same sentence."

"Why? I'm already dead."

He stared at me and then barked a laugh. "Good point." He looked down at the papers. "Okay. So, Elizabeth died first. Then Mary and Catherine."

"Wait," I said. I dug around in my memory. "My grandfather was born in the spring of 1890 . . . and he was two years older than his brother. So, that means Josiah was born in 1892."

"Good job, Ellie Bee. That means your great-grandmother died in either 1893 or 1894."

"Someone killed her," I mused, "but the other two women died by their own hand. They committed suicide, and both claimed their husbands were unfaithful. Sound familiar?"

"Just like your friends."

"And there's no convincing them otherwise, either, even though it's patently untrue. The shadow demon is messing with their minds somehow."

"We might be looking at some sort of hysteria," said Tez. "Maybe along the lines of the Salem witch trials."

"He's targeting the women of the first five families. He's the curse of Broken Heart."

"Doesn't explain Patsy," said Tez. "She's not part of a founding family."

"He needed access to the house, to his little treasure room. She was just . . . collateral."

Tez nodded. "Let's see if we can find some proof."

He returned his attention to the newspapers, and I dug through the crates.

The first one was filled with old-fashioned women's clothing wrapped in parchment and tied with string. I assumed they all belonged to my great-grandmother. They were in remarkable condition, and none was stained or torn. Most likely, a servant had packed and stored her clothing after her death. Again, it wasn't something I felt should've been hidden for nearly a hundred years. I saw nothing thus far that indicated anything other than sentimentality.

Then I removed the last wrapped item, and opened it.

It was a brown hat with copper roses along the brim. I must've made a sound of distress because Tez was at my side in an instant gently untangling my trembling fingers from the hat.

"It's hers," I said. I knew Elizabeth was communicating with me. She wanted me to find out the truth. She wanted peace, for herself and for all the troubled souls of Broken Heart.

I reached out for the hat, but Tez shook his head. "The man who killed her grabbed it right out of her hands and tossed it to the floor of that room. Right before she died she'd wondered what happened to it." I stood up and started to pace. "She was thinking about her new dress, about her duties as a hostess and a mother." I pressed my hand against my quivering mouth, and lamented my inability to cry. "She died so young. And she never got to raise her sons. It's tragic."

"Death often is," said Tez. He perched the hat on the corner edge of the crate and then took me into his arms.

I laid my head against his chest and listened to the

comforting sound of his heartbeat. "How did you do it, Tez? How do you face the gruesomeness of murder every day and still have any hope at all?"

"Who says I do?" He rubbed my back. "Humans can do really vicious things to each other. They get greedy or jealous, or just go crazy. It's been hard for me, Elizabeth, because I've wanted to separate the just crimes from the unjust. If an abused wife gets sick of being beaten and stabs her asshole husband in the heart, I secretly applaud her. I'd still arrest her and charge her, but I wouldn't like it. I've always judged my cases that way. It isn't looking at the messiness of death that bothers me; it's the motivations for murder that sicken me."

I pulled back and studied Tez's face. His voice held anguish and fury, and his eyes echoed that pain. "You didn't just go on sabbatical to find Broken Heart, did you?"

"I quit."

"Why?" I asked.

"I'll tell you someday."

I tightened my arms around him. "Okay," I said. Then I rose up and kissed him.

My attempt to comfort him flared into passion. I could sense he needed the distraction . . . that he wanted to lose whatever memories had surfaced, to quiet whatever inner demons roared inside him.

He had given me so much, and I wanted to give back to him, too.

I lowered myself to my knees and grasped the waistband of his sweats.

"Elizabeth." His voice was hoarse, his gaze darkened by his pain and his need.

"Let me." I pulled down the sweats, and his already hardening cock sprang free. I kissed the length of it, and then sucked the tip of his shaft into my mouth, swirling my tongue around the ridged edge. He tasted earthy, and oh-so-male.

Excitement pulsed through me.

His fingers slid into my hair, and rested lightly on my scalp.

I wasn't experienced with giving fellatio, but I was certainly enthusiastic. Tez seemed to enjoy my efforts. I created a rhythm with my hand and my mouth, stroking the base of his shaft while I was also, as Jenna Jameson might say, *going down* on him.

"Elizabeth. God, baby." He sucked in a breath, and his hands tightened my hair. He moved his hips in conjunction with my stroking. "I'm gonna come!"

Then he did.

His cock jerked as his hot seed spurt into my mouth, and I swallowed the salty essence, holding on to him until he was finished.

I was quite pleased with myself. I kissed his length, running my tongue up and down his cock until he scooped me under the armpits and lifted me. I squeaked at this sudden change in position. My feet dangled off the floor.

"What are you doing?" I asked indignantly.

"Marry me," he said.

"Humph. You just wanna have sex."

"God, yes." His eyes got a calculating look. "You can't be penetrated at all?"

"Not by your . . . uh, you know." I said, suddenly disturbed by the glint in his eye.

"No penis. Got it. But we have other options."

"What are you thinking?" Then I narrowed my gaze. "Undead isn't alive, and that counts, too. Penetration with another being means a hundred years together."

"Don't worry, princess. I have no intention of bringing a donkey into our bedroom."

I gaped at him. "That thought never even crossed my mind. I was thinking you being undead wouldn't help our situation. In case you're thinking of . . . I don't know, being Turned or whatever. I'm not even sure full-blood shifters can be Turned."

"I like having a heartbeat," he said. "Besides, I'm your meal ticket."

"Are not." I sounded petulant, which only made him grin. He gave me a smacking kiss and then put me down.

"Not that I'm complaining," said Tez, "but why is it that you can swallow come?"

"What?"

"I don't know. Is it considered a meal? I thought vampires could only drink blood. Unless you're in Broken Heart."

It hadn't even occurred to me. "Essence is essence, I suppose. Blood, semen, saliva. Living cells."

"So, I was like dessert?" He pulled up his sweats, giving me a very lascivious look.

"You're incorrigible." I narrowed my gaze. "Why were you asking about penetration?"

He lifted one eyebrow.

I rolled my eyes. "You know what I mean."

"Yeah, I know what you mean."

Tez was scheming about something, and I wasn't sure

I would like it. Or maybe I should've been more worried about how much I would like it. I had discovered quite a bit about myself in the last few hours—that Tez knew what tempted me; what turned me on; and that he cared enough about me to find out what I liked, to help in a sensual exploration of my own needs—and was very much afraid I was half in love with him already. He was the most virile man I'd ever met—and all that sexual potency might well kill me. Again.

I put aside the hat and repacked the other clothing. I put on the lid and shoved it back against the wall. Then I dove into the next crate. It was only half full, but the contents made me laugh. I pulled out a bottle and showed it to Tez. "Look," I said. "Scotch."

"So your grandfather really was keeping some of his hooch up here."

"It seems so." I returned the bottle, put on the lid, and pushed the crate against the wall next to the other one.

"Listen to this, Ellie." Tez picked up a paper and read: "Dennison Clark married Wilmette Johnson in a church ceremony on last Sunday. It is the second marriage for Mr. Clark, whose first wife, Cora, died tragically six years ago."

"That's it?" I asked.

"It's on the back page under 'Announcements,'" said Tez. "Kinda weird to throw in the info about death of the first wife with the notice about the new marriage." He flipped the paper over, and tapped the top corner. "This is the winter of 1905. Six years prior would make it 1894. If we're right, then all the women died that year."

"We have four women who died the same year—the year my grandfather built the general store," I said. "Or so we can assume at this point. We may not have confirmation yet, but I would bet my Neiman Marcus charge card that Evangeline LeRoy was killed, too."

"Since we're doing a lot of assuming here," said Tez as he gathered and stacked the papers, "let's say Elizabeth is killed by her husband, after he calls forth Mammon's demon shadow. He'd obviously set something into motion, something he couldn't control, or take back."

"Because he'd already given purpose to the shadow," I said. "I don't think he intended to kill Elizabeth."

"But maybe he intended to kill the other women." Tez looked at me. "Let's say that the ghost gets trapped in the attic with the shadow demon. They're both released. The demon goes off to finish his task, and the ghost is drawn to you as Elizabeth's direct descendent."

"What I don't understand is why the focus is on making the women believe their husbands cheated, and being so devastated by it, they end their lives."

"You said it before, Ellie. The curse is about ruining love."

"Do we continue the conjecture and say that he stopped after killing five women?" I looked down into the opened fourth crate and saw files, papers, books. I knew we'd found the missing archives from the Broken Heart library.

Tez finished returning the papers to the box, then put on the lid and added it to those already against the wall. "I think we're making some pretty big leaps without very much evidence." Tez sat down next to me and helped me empty out the wooden box. We piled the materials around us. "Once he'd killed the object of his true obsession—Elizabeth—he might've turned his attention to other women."

"You mean killing Elizabeth over and over again?" I shook my head. "She died after he'd invoked the demon. I really do believe he'd planned for her to live, but . . . she took a lover and betrayed him."

"Is it possible to change the demon's purpose?" asked Tez. "Maybe he called him in for one thing, and after Jeremiah killed his wife, he decided he wanted the demon to do something else."

"We're missing some very big pieces of the puzzle."

As Tez looked through a stack of paperwork, I began examining the books. There were a couple of family Bibles—one for the Allens and the other for the Clarks. On the inside page of the Clark family Bible was a list of family names. Underneath Cora and Dennison Clark were the names of their children. Wilmette Johnson had not been added to the Bible. Then again, it had probably been stored away in this loft before the marriage.

Why would these families' Bibles be in my grandfather's possession? I looked through each one and could discern no reason to keep them. No notes were hidden between the pages, and I didn't see any markings other than names of the family. It was all very disappointing.

I set aside the Bibles, and picked up a small hardcover book. "*Leaves of Grass* by Walt Whitman," I said. I opened it to the first page, and stopped cold. " 'To my darling Elizabeth, our love will bind us in this life and the next. You are everything to me. Your loving fiancé, Paul Tibbett. June 12, 1889.' "

Tez stopped perusing the paper in his hand and stared at me. "Who the hell is Paul Tibbett?"

I grappled with this newest truth. "My great-grandmother was engaged to someone else before she married Jeremiah." I thought about my visions, and suddenly they made sense. The man in the attic, the one who'd strangled her, must've been Paul Tibbett, not Jeremiah Silverstone. He was the one mad at her for marrying my great-grandfather. Relief flooded me. Maybe I didn't have homicidal maniacs in my family. "For whatever reason, she married my great-grandfather, and came with him to the Oklahoma territory to do the land run. They stake their claim, build their manse, and Elizabeth bears her first son a few months after they arrive. Jeremiah starts financing the town, two years go by, and she has another son."

"But Paul can't let go," said Tez. "He follows her to Broken Heart. She feels guilty about the way she dumped him."

I nodded. "Makes sense."

"She lets him stay, maybe gets him a job in town, but doesn't tell her husband that her old boyfriend is in town."

"And he hangs out in the attic?" I asked. "Would she really let him live in her house with her husband and kids?"

"Maybe they were carrying on their affair."

"You mean she loved Paul, but married Jeremiah for his money?" I didn't want to think my own flesh and blood had done something so selfish, but times had been different. Courtship wasn't always about love. "She was scared of him." I rubbed my jaw. "He hit her, and knocked her out."

"His jealousy drove him crazy. He realized she was

never going to leave Jeremiah, and he decided if he couldn't have her, then no one could."

Could love really turn so ugly? How awful it must've been for Elizabeth. The hands that once caressed her with tender regard had been the instruments of her death.

"I still don't understand why he was in the attic."

"Maybe Paul did the land run, too. He could've been in town the whole time. Or maybe he was hired to help build the house and did his own project on the side so he could be close to her. Maybe she didn't know about the secret room."

"Wait," said Tez. "You got Internet on your iPhone?"

"Yes, but I left it downstairs in the bedroom."

"Damn."

"What in the world do you need to Google?"

"The date of the Oklahoma land run."

"April 22, 1889."

Tez blinked at me. "How did you know that?"

"Because Oklahoma history is a requirement to graduate high school. For some reason, the date always stuck in my mind." I paused, staring down at the book of poetry. "He dated it June 12, 1889."

"It fits our hypothesis," said Tez. "He's obsessed with her, gives her the book."

"What if Elizabeth did the land run with Paul?" I asked. "They're engaged, maybe too poor to buy land of their own. They have a chance to start over in the new territory . . . so they come to Oklahoma."

"They stake out their plot, and Elizabeth breaks off the engagement. She marries Jeremiah instead and becomes the belle of the town." Tez nodded. "That's a good scenario, too. But either way, the story ends the same. Paul gets obsessed with her, can't let go, and he kills her."

"Then he somehow forces the wives of the four other founding families to commit suicide?" I asked. "That doesn't tie in to the demon shadow."

"Well, he was the one to call it forth."

"It all goes back to why," I said, feeling frustrated. "Why would anyone go through all the trouble of calling forth a powerful ancient demon—one who thrives off greed?"

"Sounds like a rich man's demon," said Tez.

"Sounds like a poor man's demon," I countered.

Tez stood up and stretched, and those lovely chest muscles of his expanded in a most alluring way. All thoughts fled my mind. I found myself off the floor and pressed against him without even realizing I'd done so—not until he leaned down and gave me a lazy kiss.

"We've discovered a lot of useful information," said Tez. He slid his arms around my waist and pulled me tight against him. "Let's call it a night."

"But it's at least three hours before daylight."

"Yeah," said Tez, grinning. He cupped my buttocks and squeezed me so that I rubbed against his thickening length. "But I have a few ideas about how to spend those hours."

"We should at least check out the last box," I said. "I don't want to return to this room. I don't like it up here."

I wasn't sure if Tez would let common sense rule, or if he would throw me over his shoulder and march to the bedroom. I was sorta hoping for the latter. I'd never been taken to bed in such a manner, and I have to admit I liked the idea.

Tez sighed. "You're right. We'll look in the last crate, take a quick gander at the rolltop, and get outta here."

"We should take the box with the archives and give it to Eva. She'll want it for the library. Or she will once she's well again."

Tez kissed me again, dipping his tongue into my mouth, offering a promise of what delights awaited me.

"Let's hurry," I said.

"Damn right." He let me go, and then knelt down and started loading up the papers and books into the crate we'd emptied. He wasn't exactly being careful, but I couldn't blame him. We could straighten it all out later.

I was eager to leave, too, and not just because I wanted to get naked with Tez. My grandfather's secret room had tainted my memories of him. I hated the idea that he'd known about his mother's murder and helped, so many years later, to continue the cover-up. I was trying to give him the benefit of the doubt, but here was the evidence of his duplicity.

I was hoping to find just another batch of fine Scotch, but instead I found a wool blanket. Impatient, I yanked it out. Something bounced out of its folds, spun across the floor, and landed at Tez's feet.

Horrified by what I'd done, and what had fallen out, I stood there like a moron and clung to the blanket.

Tez bent down and picked up the skull. He looked at me. "Look at that, Ellie Bee. You've lost your head."

Chapter 15

"That's not funny!" I dropped the blanket and marched to him, taking the skull.

"Well, at least you've got another one for your collection."

"Oh, be quiet." I examined the skull. It was damaged, and not from its unfortunate dance across the floor. A hole permeated the back, and cracks radiated from the trauma.

"Blunt instrument," said Tez. "The victim was hit with extreme force."

I couldn't imagine to whom the skull belonged, or why my grandfather had hidden it. I prayed it wasn't the cranium of one of the women we presumed dead—but then if it wasn't . . . who the hell else had been killed?

We examined the box, and found nothing else. No other bones, no missing piece of the skull, and certainly no note indicating whose head had been sitting in my grandfather's attic.

"The plot thickens," said Tez. "I guess we need to take the skull back, too."

"Stan will want to examine it." I looked at the rolltop desk and dread filled me. What would we find in it? I was getting weary of all the morbid surprises.

Tez packed the skull in the blanket and put it on top of the crate we planned to take with us. "Tell you what. I'll empty the rolltop. Whatever's in there, we'll examine tomorrow, okay? Let's go downstairs and relax."

"That sounds like an excellent idea." I was relieved by Tez's practical suggestion, and his willingness to take over what had become a laborious task. "I need to check in with Damian and let him know what we found. I'll tell him about our theories, too. Maybe he has some good news about Patsy and Eva."

"I hope so, Ellie." Tez gave me a hug, and I didn't realize how much I wanted one. How wonderful it was to have a partner who understood what I needed and could provide it. I couldn't recall the last time I had felt cared for, and Tez did it as naturally as breathing.

We headed downstairs, and when we entered the study, we made sure the secret door was closed tightly. Tez promised to retrieve everything later, and I was grateful we'd decided to take a break. I felt only a little cowardly about abandoning the room and its contents.

I really wanted to settle down with a cup of tea. Or a dry martini.

"I'm going to run a hot bath," said Tez as we entered our bedroom suite.

"Oh, that sounds wonderful. When you're finished, I'll take one."

He laughed. "I took a peek at that bathroom. I think

the entire defensive line of the Tampa Bay Buccaneers can fit in that tub." He took me into his arms and smiled. "I meant that I would run the bath for you. I know you're stressed, and you can't drink that sissy tea you like so much, so I'll fill the tub. You soak. I'll load up the Honda with our creepy cargo."

"I can run my own bath," I said, touched by his thoughtfulness.

"It's not about you being capable. It's about you letting someone help shoulder your burdens. It's about you remembering that you're worthy of being taken care of—and you deserve to be pampered."

He was right. I wasn't very good at letting others take care of me. Granted, I hadn't had anyone in a long time who wanted to do so. It was much easier to do things myself than to rely on others. I realized there were plenty of people (relatively speaking) who would gladly help me. I was too used to taking care of everything, and it was hard to trust others to do the job right. I was used to being relied upon, to being the clear head and the straight shoulders. Elizabeth Bretton could always put things aright, and she never, ever fell apart.

"I would very much appreciate you running a bath for me," I said. "And I hope you'll join me."

"Rain check, princess." He kissed my forehead and let me go.

I stared at him, flabbergasted. "Rain check?"

"See, here's the thing. You gotta learn to take. Just ... take. You don't have to give back. *Me* doing something for *you* is not a debt. You gotta stop trying to earn a gold star for your life chart." He tapped my temple. "You keep score, princess. I don't."

I opened my mouth to deny his ridiculous accusation, but no words came out.

"God, you're cute," he said. He kissed me lightly before disappearing into the bathroom. I heard him whistling "Don't Be Cruel," and then I heard the rush of water as he turned on the faucets.

I stood in the bedroom, feeling off-kilter. I never considered myself a scorekeeper. I didn't keep track of doing nice things for other people. I never felt as though I was owed for any kindness I'd given.

But that wasn't Tez's point, and I knew it.

I did keep track of the kindnesses done for me. I never wanted to feel as though I was indebted to someone else, no matter how small the favor. If a friend dropped by and brought flowers, I'd drop off some cookies the very next day. One time, Darrius had come to my rescue in town and changed a flat tire. I sent him a case of his favorite lager. I planned to gift Lenette and her sisters with a selection of coffees for the boxes of scones. I'd already insisted on paying them for the room Tez and I had taken, though Lenette tried to refused my payment. As I recounted all the times I'd repaid every, single nice thing others had done for me, I realized my motivation had very little to do with gratitude.

I didn't want anyone anywhere to be able to claim I owed them.

I thought about Henry, and how his betrayal had cut me to the quick. Was that when I started paying attention to who did what for whom? We stayed married, we even stayed friends, but I made damned sure he could never hurt me again. I had no faith in him, and, somehow, I had transferred that lack of faith to every relationship.

Deep down inside, I had decided that no one wanted to help me just to help me. That was too simple an explanation. Everyone had a motive; everyone had an angle. Tez had figured out this facet of my personality; he'd seen it clearly even when I had not. He didn't seem bothered by it, and he hadn't been cruel when he called me to the carpet, either.

I felt ashamed about how I had dishonored the genuine affection of my friends by overcompensating with gift giving. If I didn't keep score of what I happily did for others, then why couldn't I believe that my friends did the same? Was I so caught up in my own insecurities I couldn't even accept Tez's offer of running a hot bath without thinking about how to repay the gesture?

"You still having that epiphany, princess?" Tez leaned against the doorjamb of the bathroom, and studied me.

"I'm afraid so," I said. "It's quite disturbing to see such a glaring flaw in one's own personality."

"You gonna need therapy?" He stayed in the doorway, his arms crossed, his expression inscrutable. But I saw the glimmer of humor in his eyes.

"Quite possibly."

"I got my own flaws." He shook his head slowly, as if pitying himself. "Maybe we could share that therapist."

"Do you take anything seriously?"

"I take how I feel about you very seriously."

I realized I'd left the door open for that response. I wasn't sure what to say next, but Tez did. He crossed the room and took my hands in his. "No one's perfect. And seeking perfection isn't the path to happiness. Believe me, princess. You know what people want more than anything? The one gift we all really need, but never seem to get?"

"What?" I asked softly.

"Acceptance. We want someone to look at us, and really see us—our physical flaws, our personality quirks, our insecurities. And we want them to be okay with every square inch of who we are. We're always afraid we might be too needy or too much work. We put all these limitations on ourselves and our relationships because we're afraid that we're not really loved. That we're not really accepted. We hide little pieces of ourselves because we think that might be the one thing that finally drives away the person who's supposed to love us."

I was awed by his insight. That was exactly what I wanted—to receive and to give. How wonderful it would be to know that my lover saw me as I was, and would accept me body and soul? And that I could do the same for him?

Tez pulled me in close, his eyes glittering with the emotion I could not name because it was too soon. It was insane to feel that way now when we barely knew each other, and were worlds apart in so many ways, not least of which was our own natures.

"I can promise you this, Elizabeth. At the end of the day, no matter what's happened between us, I will let it go. I will tuck you into my arms and kiss you and let it go. We'll have a lot of good things together. We'll laugh every day. But I will argue with you. I'll make you cry. We'll drive each other crazy. You'll want to skin me and hang my pelt over the fireplace. But I will never turn away from you. And no matter how damned flawed you think you are, you are worthy of loyalty. You deserve devotion. I will give that all to you, and more."

No one had ever said such loving things to me before. I knew that Tez meant every word, and I was humbled by his sincerity. It very much sounded like a marriage proposal, though he couldn't mean it to be so. This wasn't the end of a romance novel where the heroine threw herself into the hero's waiting arms and agreed to marry him.

Sometimes, people didn't get happily-ever-afters. Look at my great-grandmother, and the other women of Broken Heart. A hundred years ago, what love they had known was stolen from them by Paul Tibbett.

"Thank you," I whispered. "You make me feel . . . Well, that's just it. You make me feel." I wished I could say something as beautiful and profound as he had, but I didn't have it in me. Not yet. I wanted to make that leap of faith—just dive off the cliff and know that I could fly. But I was standing at the edge of it still, weighing the pros and cons.

He kissed me lightly. "C'mon." He led me into the bathroom and turned off the flowing water. Then he undressed me, and scooped me up in a sudden whoosh. I squealed.

And he laughed.

Then he lowered me into the warm water, not caring how wet he got from the effort. "You're a beautiful woman."

"Lonely, too." I sniffed. "Look at all this tub, and just little ol' me inside it." I batted my eyelashes outrageously.

"Nice try, princess." He tapped my nose. "Enjoy your bath. I'm gonna load up the car, and run a little errand. I promise I'll be back before dawn."

I immediately wanted to know where he was going, but then I realized if he'd wanted me to know, he would've said. I trusted him—and I knew he would return. That was all I really wanted: To know the man I loved would always come home to me.

Not that I was acceding to loving Tez.

But I liked him very, very, *very* much.

Tez ran his finger over my shoulder, his gaze dipping toward my breasts. Then he heaved a great, anguished sigh. "I better go before I ravish you."

I opened my mouth to issue another invitation, but he held up his hand. "Don't go there. I'm one second away from giving in to temptation."

One more kiss, one more sweet touch, and then he was gone.

Tez hadn't returned by the time I finished bathing. I toweled myself off and poked through the lotions and powders Martha stocked in every bathroom. I took my time lathering the jasmine-scented lotion onto my body, hoping Tez might come back and find me naked and willing.

Unfortunately, his errand was taking much longer than I'd anticipated. I slipped on the black nightgown, the one I had rejected earlier in the evening as too distracting. I now had every intention of using my feminine wiles on Tez, rusty though they were.

I blew my hair dry and did a quick facial.

Still, no Tez.

Utterly disappointed, I wandered into my grandfather's library and tried to find a suitable book. It was too much to hope for a romance novel, much less some juicy commercial fiction. After a few minutes of perusing his collection, I decided I was too keyed up to read. I stared longingly at the lemon cake that beckoned from its china plate. I left the coffee on the tray, since it was now too cold to enjoy, and brought the cake into the bedroom. I might not be able to have any, but there was no reason Mr. Metabolism couldn't enjoy the rest.

I realized I hadn't talked to Damian yet, so I dug through my purse and pulled out my iPhone. Three seconds later, our call connected. I told him everything we'd found, and then discussed our theories about the killer, whom we suspected was the malevolent spirit of Paul Tibbett, and his motives for not only murdering Elizabeth Silverstone, but also for causing the suicides of four other Broken Heart women. This was, of course, assuming Evangeline LeRoy had died mysteriously, too. How the shadow factored in to the new theories was still unknown.

After I finished telling him everything, I asked, "How are Patsy and Eva?"

"Sedated in the prison," said Damian. "We've closed up the entrance to the room and posted guards. So far, no one's attempted to entry, but . . ."

"What?" I asked, dread pooling in my stomach.

"The trunks in the back room are missing," said Damian. "All five of them. We don't know when they were taken or by whom. But it does not bode well, *Liebling*."

"And no one else has found the missing items from those shelves?"

"Nein." He sighed. "We will see what we can discover about Mr. Tibbett. You will bring back the skull and papers?"

"As soon as I wake up," I said, "Tez and I will head back to Broken Heart."

"Ah. One more thing, Elizabeth. Have you seen Phoebe?"

"Not since I saw her and Connor at the manse," I said.

"She hasn't returned my calls. I can't get through to Connor, either," said Damian.

I looked at the clock and calculated how much time I might have before dawn. "I could swing by the hotel tonight, and see if they're there."

"You will call me as soon as you find them?"

"Yes, of course."

We said our good-byes, and I tucked the phone back into my purse. I hurriedly dressed in a blouse and slacks, slipping on a pair of beaded mules. I pulled my hair back into a ponytail, and checked the clock again. It was about an hour and a half before dawn. If I ignored the speed limits, I could make it to the hotel in twenty-five minutes. As I gathered my purse and headed out of the bedroom, I wondered why Damian hadn't just asked Patrick to pop in. He had the ability to transport himself in the blink of an eye. So did Lorcan, but I supposed that he didn't want to leave Eva. And Patrick was terribly busy with Patsy's triplets and his own children.

Still, I couldn't shake off my trepidation.

If I couldn't return to the house before sunrise, I could easily bunk with Phoebe and Connor. All I needed to do was contact Tez and let him know where I would be.

"Elizabeth."

I stopped and turned around. Tez was walking toward me from the direction of the study. The expression on his face made me wary.

"I thought you were gone," I accused him. "You've been here the whole time?"

"I was emptying out the rolltop and I found some letters, an envelope with newspaper clippings, and your great-grandmother's diary." He was holding a small box filled with papers and a leather journal. He looked like he'd been chewing on lemons. "You're not gonna like it."

"I'm sure I won't," I said. "But it'll have to wait. I promised Damian I would track down Phoebe and Connor. He can't get hold of them."

"I know that's important," he said impatiently, "but so is this. Paul Tibbett didn't kill your great-grandmother." He paused, his gaze on mine. "Jeremiah Silverstone did."

Chapter 16

*N*o. I wanted to absolve my great-grandfather of any wrongdoing, and here was Tez confirming my fears.

"You ever see a picture of Jeremiah Silverstone?" he asked. "There wasn't even a sketch of him in the newspaper article. He built half the town, but there's not a picture of him anywhere, is there?"

"I'm certain I've seen photos of him," I said. But I wasn't certain at all. "Family portraits . . ."

"You know, the only crap your grandfather took from Broken Heart was what he stored in the attic here in Tulsa. Everything else was left there, with Josiah. You wanna know why?"

"No," I said faintly. I scrambled through my memories. Hadn't I seen a photo of my great-grandfather somewhere? A sketch? Any kind of rendering of the man's face? I couldn't recall.

Tez pushed the box at me, but I was shaking too much

to take it. "Go on. Read through everything. I know you don't want to believe it, but it's true. Facts don't lie."

"But people do!" I snatched the box out of his grip and marched into the bedroom with it. I put it down on the bed, and then I dug out the iPhone from my purse to call Damian. The phone rang before I could touch the screen.

"Hello?"

"Have you left yet?" asked Damian.

"Just on my way." My gaze strayed to the box with its insidious contents.

"We heard from Connor. Phoebe has disappeared. They've been searching everywhere for hours. There's no sign of her. And Connor says she's not responding to his telepathy. He says she is silent, and he assumes she is unconscious."

"Oh, my God."

"I suspect the shadow," said Damian. "He has gone after all the descendents of the founding families, *ja*? So, maybe he got to Phoebe."

"That's not very good news."

"She is protected," said Damian. "Her immortality is tied to the talisman. Nothing can harm her. At least nothing we know about. Out of all of you, she is the safest.

"In the meanwhile, we are tracking down the grave of Paul Tibbett. It seems he died not long after Elizabeth did. Lorcan is helping us. I'm afraid he's not taking his wife's confinement very well."

"We'll resolve this situation soon," I said with a confidence I didn't feel. I also held off on telling Damian that Paul Tibbett might be the wrong man. *Oh, Jeremiah. How could you?* "I'll see you tomorrow."

Damian hung up, and I disconnected and tossed the phone back into my purse. I sat heavily on the edge of the bed. "I can't believe my own flesh and blood would do something so terrible."

Tez sat next to me and took my hand into his. "The thing is, Ellie, he's not your flesh and blood."

I glanced at him. "How can that be?"

"The Silverstone line died with Josiah. He was the only son born of Jeremiah and Elizabeth Silverstone." He slipped the journal out of the box and handed it to me. "Looks like your grandfather marked the relevant passages. But before you read it, you might want to check out the newspaper articles."

He stood up. I noticed he had gotten dressed, in anticipation of running his mysterious errand.

"Where are you going?" I asked.

"I'm going to finish loading up the car. And I still have a surprise to get." He leaned down and brushed his lips across mine. "I'll be back soon. You're gonna need some alone time to process everything."

I didn't really want to be alone. I'd spent a great deal of time by myself over the past few years, and was usually satisfied with my own company. But relying on Tez for the last seventy-two hours had made me realize how nice it was to share my burdens, my worries, my fears with another soul—with someone who offered comfort and support without question. I was afraid I'd gotten rather used to it, and I loathed the idea I might have to let him go.

He touched my face one last time, and then left me alone with my family's past.

I curled against the headboard with the box in my lap, and took out the yellowed articles snipped from a paper called the *Missouri Statesman*. There were three columns attached by a rusted paper clip. The first one was about the disappearance of a wealthy oilman's young wife. Her name was Bethany Silverstone. And the oilman? Jeremiah Silverstone. The second article detailed the gruesome discovery of her remains: A little boy's dog had uncovered the shallow grave in the woods.

Bethany had been strangled to death.

The third article was just a snippet about how the murderer of Mrs. Silverstone was none other than her gardener, Wilson Caper. As punishment for his crime, he got the noose. Mr. Silverstone, devastated by the loss of his bride, moved to Tulsa. Penciled in the margin was a year: 1886.

I felt sick to my stomach. Had my great-grandfather killed his first wife and somehow framed the gardener? Had poor Wilson Caper paid for a crime he didn't commit? And when my great-grandmother dared to love another, had Jeremiah killed her, too? Then he framed Paul Tibbett, her former fiancé?

It all made horrible sense.

If my great-grandmother had loved Paul, why on earth did she dump him to marry Jeremiah? For the money? Surely she would've chosen love. I had to believe it.

Yet, her choice to be with Jeremiah was proof enough.

I let the papers flutter back into the box.

Dawn was approaching; I could already feel the pull of sleep. I took a minute to put my nightie back on, and then I checked the blackout curtains on the windows on either side of the bed. I also closed the thick curtains around the bed itself. Then I crawled under the covers. I picked up the journal. As Tez had pointed out, several pieces of paper poked out from the top, marking the pages my grandfather had probably thought to be important.

What had Tez meant about me and Jeremiah not being flesh and blood? Nothing would please me more than to not be related to a murdering psychopath—a serial killer who had the power to continue tormenting his victims after his own death. And what power he had, too, if he could figure out how to call forth a demon—and if he could return in ghostly form to reenact murder.

I opened to the first marked page of Elizabeth's journal. I read about her excitement of being in the land run, how Paul set up a tent and lived on their parcel while she stayed with a cousin in Tulsa. She was obviously very much in love with Paul Tibbett.

So much so, she was already sleeping with him. The land run was in April 1889, and in the next entry, which was June 14, she mentioned the book of poetry Paul had given to her. And how she knew she was pregnant with his child.

With my grandfather, Stephen Paul Silverstone.

Elizabeth and Paul wanted to get married quickly, and made plans to wed at a small church in Tulsa.

I ached for these two people. They had a bright future together, a new life to build on that Oklahoma soil, a child to raise together, and love, so much love.

The third entry shed light on why Elizabeth chose to marry Jeremiah. Paul had been accused of thievery, and arrested—and "arrested" was a loose term. There wasn't a sheriff in those days, certainly not in what was still considered Indian Territory. They tied him to a tree and debated about whether or not to hang him.

Hanging won out.

Then Jeremiah had approached her.

"Marry me," he said, "and I will vouch for Paul. He will live, and I will take care of you and your child. I will give the babe my name, and my wealth. All I ask is that you pledge your heart to me, Elizabeth."

I could not sincerely pledge my heart to Jeremiah, but I would have said anything, promised anything so that Paul would live. When I agreed to be affianced to Jeremiah, he kept his word. He vouched for Paul, and the money that had been stolen from around the camps was mysteriously returned.

When Paul found out what I had done, I thought he would be angry with me. But Paul understood— he knew me like no other, and loved me without question. I did not want to marry Jeremiah, and I would rather live poorly with the man I loved than spend a minute in the opulence promised by a man who did not hold my heart.

Paul and I decided to wait until nightfall and then leave. I admit I was a coward. I had never broken a promise, and before I lied to Jeremiah Silverstone, I could say I was a woman of my word. Living with my shame was worth the price. Is there any cost you would not pay for love?

We never got a chance to leave. Paul disap-

*peared. And I was alone, and pregnant. Without a
husband, I would be destitute and ostracized. This
was my first lesson in learning that Jeremiah never
took chances. He trusted no one. He wanted me, and
he would have me. I thought Paul was dead, and I
grieved for his loss.*

Then I married Jeremiah.

I almost couldn't bear to read anymore. Love opened
all the doors a woman needed to walk through, and duty
opened none. And her love for Paul forced Elizabeth
into the life she did not want. I knew well how that felt.
But I couldn't blame societal pressures (other than my
mother's not-so-subtle trust fund hints) for my choices. I
chose to stay in the good graces of my parents; I chose to
marry Henry despite, as my great-grandmother so elo-
quently put it, he did not hold my heart; and I chose to
stay in a marriage with an unfaithful man.

I could not unravel the past and weave it into a more
beautiful representation of my life. What was done was
done, for me and for the other Elizabeth. Sometimes, no
matter how badly you wanted to, you couldn't stop what
had been set into motion. The inevitability of Elizabeth's
life, and her death, made me want to weep.

With my heart in my throat, I turned to the next
marked section. Elizabeth apparently settled into her
role as a wife and mother. She was scared of her husband, and suspected him of "unsavory acts." She'd heard
rumors in town about Jeremiah pursuing the affections
of married women. Because he owned most of the buildings, and had loaned money to nearly everyone within a
ten-mile radius, no one challenged his ill-behaved ways.

Then one day, Paul returned. He kept his presence in town a secret. He told Elizabeth an incredible story. He'd been shanghaied by some of Jeremiah's cohorts and taken to the Gulf of Mexico, indentured on a ship to pay off a debt Jeremiah had owed. He'd been gone six long years, imprisoned, forced to work every day until the debt was repaid. It had certainly suited Jeremiah's streak of cruelty to make his wife's former fiancé suffer, and get a financial reward as part of it.

Together, they made plans to leave, and take the children. Elizabeth snuck out food and supplies. They waited until the evening of the party to put their escape into motion—Elizabeth believed that no one would notice she and her sons were missing until it was too late.

She'd written it all down in an incriminating diary. Maybe she needed the outlet since she had no one to whom she could tell the secret. Maybe she kept it so that if she came to harm, people would know of her fear of Jeremiah. Maybe she was just naive.

Little had she known, her husband was not as ignorant of her activities as she'd hoped. The night of the party, she'd followed him into the attic at his request because she was trying act as if everything was normal. What would her life—not to mention my life—had been like if she'd escaped with Paul?

"Well, *that's* not depressing at all," I whispered. I put the journal back into the box. The spirit of Elizabeth had shown me how her plans had turned out. Her husband had taken her to that awful room—and revealed the demon spellwork he'd performed. What nefarious purpose did he want fulfilled? Was he really a serial killer?

Jeremiah strangled his wife. Maybe he'd done it because he was obsessed with her, and his brand of suffocating love couldn't tolerate the idea of her running off with her soul mate. Maybe he'd done it because he was a coldhearted killer and used Elizabeth's infidelity as an excuse to end her life. Or maybe she became the required sacrifice to Mammon.

What a bastard.

I was glad to know his blood did not run in my veins. Josiah had been his biological son. Thank heavens the man had never married or procreated. Who knew what terrible things lurked in the Silverstone DNA?

I could feel it getting close to sunrise. Soon, I would go to vampire slumberland whether I wanted to or not. Tez had not yet returned from his mysterious errand and I was feeling anxious.

I dug into the box and plucked out a folded sheet of paper. I scanned through the elegant masculine lines scrawled on the yellowed page, and felt cold shock sweep through me.

> *In the month of September, on the day of the 17th, in the year 1894, we five judged and convicted Jeremiah Silverstone of murdering Elizabeth Silverstone, Catherine Allen, Mary McCree, and Cora Clark. We confess that it was us, and us alone, who meted out his justice. Should there be consequences, either from the law or from God, we willingly accept them.*
>
> *We kidnapped Jeremiah from his mansion, bound him, gagged him, and took him to Sean McCree's barn. We forced him to his knees and beat him. It was Dennison who knocked him in the head*

with a board. Finally, Jeremiah admitted to being in league with the devil. He said it was his demon servant who killed our women as sacrifices to the prince of evil, so that Jeremiah could continue to prosper.

He showed no remorse for his crimes, and he refused to tell us where Elizabeth was buried. He was a hateful man, evil to the core. He brought to us only pain and suffering, and cursed us all with his greed.

Killing him was a mercy—and a necessity. Surely he was not a man, but himself a demon, and no one would be safe for so long as he lived.

We made a noose and strung the rope over the rafters in Sean's barn. As we placed the noose around Jeremiah's neck, he cursed us all, and swore that he would have his revenge, and that the demon who served him would never relent.

We hung him, and bore witness to his last breath on this earth. Then we removed his head and cut the rest of his body into four pieces. We each took a part of his body, which we agreed to bury on each of our properties.

Then we went to the attic, to that terrible place evil had created, to deal with the demon. We are Christian men, but we took part in Paul's heathen rituals—using things he'd learned from his time in Mexico—and called the demon into his circle, binding him to it. Paul sealed the doors with black magic. Then we boarded up the room, and prayed none would ever discover it.

We hope that the spirit of Jeremiah burns in hell.

We believe the best course of action is for Paul to "die" and be reborn as Jeremiah Silverstone. We will bury his coffin in the cemetery, along with this confession of our deeds. Paul will raise the young sons of his precious Elizabeth. He has promised compensation from Silverstone's coffers for our losses, though no amount of money can replace the women we loved so well.

Jeremiah wished for our town to be called Silverstone Shadows, but we will never honor that man's memory. We've agreed the name should be Broken Heart, a testament to the loss of our beloved wives, and a reminder of our sins.

We write these words as penitent men, and pray that when Judgment Day comes, God will have mercy on our souls.

Signed,
Paul Tibbett

Dennison Clark

Michael Allen

Sean McCree

Jonathon LeRoy

Chapter 17

"I can't believe this," I whispered. I laid the letter on top of the other items. "It's like the Pandora's Box for Broken Heart." I scooped the letter up again and stared at the signatures.

Four victims.

The demon had been obsessed with the number five, but he'd only gotten four women before he'd been bound into the circle.

Then when he'd been released from the attic prison, he'd just started all over. Except no one had actually died yet. Would he keep trying? And what about Jeremiah? If his ghost was attacking me, then . . . where had he been all this time? Trapped with the demon? Or called back from the other side when his pet was unleashed again?

All the questions swirled and tumbled until I couldn't think about it anymore. Instead, I wondered how in the world they'd gotten away with simply switching out Jeremiah with Paul Tibbett. Surely other people noticed? Or maybe he'd been such a terror, they didn't care some-

one else had taken over his identity. The town started
to really prosper after Jeremiah's death. I bet Paul was
generous with the purse strings; he'd funded Jonathon
LeRoy's newspaper—and he'd probably invested in the
other men's endeavors, too. How had the story about
Mary McCree gotten started? Had they done that to
throw off suspicion? Or had some pioneer gossip started
the tale?

Broken Heart really had been cursed. By Jeremiah
Silverstone.

Obviously, my grandfather and his brother had discovered the truth. Surely the information had driven
my grandfather, Stephen Silverstone, to Tulsa to begin
a new life while his brother felt somehow compelled to
stay in the mansion. Why had Josiah suddenly decided
to abandon the house in the 1950s? Did he have a run-in
with Jeremiah's spirit? At least I knew why he had never
wanted another Silverstone to occupy the place; he was
trying to protect his family. Biologically, he was the last
Silverstone. I wondered if he'd chosen to not to marry or
have children because he was afraid he might be more
like his father than he could help? The very idea that my
great-uncle could have serial-killer impulses froze me
to the bone.

Poor Josiah could've never foreseen his great-niece
would become a vampire. Nor could he have known
it didn't matter who lived in the house. No one could
be protected from Mammon's shadow, or Jeremiah's
vengeful spirit.

It was enough to make my skin crawl.

My phone rang, and I lunged for my purse. I took it
out and said, "Hello?"

"I'm turning down the street to your house," said Tez.

"Not going to make it," I said, yawning. "I'm this close to passing out."

I checked the curtains on the windows again; the thick fabric covered them quite well. Then I pulled the draperies on the bed shut again, glad there was an extra precaution against errant sunlight. I didn't think Martha would be pleased to find a pile of ash smeared on her freshly washed sheets.

"How did your errand go?" I said, trying to keep the petulance out of my voice. "At six a.m.?"

"The store I went to isn't the kind of place that closes, princess. I'll show you all the goodies tomorrow evening when you rise from your coffin."

"Oh, ha, ha."

"I'm parking. Then I'm running into the house. Bet I get there before—"

I yawned again, falling back against the pillows. "Before what?"

"You're not gonna believe who's sitting in the damned driveway." I heard him turn off the car and open his door. "Tawny. What the hell are you doing here? Hey!—" Tez's shout ended abruptly and the dial tone buzzed in my ear.

Tawny? I couldn't drum up the necessary energy to get out of the bed. "Tez?"

Darkness crimped the edges of my vision and I struggled to stay awake because Tez was in trouble with a real man-eater.

That was my last thought before I passed out.

*   *   *

When I awoke, I was tucked in up to my chin, the items that had been on the bed cleared away.

Tez had not crawled in beside me, and the memory of his exclamation and sudden end to his phone call filled me with dread. He'd left with Tawny?

Not willingly. Not unless something had happened to Calphon, or she'd kidnapped him at gunpoint. If Tez wasn't here, then it meant Martha had been the one in my bedroom checking on me and doing her duties.

I feared she might've read the damning items in that box, and then I calmed down. She would never commit such an impropriety. However, she might've noticed I wasn't breathing. *Good Lord.*

I pulled back the curtain and scrambled off the bed. My iPhone had been put into its charger, no doubt by the ever-efficient Martha. I unplugged it and dialed Damian immediately.

"Ja."

"Have you seen Tez?" I asked. I wiggled out of my nightie and dug through my suitcase for a bra. "That sounded rude," I said, rushed. "I'm so sorry. But have you, I mean? Seen Tez?"

"No, *Liebling*. He is missing, too?"

Something in the tone of his voice made me pause. "Are you going to tell me someone other than Phoebe had disappeared?"

"Eva has disappeared from her cell," he said. "And we cannot find Dr. Clark. He dropped Marissa off at Lenette's, but he never showed up to the hospital."

I couldn't manage the phone and the bra, so I dropped the bra and found a pair of jeans. I shoved my legs through them. "Damian, we're not looking for Paul

Tibbett. The shadow demon was called by Jeremiah Silverstone." I summarized the contents of the box, telling him about the confession of the five men, and how I believed the shadow was trying to complete his purpose—the sacrifice of five.

"We are searching every inch of Broken Heart. We discovered the empty coffin of Mr. Tibbett. It appears it was opened some time ago."

That would explain why my grandfather had the confession—and the skull. Had he dug it up to make sure he kept the Silverstone fortune? Or was he only trying to keep the secret of Broken Heart?

"The shadow's targeting descendents." I paused, one shoe dangling from my foot. "Phoebe is an Allen, Eva is a LeRoy, Marissa is a Clark—"

"He did not take the daughter," said Damian. "He took her father. He's the Clark. Darlene married into his family."

"Oh. Right. Hang on." I put down the phone and quickly put on my bra and one of Tez's T-shirts. Then I grabbed the phone and headed into the bathroom. "Do you know where Jessica is? She's a McCree."

"At her home with the children. Darrius and Drake are with her. That just leaves you, Elizabeth. You remain unprotected."

I ran a brush through my hair as I replayed the conversation with Tez the night before. *You're not gonna believe who's sitting in the damned driveway.* I swear I was going to rip out Tawny's hair by the roots! "I'm coming back to Broken Heart."

"And Tez?"

"I know where he is," I said grimly. "I'll handle it."

"Check in when you return to town," said Damian. "If Jeremiah wishes to harm to the descendents of the ones who killed him, you are not safe."

"No one is," I said. "That's the real curse of Broken Heart."

I hung up with Damian, grabbed the box of evidence, and hurried out of the bedroom. My mouth tasted tinny and felt fuzzy, but I'd wasted enough time already, and didn't even want to take thirty seconds to brush my teeth. If it were possible for me to do the zap-home magick, I would've done it already. Unfortunately, I had to drive really, really fast.

Martha waited in the foyer. She handed me two Tupperwares, a pack of peppermint gum, and the keys to my father's Mercedes.

"How do you always know?"

"It's my job," she said. "I noticed Tez had already left. The dessert is for him. Chocolate raspberry and cherry cobbler. There's plenty of gas in the tank, and you know your father won't care if you keep the Mercedes for a bit." She kissed me lightly on the cheek. "By the way, when were you going to tell me you're a vampire?"

Startled, I nearly dropped the Tupperware. "Never," I managed, feeling the same I did when I was five years old and she'd caught me eating chocolate-chip cookie dough straight out of the mixing bowl. "How'd you know?"

She arched a silver brow. "I figured it out when I noticed you weren't breathing. And the curtains were drawn on the windows and the bed."

"You seem to be rather accepting."

"My grandson was Turned a few years ago," she said.

"He runs a night club in Miami, Florida. You wouldn't believe how many vampires live there."

"In the Sunshine State?" The idea boggled my mind.

"I think it's the night life they're interested in."

"So, you've known about vampires all this time?"

"You might be surprised at how much us humans know about the supernatural." Martha narrowed her gaze. "I found blood on the library carpet."

"Oh, dear. I'm terribly sorry."

"I taught you better table manners," she agreed mildly. "You're meeting Tez, right?"

"Uh, yes. Yes, I am." I hugged her quickly. "I hope you understand why I didn't tell you about my undead-ness."

"Of course. And no, I will not tell your parents. I believe your mother still labors under the hope you will have children."

"I'm a little past child-bearing years. Technically, I'm forty-eight."

"Not to her, dear." She nodded toward the door. "Go on, now. I'll see you soon."

I hurried out the front door. As I suspected, she'd already parked the Mercedes in front. I really don't know how my mother would live without Martha. She was a one-in-a-million lady.

I opened the door, piled everything into the passenger seat, put on my seat belt, popped a piece of gum, and started the Mercedes. My urgency had me peeling out of the driveway.

Oops.

The usual two-hour drive took me a little more than an hour. The minute I hit the open highway, I rammed down the accelerator. I had no intention of stopping for the police if they attempted to pull me over. Luckily, there was little traffic and no cops.

The second I hit Broken Heart's borders, I phoned Damian to let him know I was back in town. Then I headed for the were-cat colony. The Mercedes offered a smoother ride than Tez's Honda, but it was still bumpy, and very dark.

Even with my vampire vision, I had to hit the high beams and drive more slowly than I wanted. After a few minutes, the headlights illuminated the single long building. This time it looked even more austere and un-welcoming. I parked and got out of the car.

Belatedly, I thought of a weapon. I didn't have a gun, and even if I did, I wouldn't know how to use it—unless I drew upon the lessons learned from the *Lethal Weapon* movies. I didn't have knives, and I really didn't want to have to dig out the tire iron.

Well, then. I was a vampire. I had speed, strength, the ability to control minds, and I could make beautiful jew-elry. Ah, yes. *No reason to be nervous, Elizabeth, maybe you can whip up some shiny trinkets and trade 'em for Tez.*

I pocketed my iPhone and the car keys. I activated the locks manually because I was too afraid that the beep of the alarm might alert the were-cats of my arrival. Not that I was being all that particularly stealthy.

I heard the snap and snicker of fire. As I crept along the side of the building, rhythmic drumming started. The soft, primal beats were accompanied by chanting. Heart in my throat, I dared a peek around the corner.

Just like the evening before, a bonfire raged. The

drumming was courtesy of two women on the far side of the flames. They were naked, their bodies painted. Three other women, also naked, their bodies painted with different colors and patterns than the drummers, swayed and chanted. I couldn't understand the words, but they were rife with sorrow.

I didn't see Serri among any of these women. Nor did I see any men featured in these proceedings. But I did see Tawny. She was naked, too, and did her own dance on the opposite side of the chanting women. Her dance was far more sensual than grief-filled, however.

My gaze flicked to the top of the fire; that was when I realized this wasn't just a were-cat party. It was a pyre. A large body sat amid the roaring flames, already blackened and withering to ash.

That was when I realized the alpha must've died.

And this was his funeral.

I scooted backward and pressed my hand against my chest. *Good Lord.* Had I been mistaken in my assumption that the were-cats had kidnapped Tez? I'd nearly blundered into a sacred rite. I felt like a fool for all of two seconds. Then worry gnawed at me. Where was Tez? Who had taken him? I was sure he'd recognized his captors; in fact, he'd sounded annoyed rather than fearful. Not that I could imagine Tez sounding fearful.

I heard a growl.

I froze, panic welding my feet to the ground. I was certain one of the women had changed into their cat form in order to attack. But neither cat nor woman slunk around the corner to claw at me.

Another growl, this one loud and pissed off.

I peeked around the corner again. Tawny was continuing her dance with undulating hips and pendulous swinging breasts. In her hand was a thick gold chain and it was attached to a bejeweled collar around a beautiful black jaguar's neck.

Fury slashed through me like hot knives.

I would kill her.

I stepped forward, fists clenched.

I heard a step behind me and I whirled, baring my fangs.

Serri put a finger to her lips. She was pale, her clothing stained and torn. Shadows smudged eyes; her lips were a disturbing blue. Her arm was cradled at an odd angle.

"Are you all right?" I asked, which was a silly question because obviously she was not. "Let me help you."

"Later," she said. "Tawny is trying to claim Tez. It's a very old ritual, one that must be done on the night we offer our alpha back to the gods. It's an ancient binding magic, and it's not used anymore. Some of us still believe in free will." She smiled sadly. "Trak and I tried to stop her, and she . . ." Her gaze flickered toward the small house. "You've been very kind to me. You gave me hope, when I had none. I wish I'd had an opportunity to speak to your queen."

"You still do," I said. "Tawny will not get away with this nonsense."

"I'm not worried about me anymore," she said. "You must demand the *upendo* challenge. If you do, she cannot bind with Tez unless she defeats you. Everyone's afraid of her. They won't defy her wishes. She'll be very powerful as the jaguar's mate."

"The hell," I hissed. "How will this work? I'm not a were-cat."

"All challenges must be answered. It doesn't matter that you're a vampire. But if you win," she said, her gaze intense, "you will belong to Tez, body and soul, for all his life. If you do not want that, you must let Tawny have him."

Oh, the irony. Here I'd spent all this time protecting Tez from a hundred years of vampire marriage—and now, if I won this *upendo* challenge, I would end up his wife forever.

"There's something else," said Serri. "I choose you as Dayton's *mama pili*. His second mother."

I blinked. "Oh, Serri. I . . . That's lovely." It was incredibly bad timing, but I was touched all the same. "Is that like a godmother?" I looked over my shoulder, and gauged the ongoing ritual. If I didn't get over there and issue my ultimatum, Tez was going to end up married to that harlot.

"If something happens to me, you will be his first mother." She grimaced. I realized she was in pain, and I reached out to her. She shook her head and backed away. "If anyone tries to challenge your right to him, tell them it is my *iliyopita unataka*. Use those exact words, Elizabeth. It's important."

"Yes," I said. "Of course."

She offered me a tired smile. "Go fight for the man you love."

Well, that summed it up exactly. I wanted Tez, and even though it was ridiculous to think I could love him . . . I did. Sometimes, the heart knew and the head argued. I was tired of logic. I wanted to trust my feelings. Every atom of my being was screaming that Tez was mine.

I'd be damned if Tawny got her claws on him.

I was stepping off the edge of the cliff, uncaring if I fell or if I flew. The point was to take the leap, and keep the faith.

"Elizabeth?"

I glanced over my shoulder. "Yes?"

"Kick that bitch's ass."

Chapter 18

I kicked off my shoes and ran into the clearing. The grass was soft beneath the soles of my feet. I skidded to a stop in the soft dirt surrounding the pyre. The fire was intense and very bright. Unease shot through me. If I got too close, I'd turn into ash along with the alpha.

The mourners saw me first, and stopped chanting, obviously shocked to find a vampire within their midst.

The drummers stopped as soon as they noticed me, their expressions mirroring the surprise of the others, and moved to join the singers. Everyone's gazes traveled from me to Tawny.

Tawny ceased her stripper routine and whirled around, her expression melding from mere annoyance to pure rage.

"You!" She marched toward me, jerking on the chain and forcing Tez to follow her. He yowled, reluctantly padding along behind her, his gold eyes glittering with fury. "This is a private funeral, and outsiders are not welcome. Tonight, I mourn the passing of our alpha, and my mate."

"Don't forget the part where you try to steal *my* mate," I cried. "I issue the *upendo* challenge."

The other women gasped, and Tawny's gaze went wide. "You can't. You are not were-cat."

"She can," said one of the singers. She looked like the youngest of the bunch, maybe sixteen or seventeen. Her hair was gold-blond and her eyes velveteen brown. She was too thin, and looked as delicate as china. Did the girl not eat? "Anyone can challenge you," she said to Tawny. "If you refuse her, you forfeit the right to claim your new mate."

Tawny did not like this news. It was apparent that she'd bullied everyone into the ritual, going so far as to incapacitate the second and his mate to get her way. She had kidnapped Tez, who'd already made it clear he wasn't interested—in her or in the leadership of this were-cat pride.

"Fine," she said. "I accept the challenge. Prepare for death, bitch."

She yanked on the chain, and Tez protested even as he walked to sit beside her. She stroked the head of Tez, her fingers sifting through his fur possessively.

I wanted to punch her. Hard. In the face. I couldn't recall ever wanting to physically harm another being, but this girl caused within me a need to claw and scream and damage.

"Perhaps, Emma, since you've been so kind as to help a stranger keep our ways, you can ally with her."

"Gladly," said the girl. Emma joined me, her shoulders straight, her gaze refusing to turn away from Tawny.

I applauded her bravery. I only wished she was wearing some clothing.

Her proud acquiescence only served to further infuriate Tawny. The bimbette turned to me and smiled hatefully. "She doesn't seem to value her life. You see, if she chooses to align with you, then as soon as I'm done killing you, I get to kill her."

"Well, aren't you Little Miss Sunshine," I said. "If *you* value your hands, you might want to take them off my jaguar."

"See this?"—she dangled the chain attached to the jeweled collar; I could sense the power of the gold circle—"It's old magick. Control the chain"—she yanked on it and Tez's magnificent head was jerked forward—"and control the cat."

I glared at Tawny as she continued to taunt both me and Tez with her ability to make him go hither and yon at her whims. I focused on the collar. It was definitely fairy gold, which was the only metal that could bind magical beings, and it had the persnickety quality associated with ancient pieces. I glared at Tawny even as I reached out to the gold, coaxing it to me, praising its beauty and strength. The best way to describe its response was like a snake awakening, its regal head turning toward mine as it uncoiled. I didn't know if it would allow me to pet it or if it would strike.

Apparently, it wasn't too enamored of Tawny's control. It acquiesced to my power, and began to stretch into long, shining filaments. As the metal shifted in her hand, Tawny gasped and tried to recapture the chain.

But it was like shifting sand falling through her fingers, winding away from her grasp. It refused to be held by her.

Tez growled, his gaze swinging toward Tawny. The muscles rippled in his shoulders, causing his fur to ruffle all the way down his backside. I knew he wanted to pounce on the woman who dared to bind him. And he probably wanted to do much worse—like tear her throat out. I wondered how much the man controlled the impulses of the cat.

The morphing chain twisted into the air, waiting for my command. Then I knew exactly what to do.

"Bind her," I commanded. "Form a chain around her neck. Connect manacles to her wrists and ankles."

The gold eagerly obeyed me. It detached from Tez's collar and flowed like water around Tawny's neck.

"No!" she screamed. She tried to pull it away, but the gold outmaneuvered the panicked motions of her hands. It formed a solid circlet around her throat and then delicate loops sprouted from the middle, one after another, until the new chains were long enough to touch her wrists.

Tawny yanked her arms around from the persistent gold and tried to run, but Tez clamped his massive maw around her calf, and, obviously terrified he might chew off her leg, she stayed still.

The gold formed manacles, about two inches in width, around her wrists. Then more loops dripped from each bracelet until they touched her feet. The gold stretched around each ankle and solidified into cuffs twice as wide as those binding her wrists.

Tears dripped down Tawny's face, and she stood there, mute, her expression pitiful. I wasn't one bit sorry about her predicament. She was a selfish, cruel, man-stealing, big-breasted terror—and she deserved whatever fate she got.

"Well," said Emma as she surveyed my handiwork. "I was going to tell you that most *upendo* challenges end with one of the participants being killed, even though a winner can be declared without the loser dying." She glanced at me, her eyes twinkling with humor. "I was also going to offer you some tips about Tawny's fighting weaknesses, and what to do if she shifted into her were-tiger form."

"You mean I won?" I asked. "We didn't even fight."

"You challenged her," said Emma. "Then you defeated her. That's all that is required."

"Oh." I knelt down and Tez padded to me, and nuzzled me under the chin. Then he licked my face. "That tickles," I said. Then I kissed him on the nose. He purred loudly.

"What happens now?" I asked, looking up at Emma. "Serri told me winning the challenge meant were-cat marriage."

"The collar hasn't been used in our pride in a long time," said Emma. "It's only used when the alpha chooses one mate and together they rule the pride. There is no second, and women are free to choose their own lovers." She looked sad for a moment. "I'm sure you can imagine why it hasn't been used. Rare is the alpha who only wants one woman."

I thought about Trak and Serri, and how the collar might've benefited them. It was too late to offer it, though. I had made my choice.

"Its magick binds mates together for the rest of their lives," said Emma softly. "Look."

Without my Family power guiding it, the collar around Tez's neck shone brightly. I felt the power of it buzzing, and the air went heavy and electric as though lightning were about to strike.

Tawny was openly weeping, and Emma grabbed her by the chains and drew her away. She paused and said, "When this part is over, Tez will be driven by the urge to mate with you. There's no stopping him, and you must let him take you. It's the only way to finish the ritual."

I really should've gotten more information about this endeavor before rushing headlong into it.

The collar around Tez's neck unclasped and rose into the air between us. As it began to spin, it grew brighter and brighter. I was staring at it in awe, so I nearly jumped out of my skin when I felt a male hand caress my hair.

"Princess," whispered Tez. "You rescued me."

"Looks like I married you, too."

"About time."

I looked down at his virile, naked form, stretched out next to me. If I had grapes, I could've plucked them one by one and offered them to his succulent lips. But this was not a Roman fresco. I stood up, and he joined me, taking me into his arms. His hazel eyes were smoky with desire, and an answering need began tapping out a primal rhythm in the pit of my belly.

There was a tinny noise—like two swords clanging against each other in battle. The big spinning light broke into two smaller lights.

Slowly, the sparkles descended, and as they did, they stopped spinning. Now there were two collars. His was larger and dotted with emeralds; mine was far more delicate and feminine, especially with its smaller, twinkling rubies.

The collars slipped around our necks at the same

time. I heard a clap of thunder, or maybe it was the roar of approval from the were-cats' gods, and then the collars snicked into place.

Tez growled.

I looked at him, and saw the diamond shape of his pupils. I gulped. Lust emanated off him in waves. I was so stunned by the sudden change of his demeanor that I stepped out of the circle of his arms.

"It's okay to run," yelled Emma from the porch of the bunker. The women had gathered there, and were unabashedly watching the events unfold. "In fact, you might want to start now."

The other women screamed and hooted, and I, being no fool, took off toward the edge of the woods. I ran by the pyre, skirting the side of the little church, and dove through the trees. I used my vampire speed, too. If Tez wanted me, I thought giddily, then he would have to catch me.

He did.

The chase ended when he took me down with a flying tackle. He held on tight and rolled so that when we landed, I was on top of him.

"Take your pants off," he gritted out. "Or I'll shred them."

I was caught between excitement and fear. I'd never seen him like this, and I knew he wasn't playing a game. Whatever magick created the collars, it compelled him to complete our binding.

I stood up and quickly wiggled off my pants and underwear.

Tez knelt before me and pressed his face between my thighs. He sniffed me, and a little growl issued from his

throat. Then he started to lick me. I was already aroused
by our game of chase, and it didn't take long before my
thighs were slick and pleasure was coiling hot and deep
within me.

"Hand and knees, Elizabeth. *Now.*"

I did exactly as he said. He caressed my buttocks, then
I felt him guide his cock inside me. I was wet and ready,
or so I thought. He was really big, and I was grateful he
tried to be gentle with our first real consummation.

He worked his way inside until he was fully sheathed.
For a moment, there was no movement, no breath. It
was a second, maybe two, of feeling that wonderful connection. It had been so long since I'd known the physical
pleasure of a man's penetration.

And to think, I would have several lifetimes of making love with Tez.

He began to thrust inside me. His hands gripped my
hips, his nails digging into my flesh. I could tell he was
holding back, trying not to give in to the wild urges that
surged inside him.

But I didn't want him to control himself. I didn't want
him to think he had to be careful with me or that I was
too delicate a thing to handle his true passions. We were
partners now, in every way, and I wouldn't let him hold
back. I wanted to fulfill his real needs. I didn't want protection from his animal side.

I wanted to embrace it.

"Harder," I said. "As hard as you can. Please, Tez."

He growled, and that noise of possession thrilled me.

"You turn me on so much," he whispered in a whiskey
voice. One of his hands crept underneath and started
stroking my clit. "I can't get enough of you."

I wasn't a prude (Obviously. I was half naked in the woods having sex with a were-jaguar). But still . . . good manners had been drilled into me since I could talk. I wanted to say earthy things, and be naughty in word and deed, but I just couldn't manage it.

He increased his pace, and I knew he was still holding back. At least for himself. He was doing quite fine revving my engine. In fact, I was getting very close to orgasm, and I didn't want to go over before he did.

"Let go, damn it," I demanded. "I can take you."

He groaned, his fingers working my clit, and finally—*oh, finally*—he stopped trying to control his lust. He pounded into me so hard that it was difficult to keep myself pinioned to the ground. I dug in with my fingers and pressed my knees hard against the packed earth.

My senses went into overload.

I flew over the edge into sparkling waves of bliss, and then Tez cried out my name and came with me.

I don't know how much time passed before Tez slipped out of me and helped me to my feet. The experience had been so intense, and I was shaken by it.

"You okay?" he asked.

I nodded. "You?"

"Best day of my life." He hesitated. "I know it's too late to take this all back, Elizabeth, but . . . you don't regret it, do you?"

"I love you," I said simply.

Relief entered his gaze, and then he grinned. "I love you, too." He picked me up and swung me around. "Just think of the fun we're going to have, Ellie Bee."

I realized that he only called me Elizabeth when he was being serious. Otherwise, he used all those pet nicknames. I wasn't sure I'd ever be too fond of Ellie Bee, but since I was extremely fond of the man uttering it . . . well, I guess I could live with it.

"We should get back," I said with some reluctance. "Several people are missing, and we need to give Damian everything we've found."

"Okay," he said. "I know we're bound the vampire way because of the sex, but are there other things you're supposed to do?"

I cupped the back of his neck and said, "I claim you."

When vampires claimed anyone, which could be their children, their donors, or their mates, their symbol was imprinted onto the person. Other vampires could see it; then they knew the human, or whoever, was protected. My symbol was simple: a heart.

"There's another part," I said. "It's called the word-giving. It's sorta like saying vows. The most profound sentiment I can offer you is that I love you like I've loved no other. And I'm so very glad you're mine."

"I'm glad we're together," he said. "I'm happiest when I'm near you. You are my heart, Elizabeth, and I love you."

We kissed, sealing our words and our bond.

"But as soon as we solve this mystery, you and I are locking ourselves in the bedroom and not coming out for a week."

"Good thing Martha packed you some dessert," I said.

He grinned.

"Aren't you supposed to say something romantic, like 'You're all the dessert I need,'" I pointed out.

"Well, I could," he admitted. "But we're talking about Martha. That woman can cook. You know, I'm thinking about becoming a polygamist."

I socked him in the shoulder, and he laughed. Then he pulled me in close, looked me in the eyes, and murmured, "You're all the dessert I'll ever need, Elizabeth."

He kissed me.

And I melted.

I could get used to a lifetime of this.

He helped me put on my panties and jeans. There was something very sensual about the way he helped me slide on my underwear, and even in the way he tugged up my jeans and buttoned them for me. I never imagined getting dressed was nearly as sexy as getting undressed. But I think Tez was capable of making any mundane act a sensual one.

We were soiled, leaf-strewn, and badly in need of showers, but we were happy.

When we entered the clearing, the women were waiting for us. I was relieved to see that during our tryst, they had managed to shower and dress. I didn't see Tawny, so I assumed she was locked up somewhere. I hoped it was a basement filled with mold and spiders.

All the women knelt before us and bowed their heads.

"Hail, the new alpha and his only mate," shouted Emma.

"We pledge our loyalty," responded the women.

"Aw, crap," muttered Tez.

Emma clutched a pair of pants in her hands and she moved from her place of supplication to give them to Tez. He slipped them on, and I looked at her gratefully.

The were-cats might not mind running around naked, but I did—especially when my husband was the one on display. Frankly, I wanted to be the only woman ever who got to ogle him naked.

"Okay, um . . . you." He pointed to Emma. "You're in charge or whatever until I get back. Wait. Isn't there another guy around here? Where's Serri?"

The women looked at each other, and I had a sudden chill. How in the world could I have forgotten poor Serri?

"She was hurt when I talked to her," I said to Tez. "She's the one who told me about the *upendo* challenge. Oh, I feel terrible!"

Guilt flashed across Emma's features. "We didn't think to check the house. Tawny told us they had dishonored the pride by leaving to live on their own. We thought they were gone."

Tez and I strode across the clearing. The pyre was dying down, and the alpha body had finally succumbed to the flames. When we got to the porch of the little house, I smelled something foul.

"Shit," said Tez. He opened the door and crept inside. I followed him. We found a young man in the living room facedown in a pool of blackened blood. Trak.

"Oh, no!" The man had paid the ultimate price for trying to protect his family, and his pride. We followed a trail of blood spatters down the hallway, and found Serri. She was sitting in a rocker, her arms around a baby boy fast asleep.

She was chalky white, her lips blue. And she was horribly still.

"Tez, is she . . ."

He pressed two fingers against her neck and shook his head. "Faint pulse. We need to get her to the hospital."

She'd known her husband was dead when she approached me, and that she might be dying, too. She was protecting her child, waiting for . . . me? Had she known I would win the challenge, or had she just hoped I would?

"C'mon, baby," I said, gently scooping out the boy from his mother's arms. His eyes opened sleepily. The back of his shirt was sticky with blood.

"It's not his," said Tez.

The blood had seeped from the wound in Serri's belly. It soaked her clothes, and her baby's, too. Horror washed over me.

Dayton stared at me with big brown eyes, and then he yawned and snuggled into my arms. My heart turned over in my chest. He was so precious. I wanted to rip off Tawny's head for ruining this beautiful family.

"Alpha?" Emma stood in the doorway, the only one brave enough to follow us in. She took in the scene, her expression hardening. "Tawny did this."

"She'll be punished," promised Tez.

"Emma, come with us," I said. "We're taking them to the hospital, and I want you to stay and watch over Dayton."

"Of course," she said. "What about Trak?"

"Tell the others to prepare his pyre," said Tez. "But do nothing until we return." Gently he picked up Serri, and carried her toward the doorway. "And tell everyone to pack their stuff and be ready to move into town. We're burning this creep-assed place down to the ground."

"Burning it?" exclaimed Emma. I didn't know if she sounded excited or upset.

"Yeah," said Tez. "That's what I said." He paused and leveled a look at her. "You got that, kid?"

Emma nodded, wide-eyed.

The alpha had spoken.

And that was that.

Chapter 19

"As soon as you're done expressing the alpha's wishes," I said to Emma (and, my, did it sound strange to say *that*), "then meet me at the Mercedes."

"I'll take Serri in my Honda," said Tez from the hallway. "We'll meet at the hospital."

I carried Dayton out of the house, and saw the women lined up outside looking pensive and sorrowful. What a terrible life it was here. It was like a cult. Isolated from others, dependent on a dynamic leader for direction, bound in sexual slavery . . . *Yuck!* The whole situation made my skin crawl. Were all prides set up the same, or was it just this one? I hoped this were-cat community was not the standard for all prides.

Tez left before I did. I cradled Dayton, not caring about the blood, and thought about how nice he felt in my arms. It made me wonder if adoption was possible. Maybe not a human baby, but perhaps there were orphaned paranormal children?

Emma was wise enough to grab a diaper bag and the

car seat. We strapped it in the back, and settled Dayton into it. Emma slid into the passenger side. Her eyes were as wide as saucers. "This is the nicest car I've ever been in," she said.

"I'll buy you one," I said. And I meant it. The lives of the were-cats were going to change. Big-time. I was surprised to be excited about having a hand in shaping the new community.

So much had happened.

I hadn't quite processed that I was married.

It didn't feel real, though the collar around my neck certainly did.

When we arrived at the emergency entrance to the hospital, several people awaited us. I realized that Tez had had the presence of mind to call Damian, who probably then in turn called in the troops.

I saw Damian, his brother Drake, Dr. Stan Michaels, and thank God . . . er, Goddess, Brigid waiting under the portico. Lorcan and Patrick's grandmother was an actual Celtic goddess who not only had goldsmithing skills; she was an amazing healer. Brigid was at least six feet tall with long red hair, and milky white skin. She had magical tattoos all over her body that changed into healing spells she needed to help the injured and the sick. She always wore a mossy green gown that certainly gave credence to her goddessness.

I had always been in a little awe of her.

Drake took Serri from Tez, and Brigid took Dayton. They hurried into the hospital, followed by Emma. Relieved that Serri and her son would get the care they so desperately needed, I joined Tez at the trunk of his

Honda, where he was giving Damian and Stan everything we found in my grandfather's attic room.

"I have the other items," I said. Emma had transferred all the stuff from the seat to the passenger floor, so I leaned down and grabbed the box with the diary and letters. I gladly handed it over. I wouldn't be sorry at all if I never saw any of it again. I just wanted the whole thing to be over with.

"Any sign of Phoebe or the others?" I asked.

Damian shook his head. "We cannot locate the trunks, either."

"Lenette has suggested that we gather the dissected body of Jeremiah and perform a cleansing ritual," said Stan. "She said that covering all of his bones with rock salt and then burning them should drive his spirit back into the underworld."

"What about the demon?"

"Connor and his sister are working on the incantations," said Damian. "They say it's complicated. It might be easier with Phoebe."

"She could invoke the talisman," I said.

Tez was worried about something else entirely. "You've got Jeremiah's skull," he said, "but how the hell will we find his other parts?"

"Flet," said Damian. He glanced at Tez and cupped his hands. "He is this tiny, annoying pixie."

"He says all the bad energy is getting worse," Stan said, "and it's making everything stink."

"Getting worse?"

Stan nodded. "Fights are breaking out, especially among couples. You know Rand got engaged to Mary-Beth?"

I nodded, pleased that he had popped the question.

"Not anymore. She broke up with him because she said he was cheating."

"That's ridiculous!"

"It's a plague," said Damian. "Anyone in love is either arguing or giving each other the silent treatment. It makes coordinating the searches difficult. We have to end this."

"Or call in Dr. Phil," said Tez.

"I don't think he could fix this," said Stan with a sigh. "Not even Oprah could fix this."

"Wow. It really is bad."

The demon's mere presence was infecting the residents of Broken Heart. We had to find and dispose of him. I wondered if Tez and I might start fighting, too. Would I begin to believe he was cheating on me? Would I let distrust and hurt worm through my love and destroy it inch by inch? I couldn't imagine such a thing and felt terrible that so many of my friends were experiencing this.

"Getting Silverstone's body back together and burning it is a good start," said Tez.

"Well," I said, feeling the funk of my dirty, blood-stained clothing, "we need to get cleaned up. Is there a search headquarters? Because we could meet you there later so we can help track down the others."

Damian nodded. "At the café." He stared at my collar. "I haven't seen one of those in a very long time." His gaze slid to Tez's neck. "You are mated?"

Had I the wherewithal to blush, I would've done so. This was not how I wanted to announce my marriage. I fingered the collar. "You're familiar with these?"

"It's particular to shifters," he said. "And they're

quite rare. You're very lucky." He nodded toward Tez. "Congratulations."

"Thank you."

"Yes," said Stan. "Congrats."

And on that note, Tez and I decided to retreat. I followed his Honda all the way to my house. I mean, our house. Or would it be? Maybe he didn't want to live here. Maybe he wanted a place we had both chosen. And how would he feel about adopting children? Maybe he'd chosen a vampire as a bride because he didn't want any kids at all.

"What are you thinking about?" asked Tez, peering inside as he opened the car door for me. He glanced at the Victorian, then at me. "I like this house."

"I swear!" I popped out of the car. "You can read my mind, can't you?"

"Nope. I'm just really good at reading your expression. You're an open book, Ellie Bee."

"Humph." I turned and reached over the seats to grab my purse from the passenger floorboard. Tez took the opportunity to cop a feel. Both of his hands grabbed my buttocks and squeezed.

"Tez!" I pretended offense, and jerked my bag so hard as I came up out of the car that it went flying. It landed with a thud near the porch, its contents spilling over the ground.

"I give it a ten," said Tez. "The arc on that was pretty good."

"Oh, hah." We walked over to the mess and bent down to gather up the items. I immediately recognized something square and silver. "How did that get into my purse?" I asked.

I picked up the box and immediately knew it was the wrong thing to do.

I heard Tez shout my name, and then I felt like I'd been wrapped into a black blanket and tossed into a tornado.

I landed on something flat and hard. For a moment, I couldn't see and then the darkness floated away like a dissipating mist.

"The gang's all here," said a female voice.

I got unsteadily to my feet and looked around. I was in the center of a circle of people who were chained to chairs. The woman who'd spoken was none other than Jessica.

"I thought you were safe." I sounded rather offended that she'd gotten caught. In fact, I think I was angry with myself for even touching that stupid box again.

"Yeah, well, you probably did what I did . . . touch some stupid object," groused Jessica. "Mine was a spoon. Can you believe that? I touched a freaking spoon and got zapped to spookville."

"Mine was this jewelry box." I was amazed to see it still in my hands. "What am I doing? We've got to get out of here."

"Not gonna happen, sister." This edict came from Phoebe. "I've been to hell. This place is worse."

"No way to leave," said Eva. "Something's blocking our telepathy. No one can find us."

"Is Marissa okay?" asked Dr. Clark. His expression held both anger and worry.

"She's fine. Lenette's protecting her." I spun around. Four people in four chairs. And I was the fifth one, the last of the Broken Heart five that the demon needed.

"Elizabeth!" The black shadow wavered in front of me. I felt the hatred, and I instantly dropped the box. I heard a howl of rage, and then the shadow disappeared.

"That happen to any of you?" I asked.

"Uh, no," said Jess.

I got a good look at everyone. "What are you all wearing?"

"He made us put on the dresses our ancestors wore when they died," said Eva. "He seemed insistent on it."

"Your ancestor didn't die," I said. "Your great-grandmother survived."

"How did he get her dress, then?"

I shook my head. Even Dr. Clark was wearing a dress, and he looked none too thrilled about it. "What does he hope to accomplish?"

"Sacrifice," I said. "Five of us, to the ancient demon Mammon, trying to complete what Jeremiah Silverstone set into motion more than a century ago."

Something kept digging at my hip, and it had been since I left the were-cat community. I dug into my pocket and pulled out my iPhone.

"Holy shit," said Jessica. "Call someone already!"

"If magic won't work, or telepathy," said Eva, "what makes you think we'll have access to a cell tower?"

"Maybe wherever we are just dampens the mystical," said Dr. Clark. "It's possible technology will work."

"Dial already," screeched Jessica, "before the psycho comes back."

I hit my CONTACTS button and, because I hadn't yet put Tez into my phone list, I dialed Damian.

"Ja?"

"Oh, my God. I can't believe this worked!"

"Elizabeth? Where are you?" He sounded relieved, and I had no doubt that Tez had immediately tracked him down.

"I have no idea. We're all here. It's some cave or . . . or something. Magic doesn't work here and it blocks out telepathy, too."

Suddenly, the air got heavy, and the hair on the back of my nape rose straight up.

"He's coming! Hide the phone!" Jessica's eyes bulged with fear, and there wasn't much that scared her. I put the phone on the ground and slid it so that it went under Jessica's chair.

We could still hear Damian talking, and then shouting. Jessica cried, "Shut the fuck up, Damian!" The lycanthrope went silent—and none too soon.

A man appeared next to me in the blink of an eye. Then his image wavered, skin sliding away from muscle, from bone, until there was nothing left but a skeletal shadow.

I could see why Jessica was scared. He emanated suffering. The feeling swirled out from him and encompassed me. I doubted everything, everyone. I knew, beyond doubt, beyond measure, I could trust no one with my heart.

He truly was the embodiment of the Broken Heart curse.

And I was not immune.

Tez had been with other women. He didn't love me. He betrayed me. He was a lying, sneaky bastard.

"Elizabeth." The voice was low and mean; his words slithered out like a snake's tongue. His eyes were empty.

"Put it on." He dropped the dress at my feet. I instantly recognized the velveteen gown with the copper roses. Elizabeth had been wearing it when he'd strangled her. I realized now what had been in the trunks. He'd kept the clothes of his murder victims, along with the stolen trinkets on those shelves of his.

He grabbed my throat and shook me. "Put. It. On."

Cold swept over me, and I felt as though daggers were stabbing me from the inside. He dropped me, and I fell to the ground, right on top of the dress.

Shaking, I put it on. It fit well enough, but I didn't like wearing it. I hated the idea he wanted to replay his last murders, with me and my friends as the victims. Vampires could live forever, but they weren't unkillable. The demon might not be able to choke the life out of us, but he could cut off our heads.

I felt sick.

"I need to finish my work. They trapped me, but I was patient. I waited, and I learned. I planned and planned, because I knew one day, I would return. And then . . . someone opened the door to my prison, and I was free."

A big thank-you to Patsy and Gabriel, I thought.

"Sit."

I scrambled to the empty chair. I was terrified. The shadow paced around the room, as if to spread his miasma. The air felt thick and tasted rotten. He oozed pain, and I knew it had been him walking around Broken Heart, in God knows whose form, spreading the disharmony.

It's time, Elizabeth.

The soft voice echoed in my mind, and I knew it was

my great-grandmother. I couldn't comprehend what she was asking me.

Just let go, my darling. Let go, and I'll do the rest.

Okay, I offered. *I trust you.* Then somehow, some way, I was popping free of my own body. It wasn't painful. I floated up, feeling rather wonderful, and then I noticed balls of blue energy hovering above each of my friends. As I watched in amazement, a white orb would rise out of one friend, and the blue energy would go in; this happened three times. Only Eva remained unaffected—because her ancestor had lived.

Then I was one of four luminescent glows lighting the darkness.

I realized that our ancestors had been waiting, too. Waiting because they'd known that this evil had not yet been vanquished. And now, they needed our bodies to finish *their* work.

I didn't know how to contact the consciousnesses of my friends. I assumed that they could see and hear as well as I could.

"You will harm no one else." The voice issuing from my mouth was not mine. It was softer, and had a little more Okie twang. "It's time to pay your price."

The shadow spun around the room, and it was as if he recognized the souls of his victims. The fairy-gold chains slipped off the captors and they all stood up, their gazes on the shadow.

"Jeremiah Silverstone," intoned my great-grandmother. "Come forth!"

"Noooooo!" The dark figure that had attacked me shimmered into view. It wiggled and wavered until, finally, the form of Jeremiah stood next to the demon. He looked wild-eyed and panicked. "Our work isn't done! Mine," he cried, pointed to me. To the other Elizabeth. "All of this, all of you, are mine!"

"I am Elizabeth Silverstone, and I accuse Jeremiah Silverstone of taking my life."

Phoebe stepped forward. "I am Catherine Allen, and I accuse Jeremiah Silverstone of taking my life."

Dr. Clark was next, and a breathy female voice issued from his lips. It was Cora Clark, and she accused Jeremiah as well. Then Jessica sashayed forward with her hands on her hips. In a strong Irish brogue she said, "And I, Mary McCree, accuse this no-good bastard of tossin' me in the creek and drownin' me." She spit on him, and he flinched away.

He turned to the shadow demon and screamed, "Do something!"

The creature was writhing, its mouth opened in a soundless scream. Was it being affected by the proceedings? Or had Connor found a way to break its tether to our world? I had no doubt Phoebe's husband hadn't stopped working on the spells to send the demon back to its master.

The four of us (er . . . them?) encircled Jeremiah, and in once voice, they shouted, "We judge you guilty, Jeremiah Silverstone. We demand punishment!"

A razor-sharp wind swept through the room. It got so cold, the breath of Dr. Clark, who was the only one not undead, puffed the air.

"We have heard your pleas," said the plethora of voices, a mixture of old and young, male and female. "We have examined your heart, Jeremiah Silverstone, and find you guilty. We banish you to the darkest pit of hell."

"Who are you?" cried Jeremiah. "You can't do this to me!"

"We are the fates," said the voices. "We have been called upon to judge you, and we have. You are banished."

Jeremiah screamed. Underneath his feet, a pit opened, and he was sucked down into it. He scrambled at the edge of the hole, his phantom fingers scrambling for purchase, but nothing could save him.

His unearthly screeches echoed as he was devoured by the darkness.

"Return to Mammon," the voices said to the quaking shadow. "You are not welcome here."

The shadow demon slithered into the floor, following his former master into the Pit.

"You are free," said the voices. "Leave this place, and join those who love you so well."

There was a clap of thunder, and the blue energies burst free of our bodies. In the next instant, I was falling as fast and hot as a star and when I slammed into the floor, I blacked out.

Chapter 20

When I woke up, I was being suffocated (sorta) by a well-muscled male chest.

"You're squishing me," I said. Or tried to. My face was so smooshed against him I couldn't actually talk.

Tez let up a little and looked down at me. "You're all right!" He kissed me until my toes curled, and then scooped me into his arms. "You scared the shit outta me. Never do that again!"

We were standing—okay, Tez was standing and I was clinging quite happily to his broad shoulders—in the front yard of the Silverstone mansion. Other reunions were going on. Dr. Clark was hugging his daughter; Jessica was smooching on Patrick; Eva and Lorcan were tenderly gazing into each other's eyes; and I think Connor was trying to perform a tonsillectomy on Phoebe. With his tongue.

"What happened?"

"Thanks to your iPhone, we were listening to every-thing that was going on and trying to pinpoint your location. Then the phone went dead. We still don't know where you went or how the hell you ended up back here. Lenette did the cleansing ritual on Jeremiah's remains. Then, all of sudden, we get a report you're here. All five of you." He looked down at me. "What's with the dress?"

"The demon made us put on the clothes of his victims." I really wanted to get out of it. And I never wanted to see the Silverstone mansion again. That place was nothing but bad luck and worse memories.

"How are Serri and Dayton?"

"Dayton's fine, and Serri's gonna make it. I'm just sorry she lost her husband."

He hugged me. "Don't worry. We'll make sure Trak gets his justice."

Patsy and Gabriel walked out of the front door and onto the lawn. They surveyed the lovefest going on, and grinned. Our queen was okay, and Gabriel looked very happy to have his wife back.

I held on to Tez, my own true love, and wished that wherever Elizabeth had gone, she was with her true love as well.

Tez scooped me into his arms and walked toward the Honda.

"Where are we going?" I asked.

"You remember when I went out to get you a present?"

"The night you got kidnapped by a crazy were-cat? Yes, I remember it quite well."

We got into the car. I turned and looked at Tez. "What is it?"

"Something with which to penetrate you."

"But you can penetrate me now. As often as you like."

"Doesn't mean we shouldn't explore other options."

"Hmm," I said. "Soooo instead of diamonds or shoes, you got me a . . ." I stared at him, and waited for him to reveal the nature of his present.

He grinned. "Buzz, buzz, Ellie Bee."

One month later . . .

The Silverstone mansion was no more.

In the end, it was Patsy who suggested we "should just blow the whole damned thing to pieces," and no one disagreed. So, with a little help from vampires from the Family Hua Mu Lan, who could wield fire, the mansion was destroyed. Then the bulldozers came in and cleared off the land. Lenette and her sisters cleansed whatever bad ju-ju might be lingering and added a few magick spells to keep it free of darkness.

I had discussed with Tez the idea of adopting or-phaned paranormal children. I should've known better than to worry he wouldn't want kids mucking up our lives. How could I have even thought such a thing? I was learning a lot about my own insecurities, and I wouldn't be ruled by them anymore. Tez loved the idea of giv-ing a home to children who'd been like him growing up—paranormal and alone in a world of humans—and needed love and understanding. He admitted to me that his human mother was not his true mother. She really had met his father on an archaeological dig in Mexico, but his biological mother had died; and his father, who was sick, had approached the human woman with his son,

Tez, and told her everything she would need to know to raise him. She fell in love with the dark-haired boy, and swore she would never let him forget his heritage.

I wanted to give that kind of guidance and love to other children. We had already put plans into place to expand our home, and we were working with Patsy on ways that we could track down children who needed us.

As for the were-cats, they were incorporating nicely into Broken Heart. Serri had moved into a two-bedroom house with Dayton and had taken a waitressing job at the Old Sass Café. The were-cats were prospering now that they had the ability to make choices for their own lives.

Tawny had been banished from Broken Heart, traded to another pride where, Emma had assured us, Tawny would remain only a concubine. I didn't think Tawny's ambitions would be curbed easily, but at least she was another pride's problem.

Today, a small group of us stood at the edge of the old property. The remains of the five couples who founded Broken Heart had been recovered and reburied in this place, as a memorial to the testament of love everlasting.

We all had different color roses, which we placed on each grave site.

The couples were buried in plots next to each other and all had new tombstones. It had been fenced off, not as a security measure but as an aesthetic element.

Tez lifted my hand to his lips and said, "I love you, Ellie Bee."

I smiled, my heart full. "I love you, too."

Just past the graves was a large marble monument,

and we walked to it, along with the other descendents of Broken Heart's original families. Together, we read the inscription:

We honor those whose sacrifice and love
created a place where all are welcome.

Paul Tibbett and Elizabeth Silverstone

Sean and Mary McCree

Dennison and Cora Clark

Jonathon and Evangeline LeRoy

Michael and Catherine Allen

"Doubt thou the stars are fire,
Doubt the sun doth move,
Doubt truth to be a liar
but never doubt thy love."
—William Shakespeare, *Hamlet*

THE BROKEN HEART TURN-BLOODS

* **Jessica Matthews:** Widow (first husband, Richard). Mother to Bryan and Jenny and adopted son, Rich, Jr. Stay-at-home mom. Vampire of Family Ruadan. Mated to Patrick O'Halloran.

Charlene Mason: Deceased. Mistress of Richard Matthews. Mother to Rich, Jr. Receptionist for insurance company. Vampire of Family Ruadan.

Linda Beauchamp: Divorced (first husband, Earl). Mother to MaryBeth. Nail technician. Vampire of Family Koschei. Mated to Dr. Stan Michaels.

MaryBeth Beauchamp: Nanny to Marchand triplets. Vampire of Family Ruadan.

* **Louise Evangeline "Eva" LeRoy:** Mother to Tamara. Teacher at night school and colibrarian of Broken Heart and Consortium archives. Vampire of Family Koschei. Mated to Lorcan O'Halloran.

Patricia "Patsy" Donovan: Divorced (first husband, Sean). Mother to Wilson. Former beautician. Queen of vampires and lycanthropes. Vampire of Family Amahté. Mated to *loup de sang* Gabriel Marchand. Mother to the Marchand triplets.

Ralph Genessa: Widowed (first wife, Teresa). Father to twins Michael and Stephen, and to daughter Cassandra. Dragon handler. Vampire of Family Hua Mu Lan. Mated to half-dragon Libby Monroe.

Simone Sweet: Widowed (first husband, Jacob). Mother to Glory. Mechanic. Vampire of Family Velthur. Mated to Braddock Hayes.

* Phoebe Allen: Divorced (first husband, Jackson Tate). Mother to Daniel. Comanages the Knights Inn in Tulsa. Vampire of Family Durga. Mated to Connor Ballard.

Darlene Clark: Deceased. Divorced (first husband, Jason Clark*). Mother to Marissa. Operated Internet scrapbooking business. Vampire of Family Durga.

* Elizabeth Bretton née Silverstone: Widowed (first husband, Henry). Stepmother to Venice. Socialite and jewelry maker. Vampire of Family Zela. Mated to werejaguar Tez Jones.

* Direct descendents of the five families who founded Broken Heart: the McCrees, the LeRoys, the Silverstones, the Allens, and the Clarks.

GLOSSARY

Ancient: Refers to one of the original eight vampires. The very first vampire was Ruadan, who is the biological father of Patrick and Lorcan. Several centuries ago, Ruadan and his sons took on the last name of O'Halloran, which means "stranger from overseas."

banning (see: World Between Worlds): Anyone can be sent into limbo, but the spell must be cast by an Ancient or a being with powerful magick. No one can be released from banning until they feel true remorse for their evil acts. This happens rarely, which means banning is not done lightly.

binding: When vampires have consummation sex (with any person or creature), they're bound together for a hundred years. This was the Ancients' solution to keep vamps from sexual intercourse while blood-taking. There are only two known instances of breaking a binding.

Consortium: More than five hundred years ago, Patrick

and Lorcan O'Halloran created the Consortium to figure out ways that parakind could make the world a better place for all beings. Many sudden leaps in human medicine and technology are because of the Consortium's work.

Convocation: Five neutral, immortal beings given the responsibility of keeping the balance between Light and Dark.

donors: Mortals who serve as sustenance for vampires. The Consortium screens and hires humans to be food sources. Donors are paid well and given living quarters. Not all vampires follow the guidelines created by the Consortium for feeding. A mortal may have been a donor without ever realizing it.

drones: Mortals who do the bidding of their vampire Masters. The most famous was Renfield—drone to Dracula. The Consortium's code of ethics forbids the use of drones, but plenty of vampires still use them.

ETAC: The Ethics and Technology Assessment Commission is the public face of this covert government agency. In its program, soldier volunteers have undergone surgical procedures to implant nanobyte technology, which enhances strength, intelligence, sensory perception, and healing. Volunteers are trained in use of technological weapons and defense mechanisms so advanced, it's rumored they come from a certain section of Area 51. Their mission is to remove, by any means necessary, paranormal targets named as domestic threats.

Family: Every vampire can be traced to the one of the

eight Ancients. The Ancients are divided into the Eight Sacred Sects, also known as the Families. The Families are: Ruadan, Koschei (aka Romanov), Hua Mu Lan, Durga, Zela, Amahté, Shamhat, and Velthur.

gone to ground: When vampires secure places where they can lie undisturbed for centuries, they *go to ground*. Usually they let someone know where they are located, but the resting locations of many vampires are unknown. Both the Ancients Amahté and Shamhat have gone to ground for more than three thousand years. Their locations are unknown.

Invisi-shield: Using technology stolen from ETAC, the Consortium created a shield that not only makes the town invisible to outsiders, but also creates a force field. No one can get into the town's borders without knowing specific access points, all of which are guarded by armed security details.

loup de sang: Translated as "blood wolf." The first of these vampire-werewolves were triplets born after their lycanthrope mother was drained and killed by a vampire. For nearly two centuries, Gabriel Marchand was the only known *loup de sang* and also known as "the outcast." (See: *Vedere prophecy*.) Now the *loup de sang* include his brother, Ren, his sister, Anise, his wife, Patsy, and his three children.

lycanthropes: Also called lycans. They can shift from human into wolf at will. Lycans have been around a long time and originate in Germany. Their numbers are small because they don't have many females, and most children born have a fifty percent chance of living to the age of one.

Master: Most Master vampires are hundreds of years old and have had many successful Turnings. Masters show Turn-bloods how to survive as a vampire. A Turn-blood has the protection of the Family (see: *Family*) to which their Master belongs.

PRIS: Paranormal Research and Investigation Services. Cofounded by Theodora and her husband, Elmore Monroe. Its primary mission is to document supernatural phenomena and conduct cryptozoological studies.

Roma: The Roma are cousins to full-blooded lycanthropes. They can change only on the night of a full moon. Just as full-blooded lycanthropes are raised to protect vampires, the Roma are raised to hunt vampires.

soul shifter: A supernatural being with the ability to absorb the souls of any mortal or immortal. The shifter has the ability to assume any of the forms she's absorbed. Only one is known to exist, the woman known as Ash, who works as a "balance keeper" for the Convocation.

Taint: The Black Plague for vampires, which makes vampires insane as their body deteriorates. The origins of the Taint were traced to demon poison. After many attempts to find a cure, which included transfusions of royal lycanthrope blood, a permanent cure has been found.

Turn-blood: A human who's been recently Turned into a vampire. If you're less than a century old, you're a Turn-blood.

Turning: Vampires perpetuate the species by Turning humans. Unfortunately, only one in about ten humans actually makes the transition.

Vedere prophecy: Astria Vedere predicted that in the twenty-first century a vampire queen would rule both vampires and lycans, and would also end the ruling power of the Ancients.

The prophecy reads: "A vampire queen shall come forth from the place of broken hearts. The seven powers of the Ancients will be hers to command. She shall bind with the outcast, and with this union, she will save the dual-natured. With her consort, she will rule vampires and lycanthropes as one."

World Between Worlds: The place between this plane and the next, where there is a void. Some people can slip back and forth between this "veil."

Wraiths: Rogue vampires who banded together to dominate both vampires and humans. Since the defeat of the Ancients Koschei and Durga, they are believed to be defunct.

Read on for a sneak peek at the next book
in the Broken Heart series,

Must Love Lycans

by Michele Bardsley,
coming soon from Signet Eclipse.

Why was the man naked?

I pressed my palms against the reinforced steel door, and peered through the small, square, shatter-proof glass window. Underneath it was an extremely narrow slot, which allowed sound to escape and let me speak to the patient inside. It was old school, but just one of many quirks about the Dante Clinic.

However, I couldn't quite speak.

Heat flooded my cheeks.

Good Lord.

He was pacing—emulating a trapped animal in a cage. It bothered me how close the analogy was to the truth. For now, the safety of the staff and the other patients took precedence over his comfort. How soon he got out was entirely up to him.

He was dirty and bruised. Scars crisscrossed his torso, and there were burns on his arms, too. He'd been tortured, though he seemed unconcerned about his injuries. In fact, I couldn't sense if he was in any sort of physical pain at all. With my empathic abilities, I could literally know about a person's pain, whether physical or emotional.

He was tall—way more than six feet. His thick black hair reached his back, and swung like a dark curtain as he whipped around, his agitation growing with each long stride.

I felt the snap of his anger. It reached out and tried to bite at me, but I pushed it away. I was used to fending off the emotions of others, but his were somehow different.

It was wrong—so very, very wrong—to watch the bunch and flex of his muscles. Every part of the man was built, and not because he was a gym rat. That beautiful body was the natural result of working hard. I pegged him for a construction worker, or maybe an outdoorsman. I could easily see him guiding backpackers through dense forests and then scaling a mountain.

I resisted looking at his genitals. For two seconds. Oh, good heavens. He was huge, and his penis wasn't even erect. *Do not imagine him with a hard-on.* Then I totally did. Heat swept through me again. What the hell was wrong with me? I was behaving so unprofessionally—even though I was doing it mentally. I needed to get focused and back on task.

Every so often he would pause to punch at the walls. He was also cursing—in German.

The walls and floor were padded. The cell—and I cringed to call it that—had no furniture. The place was often referred to as the "induction" room because sometimes new clients needed time and space to calm down before being assigned a residency. Their suites were no less secure, but when an angry psychiatric patient threatened to rip your head off—he might actually try to do it.

He stopped in the middle of the room, facing the door.

His head rose, and I saw the flare of his nostrils. He was ... scenting?

God, his eyes were so green. Like chips of jade.

"I smell you," he said.

Through the door?

He rushed toward me so fast he was nearly a blur, and slammed his entire body against the steel. The metal actually groaned.

I squeaked and backed away, forgetting that I was the one in charge here. Could potent masculinity reach through two feet of steel to taunt me? Or was it the insistence of my libido to replay the images of his gorgeous body? I shivered. He was just a man. A man in pain. A man who needed my help.

His face was pressed against the glass, and he studied me with a cold expression. "Let me out," he said. *"Now."*

"What's your name?" I asked.

His lips thinned. "What's yours?"

"Kelsey." Shit. Way to let him know I was in charge. Usually it was my first tactic to make patients feel comfortable, but I got the feeling he was too much an alpha personality. I straightened and put my shoulders back. "I'm Dr. Morningstone."

His gaze dropped to my breasts, which I had sorta thrust out there in an effort to create my "in-charge" body language. I couldn't back off now, so I tried to pretend that his gaze wasn't wandering over my boobs, or that I noticed his inspection.

"Let me out, Kelsey." His voice had gone low and smoky. My belly clenched as my disused girly parts perked up. *Stop that,* I demanded. *He's a patient.*

"Do you know where you are?" I asked.

One eyebrow quirked.

I flushed at the silent chastisement. I was screwing up this introduction all over the place. I had to get control of myself, the situation, and him. "You're at the Dante Clinic. You were brought in last night from another facility."

"Another facility?"

I nodded. I hadn't been told much, only that he'd been rescued from a private laboratory. The clinic's namesake and benefactor, Jarron Dante, had made it clear this man was a priority client. I shuddered to think about the kind of experimentation he'd gone through, much less why he'd been chosen to be a guinea pig. I hadn't asked more questions about his previous situation because: one, you didn't question a billionaire; and, two, the less I knew, the less I had to wrestle with my conscience about this job and all that it entailed.

"You don't remember?" I asked.

"No."

"Do you know your name?"

"Damian."

"Is that your name," I asked, "or is it the name your captors used?"

"Captors." He made the word sound like both a question and a statement. He pushed away from the door, his frustration bubbling through my psychic shields.

I returned to the window to watch him pace. He was frowning and rubbing his temples, obviously trying to remember what he'd forgotten.

Which was his entire life.

"As soon as you're ready, we'll get you a shower, some clothes, and a hot meal. Then we can talk."

"I don't want to talk," he said. "I want to leave."

"Where would you go?"

For the first time, I saw panic enter his gaze. His anger shot out again, and, wrapped deeply within it, a terrible sorrow. It was hard to stave off his emotions. They were so strong, and so . . . strange. Animalistic.

Primal.

Like him.

"When will you return?" He sounded as if he were chewing gravel. This man was not used relying on others. I was sure it chafed his ego to ask even that simple question.

"Soon," I promised.

He nodded. Then he turned away from me. If my gaze lingered a little too long on his buttocks . . . Well, I guess I'd just have to live with the guilt of ogling a beautiful man.

"We sure got a live one, Doc," said Marisol Brunes. "And Lord 'a' mercy, he's a hunk and a half. Too bad he's nuts."

I looked up from my clipboard so Mari could see how unthrilled I was with her assessment. I liked Mari. She was short and chubby with silver hair and twinkling blue eyes, but tough as nails. She was sorta like a biker version of Mrs. Claus. She'd been at the clinic since opening day more than ten years ago, and despite her loyalty to my predecessor, she'd been kinder to me than the rest of the staff. I was younger than of all them, and certainly younger than Dr. Danforth Laurence, who'd been a renowned mental-health researcher and a well-respected psychiatrist.

Me? Not so much.

After staying silent under my chastising glare, Mari finally caved.

"I know," she said with a sigh. "Derogatory language is a subtle but damaging way to assert our superiority over people who deserve nothing less than our compassion and assistance."

"Glad you've been listening."

I looked back down at the paperwork, but I knew she was rolling her eyes. I'd taken over the Dante Clinic only three weeks ago—four days after Dr. Laurence had died unexpectedly in his sleep. Dr. Laurence had been in his late fifties, and had died from cardiac arrest. We should all be lucky to go that peaceably. There were worse ways to die.

My stomach took a dive as an unwanted image flashed: the knife in my hand, the gleam in Robert's eye, the blood spilling over both of us.

No. You will not go there, Kel.

I stepped off that particular dark mental path, and circled back to something less soul crushing.

The Dante Clinic was a privately funded psychiatric facility that supported the care and well-being of clients handpicked by the facility's benefactor, Jarron Dante. No one knew why he chose the people he did—only that that most of the cases were hard-core and the patients had no families. Many of them had been homeless, locked up in state facilities. Dante picked up the considerable tab for high-quality care. At least until he hired me. Surely my reputation had stained that of the institution and its accomplishments. After what had happened last year, no one would hire me to give therapy to a dog. But here I was, in charge of the whole enchilada, which was unusual for a psychotherapist, especially one so new to the profession and who'd already fallen into the low esteem of her peers.

The facility was one of Dante's refurbished mansions. Located just outside Broken Arrow, it was a huge towering Gothic structure plopped into the middle of a heavily wooded ten acres. It looked like Dracula's castle and operated like a king's palace. There were never more than ten residents in the facility. With Damian added to the roster, we now had six clients. Every client had a personal maid and butler, who also served as certified nursing assistants and, when necessary, guards. They were all black belts in karate, and they behaved in military fashion. Nice enough people, I guess, but a little on the scary side. The patient suites were sumptuous, but secure. If patients got out of line, privileges were revoked, and in the three weeks I'd been here, no client wanted to be without their Egyptian cotton sheets, or nightly hot cocoa and scones. Meals were taken together in a dining room the size of a football field—or so it seemed to me.

The salary was generous, the living quarters luxurious, and the position prestigious.

I shouldn't have gotten the job.

No one would hire me after the fiasco in Oklahoma City. My own mother rescinded her invitation to last year's holiday gathering, and had not issued another invitation to anything, not even her local book signings. She no longer bothered with the perfunctory monthly phone calls, either—the ones her secretary scheduled so Margaret Morningstone could check off "speak to youngest daughter and make her feel inadequate" from her list.

My disgrace had tainted her, and she hadn't forgiven me.

I got a lump in my throat.

I wanted to believe I had stopped seeking Mother's approval years ago. But somewhere inside me was the rejected little girl who wanted her unconditional love. She had spent my entire life pointing out numerous times that no emotion was unconditional, least of all love.

After Mother's very public rebuff (on a national talk show, thank you), my brother and sister followed suit. We'd never been particularly close anyway. I'd been a surprise child, one born nearly eighteen years after my sister. Our father died when I was only two. My mother's psychotherapy practice was already well established, as was her career as a lecturer and author. Not long after my father died, Mother hit the *New York Times* bestseller list, and her entire career went platinum gold.

I was raised by a series of nannies. While I was in college, Mother married Ted Portshire. I liked him. He was the only one still talking to me; I admired his ability to blithely ignore Mother's edicts. He was as cheerful as my mother was dour, although she was a shining star when in a public venue.

"You look like you need a Starbucks," said Mari. "A triple shot."

I laughed. "Yeah. Maybe a triple shot of vodka."

She grinned wickedly. " 'Atta girl."

I signed off on the entrance paperwork for Damian No-Last-Name and handed her the clipboard. "I'll be in my office until my two o'clock with Mr. Danvers."

"Good luck," she said sympathetically. "Sven caught him cutting out paper feathers again."

"Oh, jeez. He's already sprained his ankle jumping off tables." I paused. "Do you have the shock bracelets on him?"

She nodded, and I saw the distaste in her gaze. I felt the same about the bracelets, but they were effective. Until the guy stopped believing a demon wanted him to fly or we found a more palatable way to keep him grounded, he would have to wear the bracelets. The clinic employed many experimental psychiatric tools. I was not sold on the bracelets, but Jarron Dante insisted. He insisted on a lot of things that made me uncomfortable—however, I couldn't deny he seemed to genuinely care about the well-being of our clients. It had not escaped my attention that he knew how very much I needed this job, not just for the paycheck and the living quarters, but also for the opportunity to redeem myself in the profession. He was a man who knew how to exploit the vulnerabilities of others; he was an effective manipulator. To be fair, though, he didn't have to twist my arm to take the job.

As I said good-bye to Mari and headed toward my first-floor office, I thought about Mr. Danvers. He blamed all his bad behavior on a demon he called Malphas, who supposedly took the form of a crow. He claimed the demon, which was inside him, wanted to return to hell by flying through a portal located in a Tulsa hotel—and the demon wanted to take Mr. Danvers with him. I can Google just as well as anyone, so it was easy enough to figure out how my patient had come up with both the name and the ideology behind Malphas. It was on Wikipedia, for heaven's sake. A hellmouth in a hotel was a good twist, though.

What I was trying to understand was why Mr. Danvers had created the delusion. Right now, I was still building trust between myself and the patients. It would probably take a while for Mr. Danvers to reveal anything that might allow me the insight I needed to help him.

It wasn't that I didn't believe in psychic phenomenon. After all, I was an empath; I could feel other people's emotions. It was one of the reasons I became a psychotherapist. I knew how to tease out the hidden nuances from the main emotion. Someone who was angry almost always had strands of sorrow or hurt or abandonment woven into their fury.

Nothing was ever as it seemed.

My ability usually made it easier to connect with patients, and to help lessen their distress. Unfortunately, Mr. Danvers was a particularly difficult case. Truth and sincerity emanated off him in waves. That was the problem with dealing with delusional patients—they believed absolutely in the reality they'd created.

Not long after opening my practice, I'd learned by sheer accident that I could also absorb emotions. After I figured out this new facet of my ability, I started using it to just take away the pain, the anger, the confusion, even the crazy. I didn't realize I'd made myself vulnerable, or that I'd taken away the ability for my patients to work through their issues. They didn't stop engaging in the destructive behaviors that had led them to my door— they just didn't feel bad about those actions anymore. I'd given them a magic pill. And I'd taken all their poison into myself.

I was already emotionally off-kilter when Robert Mallard became my patient. Somehow, he'd been able to creep under my skin, get inside my head, and—*no*. I couldn't go there. It had been a year. I had to let go. I had to move on.

I thought about the mysterious and very naked Damian. I picked up my phone and hit the speed dial for Sven's cell. He had an office, but he was never in it. He was a prowler, someone constantly on the move trying to anticipate problems. He was very good at his job, but not much of a talker. He was also way scarier than anyone else here, except for Jarron Dante.

"Dubowski."

"Hi, uh, Sven. It's Dr. Morningstone. Will you escort our newest patient to his suite?"

He was silent for so long, I said, "Um, Sven?"

"Too dangerous."

"He's much calmer. He needs a shower and someone to see about his injuries. Mr. Dante made it very clear he's a priority, so the sooner we get him integrated, the sooner we can help him."

Sven snorted in obvious disbelief. "Fine."

A second later, I heard the dial tone. "Nice talking to you, too," I muttered. Then I hung up the receiver.

"Dr. Morningstone."

Startled by the deep male voice, I gasped and shoved

back from the desk. When I saw the imposing figure of Jarron standing in the doorway, I took a shuddering breath. I remembered quite clearly shutting my door; I hadn't even noticed that he'd opened it. How long had he been standing there observing me?

He was a big man—a linebacker in Armani. He had wavy black hair, stormy gray eyes, and chiseled features. The scariest thing about Jarron was that I never got emotions off him. He was either completely emotionless, which was impossible, or exercised iron control over his emotional state. I believed he was very capable of encapsulating pesky emotions.

His lips flickered at the corners, and I swore he'd tried to smile.

Realizing that I'd been sitting on the edge of my chair gaping up at him, I rose to my feet. "Mr. Dante, please, come in."

He was already inside, but he didn't call me on the obvious flub. Instead, he strode to one of the wingbacks that faced my desk and sat down. I retook my seat and scooted closer to my desk. Mr. Danvers's and Damian's files were beneath my fingertips.

"Are you settling in well, Kelsey?"

I nodded. He'd switched from Dr. Morningstone to Kelsey. The informality suggested an intimacy in our relationship that made me uneasy. Was he attempting to create a more congenial relationship? Or trying to throw me off guard so he could whammy me?

Overanalyze much, Kel? Sheesh. Sometimes, being a psychotherapist sucked. I was constantly looking for motives in even the most mundane of gestures.

"What are your thoughts on our new patient?"

"He's confused. Angry. He's also very intelligent. I got the impression he doesn't react so much as act."

"He will assess his environment to determine the best routes for escape."

"More than likely."

"You asked Sven to assign him a suite."

"A gesture of trust," I said, feeling rattled. I never realized how much I relied on my empathic abilities until I conversed with Jarron. He spoke in a pleasant tone with a razor edge. He could be halfway into ripping me a new one before I would even realize it.

"I agree. The sooner Damian is able to accept he is our guest, the sooner we can begin the healing process. Do you believe his amnesia is permanent?"

"I don't know," I said. "After I meet with Dr. Ruthers to discuss Damian's physical injuries and get his assessment, I'll have a better idea. And, of course, I'll need to speak with Damian. My gut instinct is that the amnesia is temporary."

"Oh?"

"He was cursing in German," I said. "But I bet he didn't realize it. It may be an indicator that his memories are already returning."

"I see."

I couldn't tell if Jarron was pleased or dismayed by the idea Damian might regain his memory.

"Are you free this evening?"

I stared at him. I was free every evening. I never left the compound because there was no point. I had no friends, my family had disowned me, and going out into public venues, with all those people and their emotions, exhausted me.

"Kelsey?"

"I'm sorry." I blushed, and looked down at the desk. "Yes. I'm free."

"Excellent. Please join me in my private suite for a dinner."

I blinked up at him.

"We'll talk about your plans for the clinic, and your innovative approaches to therapy," he said.

His expression was bland, as usual, but there was something dangerous lurking in his eyes. It was like the wolf extending an invitation to Little Red Riding Hood. Did he really want to talk about the clinic? Or did he have something more carnal in mind?

My stomach squeezed as trepidation spun coldly through me.

That odd smile fluttered on his lips again, and then he stood up. "I'll see you tonight, Kelsey." He paused, tilting his head as he studied me. "Wear something nice."

Does drinking blood make me a bad mother?

I'm not just a single mother trying to make ends meet in this crazy world. I'm also a vampire. But though my stretch marks have disappeared and my vision has improved, I can't rest until the thing that did this to me is caught. My kids' future is at stake—figuratively and literally. As is my sex life. Although I wouldn't mind finding myself attached to Patrick's juicy thigh again, I learned that once a vampire does the dirty deed, it hitches her to the object of her affection for at least one hundred years. I just don't know if I'm ready for that kind of commitment...

"A fabulous combination of vampire lore, parental angst, romance, and mystery."
—Jackie Kessler, author of *Hell's Belles*

Sometimes it's hard to take your own advice—or pulse.

Ever since a master vampire bit a bunch of parents, the town of Broken Heart has catered to those who rise at sunset.

As for me, Eva LeRoy, town librarian and single mother to a teenage daughter, I'm pretty much used to being "vampified." But books still make my undead heart beat—and, strangely enough, so does Lorcán the Loner. My mama always told me everyone deserves a second chance. Still, it's one thing to deal with the usual undead hassles: rival vamps, rambunctious kids adjusting to night school, and my daughter's new vampire hunter boyfriend. And it's quite another to fall for the vampire who killed you…

"The paranormal romance of the year."
—MaryJanice Davidson

Available wherever books are sold or at
penguin.com

When you're immortal, being a mom won't kill you—it will only make you stronger.

Not just anyone can visit Broken Heart, Oklahoma, especially since all the single moms—like me, Patsy Donahue—have been turned into vampires. I'm forever forty, but looking younger than my years, thanks to my new (un)lifestyle. And even though most of my customers have skipped town, I still manage to keep my hair salon up and running because of the lycanthropes prowling around. They know how important good grooming is—especially a certain rogue shape-shifter who is as sexy as he is deadly. Now, if only I could put a leash on my wild teenage son. He's up to his neck in danger. And my maternal instincts are still alive and kicking, so no one better mess with my flesh and blood.

"Lively, sexy, out of this world—as well as in it—fun!"
—*New York Times* bestselling author Carly Phillips

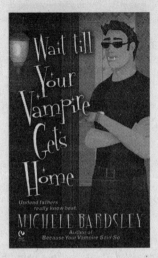

Undead fathers really do know best...

To prove her journalistic chops, Libby Monroe ends up in
Broken Heart, Oklahoma, chasing down bizarre rumors of
strange goings-on—and finding vampires, lycanthropes, and
zombies. She never expects to fall in lust with one of them,
but vampire/single dad Ralph Genessa is too irresistible. Only
the town is being torn in two by a war between the undead—
and Libby may be the only thing that can hold
Broken Heart together.

**"Has action aplenty and a free-spirited, wittily sarcastic
heroine who will delight [Michele Bardsley's] fans."**
—Booklist

Available wherever books are sold or at
penguin.com

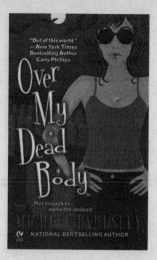

Hot enough to wake the undead...

Moving into Broken Heart seemed like the perfect
transition for Simone Sweet and her young daughter, Glory.
With her ex-husband gone after attempting to murder
Simone, and Glory being mute since the incident, it is one
place where she can feel safe, and almost forget she's a
ravenous vampire.

No one is without secrets, but Simone's are big. She'd hate to
have them interfere with what's developing with local hunk
Braddock Hayes. When not turning her legs to jelly, he's
building an Invisi-shield around Broken Heart and helping
Glory speak again. But when Simone's past resurfaces, it
threatens to ruin her second chance...

"Michele Bardsley's vampire stories rock!"
—*New York Times* bestselling author Carly Phillips

Available wherever books are sold or at
penguin.com

Everybody makes mistakes—and my first one was named Connor, a heart-stealing Scottish hottie. I thought our night together was the beginning of a love story, which turned out to be my second mistake. I, Phoebe Allen, lifelong Broken Heart resident and vampire, am now mated to a half-demon.

Thankfully Phoebe's four-year-old son Danny is safely away at Disneyworld with his human father. Because Phoebe's right in the middle of major paranormal drama, helping Connor and his rag-tag group of friends retrieve part of an ancient talisman in order to ward off Connor's vicious stepmother, an uber-demon named Lilith. Phoebe swears she isn't falling for any of Connor's demon charm. But still, he's willing to do anything to protect her and prevent demons from storming into Broken Heart. And her undead heart can't resist a bad boy with identity issues...

S0120